CANDY DON'T COME IN GRAY

CANDY DON'T COME IN GRAY

ROSLYN CARRINGTON

KENSINGTON PUBLISHING CORP.
http://www.kensingtonbooks.com

DAFINA BOOKS are published by

Kensington Publishing Corp.
850 Third Avenue
New York, NY 10022

All Kensington titles, imprints and distributed lines are available at special quantity discounts for bulk purchases for sales promotion, premiums, fund-raising, educational or institutional use.

Special book excerpts or customized printings can also be created to fit specific needs. For details, write or phone the office of the Kensington Special Sales Manager: Kensington Publishing Corp., 850 Third Avenue, New York, NY, 10022. Attn. Special Sales Department. Phone: 1-800-221-2647.

Dafina Books and the Dafina logo Reg. U.S. Pat. & TM Off.

ISBN 1-57566-852-1

First Kensington Trade Paperback Printing: August 2002
10 9 8 7 6 5 4 3 2

Printed in the United States of America

For Mrs. Hyacinth Bonair-Agard, my English teacher at St. George's College, Barataria, Trinidad, for opening my eyes to this strange and wonderful writer's world. After handing me back a particularly promising creative writing assignment, she sent my life into a tailspin with this challenge: "When you publish your first novel, remember to bring me a copy." I was just twelve at the time, and even then books were my food and my air, but like many a West Indian child I believed that books were written by old, white people in cold, faraway countries. It was only on that day, with her words, that I realized that little black girls could grow up to be writers. Mrs. Agard, I cannot thank you enough.

For my aunt, Dr. Barbara Hull, who gave me my first computer, so that I didn't have to spend my early writing life trying to decipher my own handwriting.

Mattie

Mattie collected mirrors. Her favorite was a tall, old cheval glass that balanced on brass pivots, allowing her to flip it right over until it faced the other way or to angle it so that it reflected just about any point in the room. It was bordered by large lilies etched into the glass, and its curved legs ended in brass lion's feet. She was especially fond of this one, because it was the only one she owned that let her see herself head to toe, and she usually kept it facing the bed, so that even if she woke up in a panic in the middle of the night, she could switch on the bedside lamp, look across at the mirror, and remind herself, reassure herself, that she was still there.

The one fixed to the dressing table was of little use for putting on make-up: its silver backing had been worn away with age, leaving her reflection faded, speckled, and ghostly. Apart from these, there were hand mirrors, compacts, mirrors in picture frames along the wall, and even broken bits that lined her window and glittered like sequins in the sunlight. She took a lot of care in setting them up, arranging each piece throughout her small bedroom to ensure that no matter where she passed, she could see a reflection of herself, either dead ahead or out of the corner of her eye.

What she saw didn't really matter. She never spent much time on her hair, and as far as she was concerned, her face was rather ordinary, not much different than anyone else's, with the exception of startling green eyes that were almost incongruous against her dark skin; and those she'd inherited: as unusual and as beautiful as they were, she could take no credit for that.

The magic of the mirrors was that they reminded her that she was solid, a being that reflected light rather than let it pass right through. They reminded her that the disturbing sensation she had suffered all her life, the one where her skin began to itch madly, to throb and to tingle, would not end in her gradually fading into nothingness. They were a safeguard against the threat of her fear becoming a reality: that one day she would look down at herself and notice that a ray of light, a stray sunbeam, perhaps, had pierced her body and exited the other side, as it would through a hole in the roof. That would be only the beginning. Sunbeam would follow sunbeam, gradually at first, and then more and more at a time, until she resembled a colander: part substance, part nothingness. After a while, even the substance that was left would thin and fade.

In her calmer moments, her stronger moments, she knew, of course, that this was far from possible. People didn't just disappear. Very often, her panicked rush to the nearest mirror, when the tingling began, would be followed by a stern lecture, in which she instructed herself to pull herself together. Pulling herself together was something she did well; people who knew her admired her level-headedness and confidence, while being exasperated by her stubborn side. Her man liked to tell her she could out-stubborn a mule, but he usually only said that when he didn't get his own way.

In spite of her frequent self-admonitions that she was well rooted in this world, and in this world she would stay, she still couldn't bring herself to take a single mirror down. In fact, she had developed a second line of defense—just in case. This line of defense was color. She surrounded herself with it, wrapped herself in it, hoping that her very brightness, the assault on the eye that she launched upon onlookers simply by walking into a room, would keep her fade proof. Hers were the sugar-drenched colors that greeted her every day, sitting on the shelves and spread out on the counters of the little candy shop tacked illegally onto the front of her house. She'd lived all her life there, in a quiet street in Curepe, a town that sat just at the point where Trinidad's northern mountain range sloped gently to flat ground.

The store was owned and run by her grandmother, Louisa, who made most of the candy herself. Mattie's grandmother spent her days in the kitchen preparing batches of old-fashioned sweets, like multicolored paradise plums or pink-tinted mounds of shredded coconut clumped together with crystallized cane sugar. For her part, Mattie worked out front, selling their wares to the dozens of children who came racing in before and after school, and who sometimes cut a class or two and needed a place to spend those precious stolen moments.

From the time she was old enough to work there and earn money of her own, she filled her life with candy-colored clothing, each item as sweet and soft as anything Louisa made. The wooden cupboard that dominated the far wall of her bedroom was chock-full of amazing dresses: lemon drop yellow and cotton candy pink, coconut cream blouses to be worn with orange soda fizz scarves. Her underwear drawer looked like a spilled heap of Jordan almonds: pastel pinks, blues, yellows, and greens, nestled among frothy whipped-cream white. Her pantyhose always matched her jellybean shoes. Her dressing table was a confusion of bright bangles and earrings, rum-ball eye shadow, and berry lipsticks.

Today, though, she wouldn't be wearing anything that fancy, even though it was March twentieth, and this was the day she turned twenty-four. Instead of the marmalade birthday dress she'd had specially made, and which had been hanging on a nail on the wall for over a week, she'd put on the darkest garment in her wardrobe: a straight-cut, almost severe affair in Concord grape, which at least covered her arms. Its neckline was decorous enough to hide her breasts, stopping just short of her collarbone. *Good enough for church*, she thought. *Good enough for a funeral*—but just barely. She wasn't stupid; she knew that convention dictated she should be wearing something somber, like black or gray, but she'd never owned a single black garment in her life, not even so much as a hair ornament. Black reminded her of licorice, and licorice was the only sweet she couldn't stand. As for gray, well . . . Candy didn't come in gray.

She bent over to secure the strap on her deep wine shoes, feeling the tension in the skirt as her bottom strained against the fabric. She was a petite woman: five-foot-two if she was lucky. Fine-boned, dark-skinned, and small-featured, with little-girl breasts and a waist you could encircle with one arm. But she had a rear end that flared behind her, which led to fleshy thighs that drew the gaze of many a man in the street, before tapering off to calves and feet that were more suited to someone of her diminutive size. She'd decided long ago that there was nothing she could do about an ass like that. You weren't going to see her getting up early to jog around the neighborhood like a maniac. Her unusual shape made her feel confident and resilient, like one of those bowl-ing-pin-type toys that you could hit as hard as you wanted, but always bounced back upright.

She was making sure the small slit at the back of her skirt was properly straight when she heard a sound behind her. She spun around. "Auntie Lou."

Her grandmother's soft, wide shape, which billowed above and below her plain cotton dress like jelly bubbling over on the stove, filled the doorway. Obviously, Louisa enjoyed her own confections as much as her customers did. Mattie didn't remember ever having called her Grandmother or Gran, or anything of the sort. Like all the other children who thronged into the storefront every afternoon jostling for attention and position, waving money in the air, Mattie had taken her cue from the painted shingle that Louisa had hung above the door: "Auntie Lou's Sweetie Parlor." (Louisa was old enough to still call a sweet shop a "parlor".) Even Mattie's own mother, Claudine, had never called her Mama.

"On your mother's soul, Matilda," Louisa said. Her hands were clasped before her, resting on the mound of her belly, twisting in an attitude of anxious supplication. "Please, don't go."

Mattie tried not to let Louisa spear her with her gaze. Once that happened, you were done for. She let her own glance skitter around the room, in any direction other than that of the doorway.

Louisa persisted. "You don't have to."

This time, Mattie did lift her head, and stared straight at her. "I *do* have to go. Today, they putting my father in the ground. I have to—"

"To what?" Louisa interrupted. "What you have to do?"

"Pay my respects." Mattie was firm. She looked around for her hat. It was deep purple, like the rest of her outfit. Not exactly the same shade, but close enough. She patted it gently onto her head, pushing it down over the thirty or forty corkscrew braids into which her thick, short hair was twisted. The hat was fitted with a fine net fascinator that she could draw down over her eyes, hiding most of her face. Did her grandmother not think she had planned this carefully? If her face were well hidden, she wouldn't cause a scandal. She'd go, sit at the back, and leave before anybody noticed her.

"What respect, Mattie?" Louisa had one of those booming, authoritative voices, just the kind of voice you would expect to come rumbling out of a body that size. This morning, she was using it. "What about respect for his family? His wife and daughter? And all his friends, all those people he knew—"

"All those people he never told about me? Everybody he had always been too ashamed to admit to that he had a bastard daughter? What *about* them?" She struggled to keep her voice level. Raising it against her grandmother was not an option.

Louisa stepped into the room and laid her arm on Mattie's shoulder. "Your father was never ashamed of you. You know that. He came to see you, every week, and left money—"

"He came to see my *mother* every week—"

"That's not true. Even after she was gone, he came. That's the action of a man ashamed of his own blood?" Her mother had been dead two years, snatched away by cancer that had not lingered, but which had pounced on her like a wild beast from the trees overhead, leaving them no time to prepare for their loss.

Mattie wanted to twist from her grandmother's grasp, but she didn't dare. Instead, she turned Louisa's own argument against her. "Then, why should I be ashamed to show up at his funeral? He's my father. I . . ." *Loved him*, she wanted to say.

"Not shame, Mattie. Compassion. For his widow and his daughter. Spare them the shock of seeing you there. It's hard enough for them as it is, him gone so sudden and all, without them having to find out about you . . ."

"I have my veil." Mattie tried to make her see it would be okay. "And I'll sit at the back. Nobody has to ever see me. Nobody has to know—"

"You walk in there with your father's eyes on you . . . lion eyes, and you think nobody gonna notice? Your father left his print on you. It's there in the way you hold your head and the way you smile. You don't think nobody gonna see?"

"It's a funeral. I won't be smiling." Mattie forced three long, pearl-tipped pins through the crown of her hat, regretting her haste with them as one grazed her scalp.

She wasn't sure she'd smiled at all these past few days, ever since Sunday, when she'd spread the paper out on the floor as she liked to do, to get down on her hands and knees over it and devour every word, only to learn her father was dead.

Big story, all the way up on page five, about this rich, power-ful man whisking his wife and daughter out to Queen's Hall where all the fancy people went, to see the Russians dance, only to drop dead in the middle of the show. Heart attack. No warning. Then Louisa finding her slumped with her fore-head on the floor, hands over her eyes blocking out the light but failing to stop her tears from leaving dark marks on the newsprint before her.

"I'm not smiling," she repeated firmly.

Louisa's mouth opened again, deliberately, taking on a shape so harsh and contemptuous that Mattie knew just what she would say next. *Whom* she'd be talking about next. Mattie scrunched up her eyes and braced herself, but the wait was mercifully short.

"I don't know what I'm supposed to do with you," Louisa said, a *tsk-tsk* sound on her tongue. "You too stubborn. That's the problem with you. You too stubborn. Nobody can't tell you nothing. And since you been hanging 'round this Blood-whatsizname, you been even worse."

"Blood Pye," Mattie corrected, but it made no difference anyway. Auntie Lou knew her boyfriend's name. She just chose not to remember it.

"What kind of name that is, me and God will never know. What you doing, picking up with some scamp that ain't got a better name than Blood—*anything*—I could never under-stand."

She hated it when her grandmother started up on her on-again, off-again man. Having doubts about your man was one thing. That was a woman's curse: to find yourself sitting in your quiet moments and asking if the man you were with was what you really wanted, and if you couldn't honestly do better. If you waited long enough, the feeling passed. But hearing those same doubts coming from someone else, espe-cially someone who had lived long enough and seen enough to quite possibly be right, was another. Mattie protested.

"You know that's not his real name. You know his mother never watched him in his bassinet and called him no Blood Pye. Reuben just likes—"

Louisa went on as if she were deaf. "Since you hook up with this no-good, can't-find-no-job man, I been praying for you. Just praying and praying, and asking the good Lord—"

"He's got a job," Mattie interrupted. *Sort of.*

"Raisin' a whole bunch of nasty fowl-cock, saying he fighting them, out in the bush behind God back, in the middle of the night, just waiting for police to come snatch him up, you call that a job? I call that one step short of bein' a bandit." Louisa placed both hands under her huge breasts and hitched them up, a gesture she always made when she was fixing for a battle.

There wasn't time for this. Couldn't Louisa see that? Arguing about Blood Pye could wait. The longer the better, actually. Right now, all she could think of was being there when they laid her father to rest. It would help so much if she had Louisa's blessing to go! Mattie searched for and found her bag, slung it over her shoulder, and made for the door. There she stopped dead. Louisa was blocking the doorway, and she wasn't a woman you could circumnavigate easily. "Please, Auntie," she whispered. Anxiously, she toyed with the broad gold bangle that encircled her left wrist, twisting it around and around, and running her thumb over the deep markings on the surface.

Louisa's eyes dropped to the band. Her dead daughter's married lover had placed it on Mattie's wrist three years ago to the day, when she had turned twenty-one. Its underside was inscribed "Matilda, love, Daddy." Mattie never removed it except to gaze at the letters carved there, and to feel the roughness of the few engraved words with a longing finger.

The determination on Louisa's face gave way to pity, and Mattie waited. "It's a terrible thing," Louisa said eventually. "Young girl like you, and no parent around, this stage in your life when you got more questions than answers." Resignedly, she heaved her bulk to one side, leaving room enough for Mattie to pass. "I know I'm gonna regret this, but you go, pet. Just be careful."

"I will," Mattie promised. She let Louisa follow her down the stairs, through the family room, to the store out front. The air in the room was filled with the perfume of sweets that had sat in large Mason jars and mayonnaise bottles through the decades, until their mint and cinnamon and ginger and vanilla filled up the pores of the wooden counter and the surfaces of the calendars that lined the walls, many dating back as far as the seventies, which Louisa kept around for decoration rather than any functional purpose.

Even with the parlor empty, its walls rang with the sound of small running feet, and little hands banging on the countertop, children arguing, demanding service, coins bouncing down on the glass or slipping from their grasp to spin away on the concrete floor. Every evening when the store closed, Mattie tidied up and wiped the glass counter free of the sticky fingerprints that her clients left behind, but doing so could not erase the echo of their high-pitched, clamoring voices.

She lifted her cherry red, three-speed bike down off its hooks on the far wall and wheeled it to the front of the store. The paint, though faded, chipped, and scratched, was the red of adventure. She checked it over for soundness, carefully avoiding Louisa's eyes, but bracing herself for her comments.

Louisa did not disappoint. "You riding to church? In a dress? Why you don't take a taxi? Come, child, let me give you money for a taxi."

Mattie heard the keys to Louisa's rusty cash pan jangle, and she protested. "I don't need any money, Auntie. I've *got* money on me."

"So take a taxi. You can't turn up at the churchyard on that thing. It's not decent . . ."

"But, Auntie Lou, I need to think. This helps me think. Don't worry . . ."

Her grandmother looked worried nonetheless, but before she could say anything more, Mattie popped open the front door, flipping over the CLOSED sign to say OPEN, and wheeled out onto the pavement. She slung one leg gracefully over in spite of her skirt and got off to a fine start, sailing out onto Xavier Street, which led to the Eastern Main Road, and from there, it was just twenty minutes west to the city. She barely took the time to wave goodbye, pedaling hard to be out of sight before Louisa could change her mind and call her back, but just before she moved out of earshot, she heard her grandmother warn, again, "Be careful!"

Mattie pretended she hadn't heard.

Blood Pye

Reuben "Blood Pye" Hinds was not a greedy man; so he had to keep telling everyone. He just wanted what he was entitled to. And considering the kind of shit he had to take every day—getting up early to prepare the right food for the cocks, food for champion warriors, cleaning up after them, keeping them free of ticks, seeing to wounds they had managed to get during practice, and most of all, trying to keep the police from crawling up his ass—he was entitled to plenty.

Cockfighting wasn't an easy career. You didn't just get up one day and *decide* you wanted to be a cockfighter—or at least, you didn't if you expected to be a winner. Fighting on impulse was for jokers, and the one or two slackers he knew who thought they could ease on through life and just fight a few cocks on the side usually got what they had coming to them: the humiliation of seeing their bird slashed into bloody strips in the *gayelle*, the fighting ring.

Amateurs, too, were the ones who usually got the police on their scent, because they were the assholes who couldn't keep their yaps shut. They always had to go trying to impress whichever air-headed, high-breasted piece of tail they were hitting at the time, with chat about what they did late at night out back of some country bar. They were the ones that got drunk and started inviting every Tom, Dick, and Harry out to see their cocks fight. Acting like it was just another sport, the same as small-goal football or wind-ball cricket, nothing more than that. Like it wasn't something sacred, noble. Like it wasn't a wonderful God-sent thing that you talked about in whispers only among the initiated.

Standing out in his backyard with the sun still making up its mind whether to get up or not, with the black-blue-purple of night slowly giving way, and the air rent with the sound of his cocks welcoming the dawn, Blood Pye sucked his teeth. There were things about the sport—about the *art*—that those slackers would never understand. They hadn't been born into the tradition, like him. They hadn't learned at their father's side how to put together a feed mix that would turn a promising young bird into a superstar. Their grandfathers had never taught them how to identify and cull the useless females from your flock early, so you wouldn't be wasting good feed on them.

The art was in his blood. There had been a Hinds who fought cocks as long as his people had been in the islands. One of his ancestors, a slave to an old Spaniard in Manzanilla, had lived better than any free black man of his day, with his own house and the liberty to come and go as he pleased. The story went that this slave even had slaves of his own that came down from the Great House every day to cook and clean for him, mend his clothes, and keep his garden going, all so that he had his time free to spend in the stables, rearing and training the most formidable fighting cocks the island had ever seen. Breeders had sailed from as far as Cuba, Martinique, Jamaica, and Santo Domingo just to buy his studs, and a medium-range cock with a good fighting history could fetch more on the auction block than a Negro.

A hundred years later, birds belonging to Blood Pye's grandfather had become so feared throughout Trinidad that those who were tired of losing bird after bird to him in the *gayelle* began accusing him of using obeah to curse their birds. His grandfather used to tell stories about the time a rival breeder had put a price on the head of Malice, a champion black-plumed demon that had won an unprecedented and still unrivaled thirty-four fights in succession, and how some rum-sucking fool had taken up the challenge. The man had been standing at the perimeter fence, so busy contemplating a way over the razor wire stretched overhead that he failed to anticipate the old man's sharp hearing. Hinds Senior had rocketed out of bed before the intruder had even begun his climb, snatched up his shotgun, and shot him in the shoulder. The man survived, but lost the use of his left arm, and Reuben's grandfather had done time for aggravated assault, in spite of having dragged his bleeding victim into his yard before calling the police, in order to plead that he'd merely been stopping a trespasser. He hadn't been put away for very long, just enough to enhance his reputation around town.

Malice was put into retirement, whereupon he happily studded with any female he was matched with (at least, those that survived his sexual confrontations, which could be as aggressive as his battles), and eventually died of old age within months of Hinds Senior's own passing. To the day of his death, Blood Pye's grandfather had insisted that his greatest regret in life was not having aimed well enough in the heat of the moment to shoot the drunken bastard hit man in the heart and be done with it.

The Hinds touch was passed down from man to boy. Father taught son, and so it went. One day, Blood Pye expected that if he ever had a son—at least one that he chose to acknowledge—he would teach him what he had learned. If he was good enough, he'd earn himself a fighting name. A name was an honor, not a right. The one he himself had taken referred to a type of plumage that made even veterans quake. Some cocks were gold, some black, some flame red or ochre. A blood pye cock was a cock from hell: chest feathers the color of heart's blood deepening toward the tail until they rose in a spume of black as dark as those few seconds in which life slipped away. It was a name filled with power and might. It suited him, he thought.

Blood Pye stood in his yard with his hands on his hips, sniffing the air. There was always a sweetness to it this hour of the morning, one that people who got up after sunrise would never understand. The cool morning air was like light fingers on his scalp, which he shaved twice a week or so. He'd started losing his hair at twenty-five. It was the Hinds curse, as much as cockfighting had been the Hinds gift. In order to avoid the emasculating sensation of watching his own hairline recede, he'd decided the hell with it; he'd shave it all off and be double damned. In the past five years it had served him well: he found that it added a little something to his image, and when he greased it up before a cockfight, the menacing gleam intimidated his rivals.

There was a tiny sound behind him, one that other people might not have heard under the riotous crowing going on all around, but Blood Pye had better ears than most. "Where you been?" he asked, looking down.

A small, brown paw patted his leather boot lightly, and he leaned forward to scoop the mongoose into his arms. The creature made an affectionate sound and butted his head against Blood Pye's palm, like a cat insisting on being petted. "I been looking for you all over, Threes," he complained, hoisting him up onto his shoulder and staying still until his pet could find his balance. "Where you went? You got a girl out there I should know about? You went walking?"

Not that he could go very far. Threes was aptly named, as he was missing his right hind leg, which had been lopped off at the hip by a trap set by Blood Pye himself. He was not a cruel man; but business was business, and mongooses and rats roaming your yard at night picking off your young cocks was bad for business. So Blood Pye had routinely set traps to catch any voracious intruders. In the morning he used to check the traps and despatch without prejudice anything he found in them. Killing didn't bother him: he couldn't allow it to, considering the line of work he was in, and it had to be done. In general, he liked animals, but not when they threatened his livelihood. It wasn't personal.

But on the morning in question, which, if he remembered correctly, was nearly two years ago now, he had gone to check the traps and found a little mongoose inside. It had been caught by the hind leg, which was now a mangled mess connected to its host by only a few strips of flesh and skin. Usually, a trapped animal would be panicked, snarling and spitting and trying to bite, right up until the moment when he snapped its neck. But not this one.

This fellow had just lain there, perhaps too delirious from the pain to protest, or even to feel fear. It was younger than the ones he usually caught; this was probably its first foraging trip away from its den. As Blood Pye had pried the trap's teeth away, the leg separated from the stump, and with the creature's blood staining his hands, he had leaned forward to put it out of its misery; but as he'd done so, something had stopped him. Maybe it was the eyes: clear, brown, unafraid. Surely it had known it was about to die! And it had to have been in excruciating pain. But even as his hands had closed around its neck, it hadn't struggled. Instead, its pink tongue had flicked out and licked his palm.

Blood Pye had been stunned. Confused, he'd pulled back, loosening his grip, and stared at the pointed face. The eyes had held his. He'd tried again, but could not get past the look in those eyes. Finally, he'd gathered up the small bundle, dripped water into its mouth with a wet rag, and placed it in the corner of an unused pen, leaving it to die on its own. At nightfall it was still alive, and so he'd fed it boiled egg and meal. And so on the next day, and the next. By the time the creature was up and hobbling around, Blood Pye had grown quite fond of it, and even let it sleep on a chair on his verandah.

He still set traps, but they were less lethal, designed to capture, not to hurt. Threes lived on eggs and whatever leftover

liver, beef, and meal he ground for the cocks. The one meat
Blood Pye never let him have was chicken, lest he develop a
taste for it, but he didn't need to be afraid. The mongoose
never ventured into the cock pens alone, and even if he had,
his diminished speed would have made him no match for any
of the birds. A well-aimed talon would have finished him off.

"You look happier than me," Blood Pye said conversation-
ally to Threes. "At least you ain't got no worries. You get up,
and you got water and food waiting for you. You ain't got to
stress yourself like me." He stopped at the door to the first of
a series of stables. Inside each stable were half a dozen separate pens, built so that the single cock inside had ample room
to walk about, exercise, and keep its legs strong. He placed
his hand on the lock, but couldn't go farther.

He was scared. Big man like him, afraid of what he might
find once he opened the door. It would be funny if it weren't
so serious. Last night, two of the cocks inside had been looking poorly, and try as he might to treat them, something in
his spirit had told him that they wouldn't be alive by morning. These weren't the first. For three whole weeks he'd faced
each morning with a sickening rolling of the stomach that
only came when a man was seeing his livelihood slipping
through his fingers. Something was killing his chickens.
Something virulent, something fast, and something that he
had never seen before, a malevolent microbe that was moving—how? From pen to pen? Beak to beak? By water or
air?—until, if he didn't stop it, it would touch and destroy
every dream he had ever had for himself.

He'd brought an old vet in, a man who knew about the
business and understood the importance of keeping his
mouth shut, and he had some ideas; but none seemed to go
anywhere. To find the truth, they would need tests, and tests
meant money. The solution, when it came, would mean more
money still.

But where would the money come from? Cockfighting
could be profitable if you knew what you were doing, but it

was managing the money afterward that was hard. He'd had a bit of bad luck at the cards lately. Mattie, this chick he was checking, had told him more than once that only a fool would win a fortune on the cocks and then lose it at the card table; but she was a woman, and women didn't understand. Cockfighting was about being a man. Card playing was about being a man. It was that simple.

He steeled himself and opened the door, moving quickly from pen to pen, checking for sound and movement, knowing without needing proof that it was too quiet in here. Threes leaned forward, balancing expertly on his shoulder, peering down to see what he was looking at, and Blood Pye was sure he understood what was happening.

Two dead. Two bundles of feathers, each in its own cage, each contorted, neck arched, claws rigid, as if the final agony had been greater than an honorable death in the *gayelle*. Blood Pye acted swiftly, letting his speed obliterate the pain he felt. He placed the two bodies in a crocus bag and then, hesitating only briefly, twisted the necks of the other four cocks in the stable, trying not to cry out as he felt the bone give under his hands. His cocks were like his children; he knew them each by name, weight, habits, and personalities. This was murder. But it would not have been long before whatever had killed the other two would take these four as well, and if he dared to let these outside for exercise or practice, what was stopping them from contaminating the rest of the flock? Maybe if he acted now, the disease that crawled the walls and floors of this stable would stay here, until he had time to purge it.

He slung the crocus bag over his other shoulder, feeling the final frantic convulsions of the dying birds inside. At the far end of his yard he doused the entire heap with gasoline and struck a match. The stench of burning feathers made his eyes water. When there was nothing left but ashes, he attacked the stable with brown disinfectant as thick as blackstrap molasses, diluted in water, sloshing it on all the walls and scrubbing it into his floors until his hands hurt, while Threes watched from a rafter. As he launched attack after attack on this invisible enemy that was taking his livelihood away, his mind ran on Mattie again. He wished she could be here with him now, in his time of distress.

This surprised him, as women rarely came to mind unless physical need drove them there. But his heart was hurting, and Mattie was soft and sweet and would listen. But she would be burying her father today; even he wouldn't call on her, at least not right away. He was a gentleman, after all. But when he did see her, he'd need to talk.

Jonah

"You're going to spoil the knot."

Jonah looked at his wife in surprise. He hadn't even realized he was tugging at his tie. The damn thing was choking him. Port of Spain was hot, and the navy suit he was wearing, though lightweight and well cut, made him even hotter. The tie was pale lemon, a color he would never have chosen for himself; but Justice had an eye for these things, so he left all such decisions up to her.

What had surprised him was not the fact that he'd been fiddling with the constriction around his neck, but that Justice had actually spoken. She hadn't said a thing all morning. As a matter of fact, she hadn't said a whole hell of a lot since her father died three nights ago. He'd done all he could to comfort her, but she had a way about her of receding when she was thoughtful or sad, to a place he could never reach. Although she had known him almost her entire lifetime, and been married to him for three years, she still wouldn't let him in at her times of greatest pain. From deep inside himself, Jonah sighed.

Her hands were soft against his throat. "Look," she chastised, "you messed it up. It's all crooked now."

"I'm driving, Tish," he protested gently, but held the steering wheel with one hand and leaned as far back in his seat as he could to allow her access to his neck without obscuring his view.

"What?" The voice came from behind his head. "What is it?"

Jonah lifted his eyes to the rearview mirror to meet clear, cool ones half hidden by a black lace veil. His mother-in-law was playing her unexpected role to the hilt: black broad-brimmed hat, veil, scarf, gloves, oiled-silk dress, stockings, and patent-leather shoes. Hair freshly straightened, dyed ebony, and drawn back smoothly in a roll, sprayed so stiff a good wind wouldn't budge it. Make-up flawless, all done by a beautician hired to make a house call at seven this morning to ensure that the new Widow Evers was presentable when she faced the wives of the financiers, politicos, lawyers, doctors, and the rest of the Port of Spain elite who would be swarming down upon her husband's funeral. The only trace of brightness about her was the double circlet of pearls that shimmered at her neck, enhanced by the single settings in her ears. Not yet fifty, she dressed older, like the society ladies Jonah always felt so uncomfortable around, and whom she was so eager to emulate. "What is it?" she repeated. He felt the pressure of her satin-gloved hand against the back of his leather seat.

"Nothing, Faith," he murmured.

"Jonah messed up his tie, Mama," Justice explained. There was not a trace of malice or condemnation in her voice.

A stab of annoyance came directly from Faith, hitting him like a thumbtack at the base of his neck, and then it was gone. Back into her own thoughts. Quiet.

As Justice finished with her fiddling and settled back into silence, Jonah reached over and caught her hand before it could fall into her lap and gently laid it on his thigh. He kept his own lightly over it, letting his fingers trace its shape, down to the pink polished tips of her fingers, and back again to the slender wrist, where a band of beaten gold sat snug.

She'd gotten so thin lately. He could just about encircle her arm below the elbow. She'd begun to worry him. There had been a soft sweetness about the girl he'd married. Not fat, not nearly, but a tender roundness to her limbs and waist that he could still remember against his own flesh when he got out of bed in the morning. Then she'd started dieting. Slowly at first, giving up treats she liked. Ice cream. Puffs. Last Valentine's Day he'd bought her Belgian chocolates filled with orange liqueur: there was a game they often played where they passed that giddy stuff from mouth to mouth, and he'd been looking forward to playing it again. But although she'd thanked him and smiled, the box had sat unopened on her dressing table until the ants came.

Later, she gave up bacon and sausages. Then butter, then sugar. Nothing he said or did could convince her that she was fine as she was. When she started weighing her food, he'd taken away her scale. She'd gone out and bought herself a new one.

He took his eyes off the road long enough to look down at their joined hands. Her self-imposed restrictions had made her paler than usual, and the contrast between their skin tones was sharp. Hers, a mellow beige, her bloodline having been thinned over the generations by commingling with the old-time French Creoles and Portuguese, leaving her just enough color to still legitimately lay claim to African ancestry, yet not enough to provoke the unspoken racism of the exclusive and protectionist high-brown circle into which she had been born. His was quite a bit darker, but not so much so that it was a problem with his mother-in-law or her peers: his mother was *panyol*, bush Spanish, with a splendid head of wavy brown hair that fell to her waist, freckled skin the color of sand in the sunlight, a fine, high nose, and wide almond-shaped eyes that turned up slightly at the corners. Although, as he'd been told, his father had been dark-skinned and heavy-featured, Jonah still looked enough like Rosalie Reyes to satisfy any disquiet that onlookers might have felt at the Evers family having been infiltrated by a boy from the beach with no evident pedigree.

All this thanks to Dominic, who had not only welcomed him into their home, but had set about guiding the direction of his growth as one did a sapling, until he was suitable for membership in his family. He'd been a man of class who didn't see class, not in the way those around him did. When Jonah was eleven, a scholarship to a good Catholic boys' school in Port of Spain had changed his world from one of sand paths and wooden walls to paved roads and concrete. Rosalie, proud to the point of tears, had stitched him three sets of uniforms, bought him his first pair of real leather shoes, and packed him off to Port of Spain, to stay with her sister, Elba—who just happened to be Dominic's live-in maid.

Dominic had ignored Faith's protestations that the ragged interloper was not welcome; another mouth to feed and nothing to show for it. He'd insisted that Jonah could stay as long as he liked and brushed aside all offers from Elba to take a pay cut to compensate for the boy's room and board. In fact, he'd been intrigued by the bright youngster who never ceased to ask questions, and gave him light tasks around the garden, teaching him how to prune, mulch, and mold rosebushes so that they fulfilled their promise of glory. Their afternoons in the garden grafting hybrids transmuted into evenings in Dominic's teak-paneled study, where both could be found with their heads together, poring over old books. They later invented a game between themselves, in which Dominic would spin a huge old globe that stood on brass fixtures in a corner of the room and shout out the name of a city, mountain, or river. Jonah had thirty seconds to find it: if he did, Dominic gave him twenty-five cents. If he failed, Jonah found himself adding an extra page of reading or sums to his already heavy quota of homework. Young Jonah proved to have a head for numbers, and soon he was racing through his school assignments in order to have time left over to discuss golden rectangles and the magic of compounding with his mentor.

Dominic had stood by him, and now that he was gone it was Jonah's turn to be the stalwart in the family. He caught Justice's huge, round green eyes—Dominic's eyes—gazing at him. There was anxiety there, loss, and something very close to panic. He gave her a reassuring smile. The smile she matched his with was forced, but brave. In spite of his concern, her answer to her mother mildly irritated him, but his irritation couldn't be directed at her. Although at twenty-three she was not exactly a child, there was something about being near Faith that always brought Justice to a state where she could exercise no guile, nor keep herself from blurting whatever was on her mind or the tip of her tongue.

He'd known Justice since she was three or four and was used to seeing any composure she maintained with others crumble in the presence of her mother. Whether it had been about getting caught playing with her dolls out on the damp grass, or running across the lawn to the maid's quarters where Jonah had once made his home to beg him to come out and throw her tennis balls, or later, sneaking off the grounds to go to the cinema with boys when she was under curfew, Justice couldn't lie to her mother. Faith was not a woman to be lied to.

Unlike her daughter, Faith guarded her feelings jealously. Any detectable grief or pain was safely enshrouded in a dozen chilly layers of cool composure, tucked away behind a veil of stage fright. Anger knotted Jonah's stomach. The primary emotion to come pouring out of Faith right now was nervousness, the kind an actor felt on the day of a big performance. Could she really be more concerned over pulling this whole thing off well than she was with the fact that her man was dead?

Over the past hideous nights and days, when Jonah held his wife close to let her sob out her grief, with his own tears of loss and devastation seeping into her soft brown hair, Faith had revealed nothing. Instead, she had twittered on about flowers for the house and linens for the table, and a guest list for the post-funeral luncheon. She had consulted etiquette books to determine whether it was appropriate to transfer the engagement and wedding rings Dominic had given her from her left hand to her right *before* or *after* her husband was in the ground.

But Dominic deserved better than that. He was a good man, a great one, and he had a right to be properly mourned. Hadn't Faith loved her husband? She must have, although through all the years he had known them both, he couldn't think of a single definitive incident in which this woman had ever shown any feelings toward him that surpassed mere affection. Jonah was a good Catholic—at least, a passable one—and couldn't conceive of a marriage formed without love. And if so, how could you lose your life partner and not look and feel as though a part of you would be buried with him?

In Jonah's village, death was met with a great hue and cry: the whole community descended upon the house of mourning, stretching canvas sheeting across bamboo poles in the yard to make a tent, strewing borrowed chairs and tables, placing candles all along the road leading to the house, so that anyone who passed knew that the Angel of Death had visited. Every night until the burial, people played cards and dominoes, sometimes cooking fish broth or crab and dumplings in cauldrons on three big stones out in the yard, and when they were good and drunk, they played the radio loud and sang and told stories about what a great person the deceased had been, even if everyone knew he was a son of a bitch. In death, there were no distinctions. In death, you were duly grieved and feted.

But in Dominic's house, there were party planners and caterers discussing menus. What a trite end for a man who had been more of a father to him than the stranger who had left a few droplets of sperm in his mother some thirty years ago, before getting dressed and walking out into the night! This was the man who had been torn from the fabric of Jonah's life. This was the man whose wife failed to mourn him, at least in any visible way. It was enough to shake his faith. Weren't the good entitled to be honored?

As Jonah turned the low, sleek, silver car into the church lot, he slipped his fingers under the fine wire frames of his glasses to touch the lids of his eyes, brushing away the hurt, exhaustion, and futility, and feeling moisture there, too. This surprised him; he had thought he was done crying. He brought his hand up before his eyes, attention diverted from the driveway by the damp smear. And then a bump, the grinding crunch of impact, the sound of metal tearing metal, so high-pitched it made his back teeth hurt, like chalk on a blackboard.

His body tense and alert. Justice squeaking beside him, and Faith struggling to regain her balance, holding on to his headrest for support, pushing away from the back of his seat, where she had been shoved forward at the moment of impact. After glancing around to be sure they were okay, he thrust open his door and bolted round to the front, where people were already gathered, to see what he had hit.

A tangle of metal under his front wheel, a bicycle seat crushed and twisted, spokes torn from their hub and standing straight out, like a warning signal from the spines of a scorpion fish. A huddle of limbs: a girl or a woman, in a dress that was a remarkably ugly shade of purple. Strange, how even in this horrible circumstance his brain could remain dispassionate enough for him to notice and process such a detail, but the mind was funny that way.

Two men were already reaching out to her, trying gently to disentangle her from the wrecked mess on the gravel.

"Careful," Jonah warned the shorter of the two. "Her

neck. Her back. Be gentle." He brushed away the man's hands, a little too roughly, and peered down at the girl, who by now was struggling to free herself from their helping grasp. A smear of blood darkened her skirt, but where it had come from, he couldn't tell. He tried to restrain her as she attempted to get to her feet. "Don't."

She halted in midmove, both hands pressed flat on the ground, and lifted her head. She was small-boned, but from what he could tell, an adult. Her face was pointed, almost elfin, with a narrow jaw and a full mouth that was contorted with pain. "Hurts," he thought he heard her murmur. She panted like a thirsty deer.

A silly purple hat was jammed down upon her skull, its net veil obscuring the upper half of her face. Her eyes were shadows behind the fabric. A wave of irritation rolled over him. If the fool child hadn't been trying to ride with her eyes covered in the first place . . . but then he reminded himself that it was he who had been distracted. *He* had hit *her*.

"What hurts?"

She panted harder, lips drawn back so he could see her eye teeth, but didn't answer.

His eyes fell to the smear of blood on her skirt. "Tell me," he insisted. "Where does it hurt? Let me get you to a doctor."

"Nowhere." She levered herself up from the ground with both hands and stood, dusting off her clothes. "Nothing hurts." She looked down at her bike, and her mouth moved convulsively, as if it were a well-loved dog slain on the roadway.

Jonah stepped between her and the crushed bike in a bid to spare her the pain of the unpleasant sight. Inside the car, two faces were blurs behind the smoked glass, but they were both watching intently. Other cars lined up behind him, extending out into the street, and already impatient drivers were leaning on their horns. Woodbrook was a genteel old neighborhood, lined with smartly painted English colonial houses, all with near-identical lacy gingerbread trim. In the quiet of the morning, the sound of the horns hung in the air like irritated punctuation marks.

He glanced at the church and the dark oblong coffin clearly visible just within its wide double arches, flowers draped over it like a centerpiece at some lavish feast. Then he turned back to the girl again, who was bent over, futilely trying to pull the wreckage out from under his front wheels. She looked well enough, but he'd heard of people who had walked away from accidents as if nothing had happened, only to keel over later from some grievous, unseen injury. He moved to restrain her, cursing himself for being so careless, wishing this had never happened, or at least, wishing it would all be over soon, so that he could take his place under the arches, standing guard over Dominic: a son's duty.

"You can't get it that way. Let me move the car; then I'll get it out for you. And then . . ." He hesitated and looked fleetingly over to the place where Dominic lay. "Then, the hospital. You understand?"

The fat mouth took on a stubborn set. "No. I don't need a hospital."

He insisted. "A good one. A private one. I'll pay. I'll take you there." A sound from the car cut him off before he could finish. Faith was winding down the window and looking out, impatient. "Jonah? Are you going to make us late? I don't want to be late, do you hear? And there are people behind us. Cars . . ."

As he began to answer her, to say, *Please, Faith, be patient, this is a crisis*, or even, *You can walk to the church, Faith, it's just over there*, the damn girl was yanking again at the twisted wheel. Did she honestly feel that she could shift a thousand pounds of metal to set it free? Once again, irritation colored his concern, and he moved to pull her away from the bike. As he bent near, the source of the blood on her skirt became evident to him. A tear ran a good five inches down one side of it, and it had begun to adhere to the gash on her upper thigh. The stain was spreading fast, oozing across the fabric like a flower opening on sped-up film. The sight of the blood, and her nonchalance toward it, made him briefly queasy.

"I told you, you can't—" He stopped, the words drying up in his throat, turning to dust before they could leave his mouth. In an effort to stop her, his hand had come down on her wrist, closing over a band of metal that was as warm and alive as human flesh, and seemed . . . familiar.

He looked down at it, not letting her go, but turning her arm over, riveted by the trinket, the size and shape of which he knew by heart. His wife's gold bangle curved around this strange woman's wrist, with its raised carvings of dragons flying mouth-to-tail all around it, wings taut, outstretched, bodies sinuous, half lizard, half snake. He stared, his thumb obscuring a dragon's head, baffled. This was the bracelet Justice had worn since her twenty-first birthday, when Dominic had slipped it onto her wrist with a kiss.

It was heavy, hard. On their wedding night, a mere month after she'd turned twenty-one, Jonah had been making love to Justice for the first time, and she'd moved her arm in the dark, accidentally striking him across the mouth with it, crushing his lower lip against his teeth until the soft flesh split. She'd kissed him deeply, even though his mouth was full of blood, her tongue warm, relishing the salty taste. Laughing that it would somehow seal the new covenant between them. Blood for blood, she'd said. He'd drawn hers with his loving just moments before; the evidence was smeared on his thighs. It had been only fitting that she should spill some of his.

The woman in the purple dress struggled to pull her arm away, but his hand locked around it. He looked frantically over at his wife, who was still strapped to the front seat, staring at him, leaning forward until her face loomed larger. This was impossible. Justice was wearing her bracelet. He'd touched it moments before, when he'd held her hand. She never took it off, not even to shower. "Where'd you get this?" He fought to keep the aggression out of his voice, but it was there all the same. Justice's band was not store-bought. It was handmade, and one of a kind, commissioned by Dominic just for her, engraved on the inside with her name and the date.

The girl showed her teeth in a snarl and wrenched away. "None of your business. Leave me alone." She seemed anxious to go now. With a final, agitated look at her bike's remains, she spun around and skirted his car, moving surprisingly fast.

Without thinking, Jonah was after her, shouldering his way through the crowd, which had grown thicker with funeralgoers and gawkers. Before he could gain ground, Justice threw open her door, hitting him square in the chest.

"Jonah, all these people . . ." She waved her arm to indicate the line of cars that now stretched down the driveway and out into the road. Even traffic not connected with the funeral had become ensnarled, and a cacophony of horns grated in their ears. People were getting out of their cars and trying to gain access to the churchyard on foot. Others had just forced their way through the crowd to curse at the cause of the holdup.

He looked from his wife to the fleeing purple figure that was almost out of sight by now, and then again at the car. He didn't debate long. He tossed the keys in her direction, underarm, gently, as she wasn't a very good catch. Justice fumbled, and they hit the ground. She bent over and picked them up by the key chain, puzzled.

"Move it aside, and take your mother into the church," he told her. "I'll be there in a minute."

She held the bunch of keys in her hand as if they were a fat, fractious spider. Her mouth was a circle. "What?"

"Just park it, Tish." He was sharper with her than he meant to be. "I'll be back." He rushed past her, not looking at her face, because he didn't want to see the confusion he knew would be written there. Confusion justified; it was twenty minutes to start time, and in the absence of a blood son, he was to be Dominic's lead pallbearer. He could see the priest in his robes hovering at the top of the front stairs, peering out into the parking lot. This was not a time to act on impulse: Dominic needed him, and he had always been there before. But something in his gut was telling him that this woman held a secret, a message, a key, and he had to wrest it from her. He wouldn't be long.

Out on the sidewalk, he broke into a run, unhindered by the squeaky new leather shoes he had bought for the occasion, which were already gnawing at his instep. His damned yellow tie flapped in his face. The narrow roads of the old quarter of Port of Spain in which the church lay had been designed a hundred years ago for horse-drawn carriages, and the advent of the automobile had prompted no attempt to widen them or their sidewalks. He had to shift and dart between startled pedestrians, once or twice losing sight of the girl, but her anxiety left its own trail behind her, like a cold Atlantic current swirling through the warmer waters of the Caribbean Sea. By sheer determination, he gained ground. She swung a corner into an even narrower alley and would have been lost to him, but the street was empty except for a few parked cars; so Jonah abandoned the safety of the rutted sidewalk to streak up the middle, feet thudding on the bitumen. He was a tall man, well over six feet, with long, muscular, athletic legs. With three years of college track behind him, and weekly rugby games since then, he was fit, and the much smaller girl was no match for his speed, in spite of her head start. He was upon her, surpassing her, and then turned sharply to cut off her escape.

Her own momentum made it impossible for her to halt in her tracks. She slammed into him, hitting him hard in his chest, and Jonah felt a puff of air on his neck as the wind was knocked out of her. His arms came up to steady her. He had expected her to be slight, but her flesh was warm and firm. Though trapped, she was still defiant. "Easy," he murmured soothingly, as if to a restive horse. "Easy now. Steady."

She was winded and obviously tired. "What you want? Why you hunting me down like this? You mad?"

Maybe he *was* mad. Chasing after her and cornering her in an alley as if he were a mugger. Jonah opened his mouth and tried to put forth an explanation for his actions, but none came. What could he say? *I chased you across four blocks because your bracelet looks just like my wife's?* Maybe it was a stupid mistake. Maybe Dominic's jeweler had lied to him about Justice's bracelet being one of a kind, or cheated a little by waiting a while and then knocking off a copy and selling it to someone else. Hell, maybe there was a factory out there, in Taiwan or China, just cranking them out by machine. He began to feel like a jackass. He realized he was still holding her against his body, and he let her go, but remained alert, prepared to act if she should take flight again.

But somehow, she knew exactly what had caught his attention. She thrust her hands behind her back like a naughty child with jam-smeared fingers and hung her head. To his horror, he noticed she was trembling. He backed away.

"I'm not a thief," he began. "I don't want to take it from you. I just wanted to know—"

"Know what?" Aggression. Defiance. Fear.

"Where you got it. My friend gave this to . . . My wife has one just like it. I was wondering . . . This sounds stupid, I know . . ." It did. Even to him. He stopped, not wanting to make a bigger fool of himself.

The alley was quiet, as neither of them spoke. Behind her, a stray cat rummaged through garbage, and the sun beat down on them from a cloudless sky, throwing harsh shadows. In every line of her body there was mute rebellion.

This couldn't go on. He was wasting his time, and anything he tried to say now would only make the situation worse. He made a placatory gesture with his hands. "Don't bother. It's not important. Forget I asked, okay? I'm sorry. Now, please, just let me take you to a doctor."

She lifted her pointed chin, mouth set stubborn, upper

teeth still bared, making her look like a trapped fox. There was a wide gap between her front teeth, which even in her hostility was disarming. He didn't need to hear her speak to know that she would once again refuse. But with that one movement of her head, his planet shifted out of alignment. The silly purple hat, with its ridiculous old-fashioned veil, teetered and slid backward, with the tops of a plastic pin or two poking through it. The hat had been dislodged by the impact of the accident or by her impetuous flight. Either way, the fact was that it had, indeed, moved, and now her face was bare to his view. Her hand snapped up from behind her back to catch the hat and set it right, her eyes flew open, startled, and Jonah had the answer to his question.

Lion's eyes. Hers were huge, almost cartoonish, round, wide, and their tawny gold center was fringed with a green as deep as the heart of the sea. They were doubly stunning set against her dark skin and her thick, black, woolly corkscrews of hair, like unset gemstones in a box lined with black velvet. Incongruous as they were, hostile as they were now, they brought a heat to the small face that transformed it. He didn't need to be told that in the early morning their green was deep enough to swim in, or that by night their irises were like the moon in eclipse. He lived with those eyes every day; they were the last thing he saw before he shut his own. They shot sparks at him during the sweet heated battle that ensued between him and his wife among their tangled sheets. They were Justice's eyes, and this strange young woman could only have inherited them from the same person who had passed them on to her.

"Dominic," he breathed. His heartbeat thudded in his ears.

With nothing left to hide, the young woman did not let her head hang down again, but instead remained riveted, unflinching under his shocked scrutiny.

Dominic's daughter. Dominic's secret. His eyes darted about, searching her for other characteristics that would be further proof of her paternity, but saw none. Dominic had been huge, wide-shouldered, taller even than Jonah, and had fought a lifelong battle against the extra forty pounds that eventually proved his undoing. There was no evidence of his large nose and lantern jaw, heavy limbs, not even in any muted feminine translation. He searched further, looking for Justice in her, but if they were sisters—who was he fooling? There was no question about it—the similarity stopped at those eyes.

She could be no younger than Justice was and probably not much older. The thought struck him that they could be close enough in age for Dominic to have commissioned both pieces of jewelry at the same time. Ah, that was it. There had been two birthdays, not one. Two bracelets.

It was obvious, then, that this woman was not the result of a youthful premarital indiscretion, as Dominic and Faith had been married for over a quarter of a century. She could be nothing other than the living legacy of an extramarital liaison, and for some reason, this shocked Jonah to the very core.

He was not a man of little experience, as far as women were concerned. He had brought to his marriage bed as much knowledge of women and of things sexual as would any man his age. He had reveled in the flush of teenage discovery, the realization that girls were soft and sweet smelling and made him ache. He'd survived the lunacy of his college years, when young women were knowledgeable, available, and sought no more emotional ties than he did himself. Later, in his twenties, he had become more judicious, exploring not just his sexuality but his own emotional complexity, been more selective and patient. He'd had his heart crushed, more than once, but in so doing, he had learned to love and be loved. So he was ignorant neither of the world nor of the passions that lurked in the human heart.

But Dominic, he was different. A stoic, a man of few words, shrewd at business, powerful, always in calm self-control. But kind, decent, upright. For fifteen years he had served the church by helping with the collection baskets every Sunday, offering his own personal secretary for one half-day a week to manage church accounts and finances. He had belonged to the Lions, the Kiwanis, and a handful of men's clubs, and every Christmas had thrown a party on his own lawn, funded out of his own pocket, for fifty orphans. He had been a gentleman's gentleman, a doting father, and a solicitous husband, even to a wife as cool and demanding as his was. But he had not been a philanderer, not a cheat. This was something Jonah would have been prepared to stake his life on.

Until now. The woman hadn't moved, but withstood his unflinching scrutiny with an unreadable expression. When he turned his head away, reeling, numb, she spoke. "Finished?"

Finished? Not nearly. There were so many questions he needed answered. A hundred. More. The first one came unbidden to his lips. "Did you know him?"

"Know him?" Her laugh was harsh, mocking. Dismissive. She turned toward the entrance of the alley. "Did you?" She began to walk unsteadily, but determinedly, away.

Jonah made no move to follow, although everything in him screamed to do so. Shame stayed his feet. He'd run her to ground here, like an animal. He was bigger and faster, she was injured, and yet he had hunted her down. How could he press her further? Time to go back. He'd return to the church, bury his mentor, and then wrestle with his questions on his own. He pressed his fingers to his temples, discovering that his head hurt.

At the mouth of the alley, she stopped and swayed, and before his mind could tell him what was happening, before he could react and sprint toward her, she reeled, knees buckling, and thudded to the ground, her hat rolling away.

He was not quick enough to prevent the impact, but even as she hit she was in his arms. One hand behind her head, the other frantic, feeling for a pulse. It was weak, and her ashen skin incriminated him. Without any thought for her modesty, he lifted up her torn skirt, pressing down on the gash both he and she had forgotten. Blood. Smeared over his hands, her thighs, and her deep berry-colored panties, not pumping from the wound, but oozing, draining away onto the paving.

She was heavy in his arms, and limp, and as he emerged from the alley with her the astonishment written on the faces of onlookers barely registered. He ran with her out into the street—to hell with the cars that swerved to avoid him—shouting above the horns, begging someone, anyone, to show the mercy of God in their hearts and stop and help him get her to a doctor.

Justice

Man is lonely by birth,
Man is only a pilgrim on Earth . . .
Where was Jonah? Justice looked at her watch, but it was
only three minutes later than it had been when she'd looked
at it three minutes before. The service should have started
half an hour ago, and Father Shaunessy was getting restless.
He paced from the font to the steps and back, his shiny black
shoes barely making a sound on the marble floor, and had
begun to twiddle with his vestments. She could just imagine
what Mama was saying to him; what with the wrinkle on her
brow making a lie of her plastic apologetic smile, and her
fine-boned hands fluttering in small agitated gestures as she
struggled to explain her son-in-law's disappearance. The five
pallbearers, all members of one or the other of Papa's men's
clubs, were huddled near to his coffin, murmuring among
themselves.

Like the wind in the trees,
Man has been rather reckless and free . . .
At Mama's urging, the choir had begun to fill the uneasy
silence, singing over and over one of the dirges printed on the
heavy, watermarked, keepsake programs. Justice wished she
could shove her fingers into her ears and not listen. How she
hated that song! That mournful, doleful organ, echoing

through the rafters like a cry of anguish from the depths of a lost soul. And those awful words, all death and loneliness.
Like the grass on the lawn,
He will pass by the way and be gone . . .
There was no comfort in those words, no solace, no shred of consolation upon which to lay down her burden of grief. Why did they have to sing those awful, awful songs at funerals? They might comfort the dead, but all they had to offer those the dead left behind was distress.

Two gray women, shrunken with age, their handkerchiefs pressed to their tear-dampened cheeks, strained to look over into her father's coffin, which still lay on its high gurney. One actually reached in and touched his cold forehead, wet her fingers from a small bottle of bright green cologne—the kind old ladies bought in drugstores for a few dollars to splash on their faces when they were feeling faint—and let it drip onto his thin, flat hair. Justice felt her pain pierced through with a spike of jealous anger. Touched him. They *touched* him. How dare they? They were practically strangers, and here they were, taking liberties. Distant aunties, maybe, or Papa's old friends' widows or mothers. She couldn't be sure. Women who knew him in passing, but not well enough to . . . It wasn't decent. It wasn't. . . .

Jonah wasn't back yet. Justice considered walking back out into the church lot to stand again between the gates where the accident had happened, where he'd hit that girl in the hideous dress, and peer again in the direction he had run; but her high heels were narrow, and picking her way along the gravel made her feet hurt, so she stood at the bottom of the stairs, staring at the gateway and willing him to appear. When he did, it would be all she could do not to slap him for being so stupid. So soft. Why go after the girl? It was her own damn fool fault for being in the way, and if she didn't want help, well, tough. Papa was lying there, still and cold, waiting, and Jonah was out hunting down a phantom on foot. She probably hadn't been on her way to the funeral anyway.

She obviously didn't belong; Justice had asked around, and nobody knew her. Riding in here on a bike, for the love of . . .

"Justice." Satin brushed her elbow. Her mother's voice in her ear. "We're starting."

Justice spun around, almost teetering over, surprise and confusion in her eyes. "But . . . ," she floundered. Begin? How could they? They had to get the coffin inside first, and for that, they needed Jonah. He was supposed to lead, front right. Dominic's right-hand man. He who sitteth at the . . .

"We can't. Jonah's not back . . ." She scanned the entrance frantically, concentrating hard, saying his name over and over in her mind to force him to appear. When she'd been a girl and he'd been already nearly grown, she used to play a game with him from the main house, all the way across the grounds, screwing up her eyes and thinking hard and sending him messages with her mind. He used to tell her he'd received them, and it wasn't until years later that she ever wondered if he'd just been humoring her. But if there was ever that ability between them, even the smallest spark, let it be lit now. . . .

Not a glimmer. No sight of his tall frame or bright features. None of the passing, indistinct figures possessed his familiar, long-legged, confident stride. But still she waited, shifting her weight slightly from one foot to the other, drawing comfort from her body's rocking. Then Mama was ushering her into the church, with one hand in the small of her back, firm, tolerating no opposition.

Confused, it was difficult for her to find her tongue. "But who'll help carry him? We have nobody to—"

Mama cut her off. "Anton Quesnel's taking Jonah's place. Come."

"But Jonah wanted to carry him! He has to! Papa was the only father he ever . . . It's not fair! He'll be back. He went after that woman . . ."

Mama's mouth pursed, fine lines gathering at the edges. The lines were getting deeper of late, probably from a dearth of smiles. "I know where he went, child. But he hasn't come back, and we have guests. It's embarrassing enough already. Do you really want me to keep them waiting longer?"

Justice wouldn't have thought of members of a funeral party as guests, but she knew better than to contradict her mother. Back up the stairs again, through the covey of waiting friends and relatives, most of whom had abandoned their pews and begun gathering in clusters near the coffin. Father Shaunessy was patting his balding head with a white handkerchief. He was fairly new to the island, on a two-year assignment from an Irish diocese, and was struggling to become used to the heat. His face was a brilliant mottled pink, and damp spots had begun to appear on his vestments.

Mama was right, she knew, and the funeral had to go on. But still, she craned her neck toward the street.

"Eyes front," Mama snapped. "Lift your head."

Justice lifted her head. Though her father was being held high on his friends' shoulders, carried along the aisle, and guests were standing and turning to watch his progress, she couldn't bear to look, not even a sidelong glance. The dreadful organ struck up anew, much too slow, dragging out the beats, weighing down her heart. Each mournful, grievous word of every hymn sliced at her, tiny cuts from a sharp instrument, each drawing just one droplet of blood, but the droplets rolled in to meet each other, growing and swelling until at their confluence there was a flood of pain and panic.

Like the wind in the trees. What an unkind lyric. What a callous thought. That a human life could be there, then gone, like a breath. Insubstantial. Nothing. It gave words to her deepest unspoken fear.

She couldn't remember just how or when her death-fear had begun. It wasn't the kind of thing you saw on TV or read about, where somebody lost a parent or a pet in some godawful way, right before their eyes, and forever more was haunted by the specter of it. It wasn't like that.

Her childhood had been relatively untouched by pain; on the contrary, she remembered nothing but sunshine, pretty dresses, piano lessons, and birthday parties out on the lawn. No darkness, no want.

But in spite of this cloak of protection that Papa and Mama had wrapped around their little girl, keeping her from the ugliness of the world, or maybe even *because* of this, Justice lived with a thread of fear running through her. It was a tenuous thing, a ghost that defied scrutiny, like a speck in the corner of her eye that vanished when she tried to focus on it.

As far back as she could remember, she never hugged a family dog without imagining it dead, never stroked a cat without the terrible reminder at the back of her head that one day this warm, purring ball would be stiff and cold, eyes glazed over, lips pulled back in a final grimace. With people, her fear was more deeply ingrained, as there were so many more unexpected ways for humans to die. When she spoke to people, she paid attention to them with only half of herself. The other half would be struggling with a dozen graphic blood-washed images, of car wrecks and murders, earth-quakes and falling walls.

It seemed to her that the more she loved someone, the more violent these images would be. Whenever she left Mama alone in the house, it was all Justice could do not to phone every hour, just to assure herself that bandits hadn't swarmed over the high wall and smashed their way past the gates and doors and alarms, and that that perfect, long, ele-gant neck wasn't now marred by blood spurting from a slit throat. When Jonah left in that damn fast car he loved so much, all Justice had to do was close her eyes, and she could read the headlines in tomorrow's paper, already seeing it spread open on the table before her. YOUNG EXECUTIVE KILLED IN WORST ACCIDENT FOR THE YEAR, they read in three-inch type. CAR RENT IN TWO, THEN GOES UP IN BLAZE.

These fears were her own personal torment; she shared them with no one, not her husband, not her priest. And now they were real, but when death had come, it had come not for the dogs or the cat or Jonah or Mama, but for Papa, not roaring like a pouncing lion, but quietly, insidiously, stealing his spark from him like a pickpocket.

Justice lifted her wet, sticky lashes. From front row center, that cursed spot—best seats in the house, as if it were a game or a concert—she could see everything. Watch Father Shaunessy with his damn holy water, listen to the awful droning voice with its thick Irish accent, and choke on the stink of incense. She could feel the eyes of the congregation on her, and on the empty place next to hers, and hear with her mind the curious whispers. And the long box of hand-polished teak, with its top screwed shut now, and a handful of dust scattered upon it, a reminder of the dust Papa was to become. But before the dust, the decay. In an hour, he would be in the ground. In a week, the skin would begin to slide from his bloated face. In a month, the grotesque thing in the box would surpass her worst nightmare. Justice gagged, swallowing fast.

Three nights ago, the best seats in the house were theirs. Queen's Hall, with its high, barreled roof curving over her head and music swirling around her. Papa on her left, Jonah on her right, and she was happy. When word spread that the Bolshoi ballet would be in town, Papa had booked tickets. Six months in advance, something that wasn't usually possible. But Papa was a powerful man, and a phone call was all it had taken.

She'd seen Handel's *Water Musick* interpreted in dance once before, in London, when she was fourteen, alone with Papa. She'd felt so grown up, floating in on his arm in her first gown, seated by his side, with her gold opera glasses and a gilt-edged program she later took home and placed in her oak chest of treasured things, next to the ballet slippers she'd worn when she was five and the half dozen padlocked diaries she'd filled in in her perfect, rounded handwriting.

This time, she was with both of her men, Papa tall and handsome and at ease, eyes closed, soaking in the glorious music rather than watching the dancing. Jonah uncomfortable in his suit, but quiet, rock still, engrossed by the scene on the stage, enchanted by the fluidity of the dancers, whispering to her that they really *did* move like water. Mama next to Papa, more proud to be seen at the ballet than to see the ballet itself, waving at the beautiful people to ensure that they all knew she was there, too. After a while, Justice closed her eyes, letting the grand music rise and fall and wash over her, sharing Papa's pure distilled pleasure at it.

But then the curtain fell, and the applause thundered, and Justice leaped to her feet, the closing movements repeating in her ears like echoes off a cliff face. She threw Jonah a smile. He was awed, eyes bright, rising to his feet, too, glancing over at Papa, thanking him again for bringing them. And then she bent forward and threw herself on her father, arms going around his neck, saying, "Papa, Papa, it was wonderful."

But something was wrong. The music had faded, the lights were up, and people were leaving, but he hadn't moved. Eyes still shut, like one transported.

"Papa?" Her lips were against his warm cheek, but he was ignoring her.

Then Jonah shoved her aside, lifting her by the waist and pushing her into her mother's arms, hoisting Papa by the jacket into the aisle and down onto the floor, flat on his back. Slamming him in the chest, punching him with both fists like a man gone mad. She remembered screaming, "Jonah! Jonah! Stop it! Are you crazy?" She tore at him, trying to halt the insane attack, feeling his shirt collar scrunch under her hands. The fine linen held and did not tear. Her mother started shouting, first trying to haul her off of Jonah's kneeling form, then letting Justice go and running up the aisle, clawing at the few stragglers in the theater, begging them to *help, help, help!*

The beautiful people gawking, sidestepping the insanity. Jonah with his lips fixed on Papa's, blowing into his mouth, ripping at the buttons on his white pin-pleated shirt and baring his chest, and still pounding.

And even then, she didn't understand. Even then, she stood stupidly by, thinking the world had gone mad. It wasn't until Jonah had stopped his manic attack, slumping forward on his knees, with his head on Papa's chest, tears falling onto the matted hair, that comprehension came to her. Papa had left her, slipped away through a back door while no one was watching, even while they were sitting next to him. He'd not made a sound, not a gasp or groan at the moment that his heart had stopped. Cheater. He'd denied her the right to be prepared. She should have known in advance and had the time to ready herself to grieve. For that, she would never forgive him.

Mama's elbow in her side dragged her back to the present. "Stand up," she was saying. "Get up, Justice."

She blinked, confused. She looked around again for her husband, but he still wasn't there.

"Up," Mama said again. "It's time."

They were wheeling the thing that used to be Papa back up the same aisle he'd walked down to marry Mama twenty-five years before. The five men and the impostor who had taken Jonah's place flanked the box, each with a hand placed lightly on one of its silver handles. Mama urged her out of the pew. She'd forgotten; she was supposed to walk behind the thing. That was her job today, to walk with her mother out to the sleek hearse and then follow it over to the cemetery and stand there while they put it into the hole and then threw dirt on it.

Her black linen dress itched and stuck to her in the worst places. It was hot, and she was scared and alone and choking on her own panic. And Jonah wasn't there. He wasn't there. He'd put some strange woman first and left her to her misery. She watched as they put the box into the yawning black vehicle, and let people hug her and whisper things at her and her mother before piling heaps of flowers high on the top of the

coffin and the long car. The churchyard was filled with murmurs, quiet chatter, and the sound of engines starting. She
stood next to her mother and stared blankly at the open gate.

"You still have the car keys?" Mama asked.

Justice nodded.

"Drive," she said.

"But Jonah . . . ," she began.

"Drive."

Mattie and Jonah

"Daddy didn't have a son," Mattie said to the man next to her, but it was not as much a statement as it was a question. He wasn't the only one who could probe for information. Something about him told her that the two men were close, even if it was only the uncanny way he'd looked into her eyes and seen her father there and the defensiveness and aggression and shock that had come to him after. You had to know a man, love him, to be at the same time so hurt and curious and aghast by such an intimate secret.

He was definitely not a son. A nephew, maybe. Or more likely, a close friend. Assistant. Colleague. He didn't look anything like Dominic: almost as tall, but much slimmer, harder. Good looking, in a way, but the light skin and crisp, curly brown hair were closer to half *panyol* or Portuguese than Dominic's French Creole heritage. And in any case, he'd said his name was Reyes. Jonah Reyes. Spanish name, all right.

"No, he didn't," the man said. He took his glasses off—ones with wire frames so thin they were barely visible, and that meant money—and passed his hand across his eyes. "Not really."

"'Not really'? Wha's that mean?" The drugs the doctor had given her made her tongue heavy, and her words tripped clumsily out of her mouth. But at least her thigh didn't hurt like the damn devil. She slipped her hand down between her legs to touch the thick bandage that covered the wound. Five stitches. She wondered why doctors always had to tell you just how many stitches you got. Like they were proud of themselves, or they thought you needed the exact figure to impress your friends and relatives with when you got home. "Five stitches, miss," he had told her. He was a dark-skinned Indian man, small, as short as she was, and his big teeth were white in his face. "Five whole stitches." She'd given him a groggy half smile and then struggled against Reyes, who was trying to be a saint or a knight or something and lift her and carry her out of the clinic the same way he'd carried her in. But she hadn't needed him. She'd had a needle full of pain-killers stuck into her arm and drunk a glass of some nasty glucose mess and left there on her own two legs, dammit.

"Wha's 'not really' supposed to mean?" she repeated. "He didn't have a son, period. If he did, I'da known."

His mouth had an ironic twist. "And a few hours ago, I'd have said he had only one daughter."

Mattie sniffed and turned her head away, staring hard out the window of the taxi. If he thought he was going to goad her on that, he was wrong.

The taxi driver had a stretched-out old dub tape on, and the pounding bass and unintelligible Jamaican lyrics hammered away at her temples. She was too tired to tell him to turn it off, and disappointed that Reyes hadn't had the decency to ask on her behalf. Maybe he liked bad music. She turned her head so she could peek at him without being caught doing so. He was a fine piece of work. Well bred, well put together: the type she didn't quite trust. Suit neat, except for the mess he'd made of it lifting her earlier. Nails trimmed, hair freshly cut. She'd be willing to bet he flossed his teeth every day and that his underwear was stark white. She almost laughed. He probably didn't like much music at all, especially not the kind that had anything resembling a beat.

Pampered all his life; didn't know what work was. What being poor meant.

At least he'd been decent enough to hire the whole car, rather than have them suffer the usual mode of transport, squashed in with three other passengers. Three purple twenties pressed into the driver's hand and the car was all theirs.

They were on the Churchill-Roosevelt Highway, heading east, home. Their backs were to the city, with its ochre curtain of smog, and Mattie was glad of this. She didn't like Port of Spain; it was hard to breathe there: too crowded and too noisy. But to be free of the city you had to traverse the wasteland that was the Beetham, a dumpsite that sprawled on the edge of a vast mangrove swamp, where an endless convoy of trucks abandoned garbage every day. Curlicues of foul-smelling smoke rose from the dump, where scattered fires burned without cease, and where young men from the filthy, ramshackle houses on the opposite side rifled through the garbage to salvage anything worth taking, or waited at the gates to leap onto garbage trucks, scrambling into the yawning compactors to get first pick. Boys played cricket with makeshift bats in the mud at the highway's edge, and skinny dogs lolled around and watched, too hungry to take part in the games. She concentrated on the images that sped by, and as she watched, her breath made frosty patterns on the glass window. She wiped them away with her arm, so as not to cloud the reflection of herself that she could see there. The pale shadow of her own face, superimposed on the scenery that passed by, helped her feel grounded and calm.

He tried to make peace and fill their silence by giving her the information she had sought. "Son-in-law," he offered. "I married his daughter."

Of course. Dominic's daughter—she had never thought of her as her sister—had married, three, maybe four years ago. She couldn't be quite sure when. Dominic had never talked much about his other life when he visited, and that was just the way she liked it. He cut loose every memory of it the moment he crossed into her grandmother's yard, pretending that it didn't exist, or that the little house in which he'd spent one afternoon a week all her life was reality, and everything else was a walking dream. And if he could shut it all out, so could she. It was better that way, for everyone.

So she ignored the peace offering of the man who sat next to her, discovering that she didn't want to know after all, especially if it meant his being nice to her. She was tired and angry, and he'd ruined her day by taking off after her instead of letting well enough alone. And now he knew things about her that she didn't want known, so she was better off just not liking him.

He spoke again. "How's the pain?"

"Painful."

"We can stop and fill your prescription, Matilda." He said her name as though he were tasting it. "When you get home, you can take a pill and go to sleep. I can stay with you until you fall asleep if you like." He'd shifted and was leaning near her, looking concerned. The ugly vinyl on the car seat, a nasty, sticky brown that she didn't like having to touch, squeaked as he moved.

Like she didn't have anyone to take care of her! Auntie Lou would do just fine, she wanted to tell him; but that would be information, and information about her was something he'd been probing for all morning.

He misunderstood her hesitation. "I'll pay for it; you don't have to worry about that. Just tell me if there's a pharmacy you usually go to, or if we can just stop off at any one along the way." His eyes were on her: dark and patient.

There it was, that ease with money, the same nonchalance Dominic had had. She'd seen it on his face earlier when he'd paid the clinic's bill, barely glancing at it before handing over a shiny metallic card. Like a man who hadn't had to do any quick mental arithmetic, trying to conjure up his bank balance, adding and subtracting, determining exactly what he

needed to do without between then and next payday in order
to pay what was being asked.

He wasn't like her and her kind. Buying something wasn't,
for him, a matter of having to give something else up. She
knew all about that. Auntie Lou's store didn't bring in much
money, and judging from her prescription, the medicine she
needed would cut deeply into what she had. But his paying
for her would be charity, and charity stuck in her craw. Of its
own volition, her lower lip jutted. "I don' need you to buy no
nothing for me. I can fill it myself."

He leaned forward so suddenly she flinched. "I'm not asking you to take anything you're not entitled to. I hit you.
With my *car*. You got hurt. It's my responsibility to—"

"You don' have a funeral to go to?" She cut him off, distracting his attention and struggling against the hold that the
medicine had on her tongue, enunciating carefully, determined to master her own speech.

It was an unkind thing to say. Insensitive. He sat back in
his seat as if the air was seeping out of a pinhole in his side.
"It's finished already," he told her. "It's over." He looked at
his watch. It was stainless steel, heavy and smooth and glowing, not at all shiny and loud. It looked as though it had been
carved from a single piece of metal. Just like the one her father wore. Maybe they had bought their watches together.
Maybe Dominic had given it to him; he'd been a generous
man and loved giving presents. "It's too late. I missed it. He's
in the ground now." His voice was low and thick.

Mattie tried not to feel guilty. It had been her fault, that
accident. She hadn't been paying attention, lost in her
thoughts, going over her plan one last time, to approach the
last pew from the back and to stay there, unnoticed. She'd
ridden into the churchyard with her fascinator pulled down
over her eyes. She'd been clumsy and rash. She'd done a stupid thing.

"I'm sorry."

He shook his head. "No. I am."

"You missed the service. You shoulda been there with your wife. And my father's wife."

He lifted his shoulders and let them fall. His jacket was draped across his knee, and she could clearly see the bulk of his arms through the white shirt that was smeared with her own drying blood. "I bathed and dressed him this morning. At the funeral home. His wife just couldn't face it. She's not that kind of person. She wanted to let the funeral people do it, but I couldn't let him go away like that."

Mattie glanced at him, mildly surprised. Bathing the dead was such a country thing. Not the kind of thing she'd expect from a sophisticated young man such as this. His kind, her father's wife's kind, preferred to pay and have the service done by a total, uncaring stranger, rather than give the lost one the final comfort of having their intimate needs handled by someone who loved them. Grudgingly, she admired him for it.

He went on. "I've never done that before. I never lost anyone like that before. It was . . . hard. But at least I got to do *something*." He made a soft, choking sound.

"He'd have appreciated that," she tried to reassure him. She considered reaching out to touch him on the arm, but thought better of it.

Reyes nodded. "He would have." He was quiet for a while, thinking. He took his glasses and toyed with them, twisting their arms into impossible shapes and then watching them spring back. He was waiting for a moment, and his hesitation filled her with dread. She knew what was on his mind. She glanced around the inside of the taxi like someone looking for an escape hatch. The car was suddenly too small for both of them.

Then his eyes were sharp again, on her, unflinching. "Did you know him? Tell me." There it was again, that hunger in his eyes. For knowledge. For information. As if his lack of knowledge left him out of control, and loss of control obviously wasn't something he was used to. That was it: he was not hungry; he was afraid. Not knowing scared him.

Mattie glanced out of the window once more. They were ten minutes from home. Ten minutes, maybe fifteen if the traffic got any worse, and then she would be free of this man and his questions. Then she wouldn't have to tell him a damn thing. But he seemed so bereft, so needy.

"I knew him," she relented.

"How well? Did you see him? Often?"

"Every week, most of my life. Every Wednesday evening. He came over and brought food and money, and we sat in the living room and watched TV and talked. Played games. Monopoly. Chinese Checkers. Cards." She watched his face, waiting for a reaction.

"*Dominic* played *cards?*" He looked bemused, unsure that they were talking about the same person.

The memory made her warm inside. "He was a shark."

His eyes were on her, alert. Then a slow smile spread across it, rueful, understanding coming. "Wednesdays, eh?"

"Most of them."

"He told us he had meetings every Wednesday. Men's clubs, Lodge, Kiwanis, something. I can't remember now. He just came home from the office, showered, and left. He never set a business appointment for Wednesday evening, and he never stayed home. That's been going on forever. We just knew he was busy on Wednesdays. We never asked."

"Never curious?"

He shook his head slowly in amazement. "No."

Now it was her turn to smile. Stupid, blind boy. Trusting without question. That had been Dominic's gift. He had a way about him that when he spoke, he left you thinking that his words proceeded from the mouth of God. Heaven knew he'd had that effect on her mother. Enough for her to love him all her life, to the exclusion of anyone else. She wondered what this man would say if she told him that after the family coziness in the living room, after the Monopoly and the cards, Claudine and Dominic would inevitably make their way up to her room and shut the door.

"And your mother?"

Mattie flinched. Uncanny, the way he honed in on her thoughts. Or maybe not so uncanny; it was an obvious question. Still, she bristled defensively. "What about her?"

He shrugged. "I don't know. Just tell me . . . *something*. Anything."

"Dead." She didn't feel like elaborating.

"I'm sorry." He looked uncomfortable, but not enough to quell his curiosity.

"Why? You kill her?" She felt him flinch at the bitterness in her voice.

The large hand that fell over hers was firm and warm. "Matilda, I'm sorry. I don't mean to pry. I just need to know. Anything I can find out."

"Why?"

"Because this is the last thing I expected when I got up this morning. You took me by surprise, okay? And I'm trying to deal with it. And the way I deal with things is to ask questions."

"Because knowledge is power?" She grasped his wrist to throw his hand from her, but somehow didn't have the energy to do so. She left her own hand closed over the satiny metal of his watch. Its silvery coolness was like drying leaves.

"Because knowledge is understanding." He was staring at her, and she had the strangest feeling he was trying to read her as one read a book written in a foreign language: with great effort and concentration. It made her uneasy. He was staring too hard—no, listening too hard. She squirmed.

"What's there to understand? Men have children all the time. This is the real world, not some fantasy you made up in your head where everybody's perfect and just the way you want them to be. They have sex; they have babies. And not just with their wives."

Something about her words hurt him deeply. She watched unnamed emotions work their way across his face. "I know. I'm not a child; you don't have to tell me that. I know how the world works. My own father—" He bit off whatever he was going to say. "But Dominic was . . ."

"A saint?"

"No. I'm not that naive. But he was never a man to be frivolous. He was a stoic. He was strong and quiet and serious. He prayed."

"Just because he put up with his bitch wife all these years, and went to church on a Sunday and bowed before statues and gave money to the poor, didn't mean he didn't have a dick. He was a *man!*"

His brows shot up in reaction to the venom in her voice. "A good one."

"Too good for my mother?"

"That's not what I said!"

"That's what you meant!"

"No!" The bones in her hand ground against each other under his tightening grip.

"What, then? What you meant?"

He drew his hand away from both of hers, and she grasped her wrist defensively against herself. "I don't know." He sounded truly bewildered.

Mattie sucked her teeth in exasperation. Damn prissy city boy, with his fucked-up, straight-laced ideas about how other people were supposed to be. "Look at yourself. Listen to yourself. Going on about how good he was." She sneered. "What? You think the fact I'm alive make him any less *good?* You see me for the first time today, and realize who I am, and all of a sudden you love him less, because as far as you concerned, he not as *good* as you thought?"

He raised his voice in protest. "No! I don't love him any less. I could never love him any—"

"You behaving just the way he said y'all would. His family. All of you. It's people like you that had me walking in the shadows all my life. Daddy *said* you'd never understand. That's why he never took us anywhere. That's why when he came to see us he brought dinner, always some fried chicken or some Chinese shit, and we had to eat in the house. Like we were this nasty secret instead of a family. He said you people could never know, because you'd act like . . ." She waved her hand around, searching for a comparison. "Like this!"

He didn't pull his head away when she pointed her finger dead center in his face, like a gun about to go off. "That's not true. That's not fair."

She laughed. "No? So you understand? What you understand?"

He conceded slowly. "Nothing . . ." He was going to say more, and then he halted.

"Well?" she needled.

"But I would if you told me more. Tell me."

"Why? So you can keep sucking information from me? Like blood from my throat? Like a *soucouyant?*" The harsh laugh came again.

"Don't be ridiculous." Even though she'd called him a vampire, he didn't take umbrage. Even though her hand was still sticking into his face, he didn't brush it away. "Don't condemn me for not understanding and then refuse to explain it to me. Tell me more."

Outside, the traffic slowed and thickened. They were entering Curepe, her hometown, and as an access way to all cardinal points, it was jammed. Cars, trucks, schoolchildren on foot, all clogged the street. She didn't have to stay here and listen to his badgering; she could walk home from here. She leaned forward and spoke to the driver. "Pull aside, man. Lemme out."

The driver glanced up at her in the rearview mirror and put on his turn signal, trying to negotiate his way to the curb.

Reyes shot forward, his hand on the man's shoulder. "No. Take her all the way home. Xavier Street." He turned to Mattie. "That's what you said, right?"

"What I said don't count no more. I'm getting out." She grasped at the door lock, but her sweaty fingers were slippery.

"Drive on," Reyes told the man. He didn't need to raise his voice.

The man gave her an apologetic glance. "He the one that pay me, miss," he explained, and pulled back into the dense traffic.

Mattie scowled, thwarted, and didn't answer.

"One more," Reyes pleaded. "One more question. And that's all." He waited, and then took her silence for a yes. "Your mother. How long did he know her? Did he know her before he was married? Why didn't he marry her? Are you older or younger than my wife?"

"That's one question?"

"Humor me."

"Then after that, you finished?"

"Yes."

"Promise?"

He nodded.

"Okay. But no interruptions."

"Fine."

"And no clarifications."

"No problem." His eyes were steady on her, holding hers by will alone. She didn't have to push him any harder to know he wasn't backing down.

She inhaled. Her head throbbed, and though her tongue was lightening up, it tasted like drain scum. She began. "Dominic met my mother when she was fourteen. He was a student; twenty-one, twenty-two, maybe. Between classes, he used to walk out the university gates, right over there." She pointed in the direction of the sprawling college campus, no more than a mile away. "Looking for something to eat. He liked sweets."

"Tamarind balls," Reyes began. "He always kept those around. In the car, and in his desk drawers—"

She glared at him, and he shut up. "He used to come into my grandmother's parlor to buy sweets, once in a while. And then one day he saw my mother there, helping Auntie Lou out behind the counter. In her school uniform. After he saw her, he started coming more often. He probably put on ten pounds, buying things at the store. Then he used to turn up outside her school gate to walk next to her as she rode home on her bike. He used to walk with one hand on her handlebars and ring her bell for her when she wanted somebody to get out of her way. She thought that was romantic." If she were honest, she'd admit that she thought it was romantic, too. She smiled at her own story, and so did Reyes.

She went on, the facts coming easily to her mind, as Claudine, especially in her last days, had loved to tell the story, over and over, celebrating the romance that had consumed and overturned her young life. For Mattie, remembering it was easy. It was the telling that was hard. "Then instead of him following her to her home, *she* started following him to *his*. To his room on the students' hall."

"Fourteen," he cut in. "That's—"

"Illegal. I thought I said no interruptions?"

He fell silent again.

"They didn't think about it. Or if they thought about it, they didn't care. They were in love. What's right and wrong got to do with anything when you in love?"

He frowned. "You believe that?"

She didn't feel like enduring a lesson in his own personal morality. Did he come from some other world, where everything was good and right, and people always did just what they were supposed to do? "You want me to finish?"

His jaw worked. She watched as he swallowed down whatever he had been going to say next. "Go on."

"Go on where? What more I can tell you you can't already figure out for yourself? They hid it for years, this affair they were having, until she was old enough that they didn't need to hide anymore—at least not from her mother. *His* family

was a different story. Nice boy from St. Clair with a family
business and a last name. Almost high-brown enough to
pass. And my mother, barely finished school, working in a
sweetie parlor. Black as . . ." She floundered for a simile. "As
me," she finally said, pointing to her chest. "You think his
family ever got to meet her?" She glared at him, as though he
should know what she was talking about. As though he was
part of the problem.

"So he did what he had to do and worked for his father
until the man was gone and he got everything that was coming to him. But whatever happened, he made it up here once
a week. He got married, and that didn't stop him. My mother
got pregnant with me, and that didn't stop him. He still left
his wife every Wednesday night and drove to Curepe to meet
my mother. By then, my grandmother was used to the idea,
because nothing she said to stop my mother from seeing him
worked. They couldn't let go, no matter what they tried. And
after a while, they didn't want to let go."

"He could have married your mother."

She waved away his remark. It was a stupid thing to say.
Hadn't he just said he knew how the world worked? "What?
Marry a sweet-shop girl from 'round behind the bus route? A
bright man like him with a master's in business and a future?
He needed a wife who knew what side the knife and fork had
to go on. A nice, light-skinned convent girl who could give
him nice, light-skinned children that'd look like him. That'd
look right in that big house in St. Clair."

"That's stupid. Skin tone has nothing to do with anything."

"Grow up. Did it look to you like he loved his wife? You
knew him. And you know her. Did that look like *love?* Or an
investment, like long-term stock?"

"Did he tell you this?"

"He didn't have to. Every week, once a week, he came.
And gave my mother enough money that she didn't have to
work, and ate with her and me and my grandmother, and

talked and watched TV, and pretended we were a family, and then took her to bed. Sound like a man in *love* with his *wife?*"

He looked confused, floundering to hang on to an ideal that was developing cracks in its foundation. "He had to have married her for love. That's what people do."

"Where the fuck you *come* from?" She sneered. "You for real?"

He leaned his head back against the seat and closed his eyes. "Finish your story."

"That's it."

"No, you and your sister. My wife. We had a deal."

She could have told him that he broke his part of the bargain—no interruptions—many times, but it wasn't worth it. "There's seven months between me and what's-her-name," she said, deliberately obtuse.

"Justice." He knew she was being difficult, but didn't let himself get riled.

"Great taste in names, your mother-in-law."

He didn't answer.

"And *I'm* older." She said it with triumph, as if it made her more of a wanted child. They were turning onto Xavier Street. It was on the old side of Curepe: narrow, with houses scrambling over themselves to get as close to the road as they possibly could. The road hadn't been paved in years, and probably wouldn't be until there was another election due. The driver negotiated the rutted potholes and piles of garbage and hedge cuttings, cursing. Stray dogs shook themselves from their slumber and slunk out of the way, only to resume their positions in the middle of the road when the car had passed.

The day was waning, but still hot, and they could smell the open drains. The houses were for the most part livable, but paint flaked and fences needed mending. Mattie glanced at him, embarrassed by it all, trying to read distaste on his fine features. Dominic had known this street well, even loved it, but this fancy boy would certainly feel at least a glimmer of contempt. But his alert eyes held nothing but curiosity.

"Here, driver," she said.

The car squealed to a halt outside Auntie Lou's parlor, barely able to pull to the curb because of the children who stood around in twos and threes, arguing and chattering. School had been out for more than an hour, but the cluster of clamoring students had not thinned much. The yard was a popular spot, and children lingered there, meeting friends, flirting, trading bubble gum cards and music, especially the older ones, who got out later. One or two smoked brazenly, tilting their heads back to puff smoke into the air, the better to be noticed.

Mattie popped open the door and struggled to get out, but, Boy Scout that he was, Reyes was out before her, racing round to her side to hold it.

"Let me help you."

"I can *walk,* goddammit." She pushed him away. Her thigh hurt like hell, and the bandages pulled at her skin, making her wince with every step. But she was making it in on her own. She ignored him as he stopped to slip the driver an extra twenty, negotiating her way through the group of children and across the concrete covering that spanned the drain running in front of their yard.

Then he was beside her, one hand cupping her elbow, guiding her through the gate. Children made room for them, falling into silence as they spotted the blood that spattered them both. They stared, bug-eyed, riveted by the promise of drama, mouths full of sugar or sweet biscuits or sodas. She knew most of them, having served them, joked with them over the counter, slapped away those who thought themselves man enough to slip a hand near her bottom or try a fast one near the cash pan. In spite of this, she felt conspicuous, embarrassed, longing to be past the parlor entrance and into the seclusion of her home. She was bleeding, and blood was a private matter. Bleeding was something you did quietly, in your own company.

Then, with the suddenness of a thunderclap, the silence broke. The children surged forward in unison, shouting, reaching out to touch her, asking questions in that indelicate way that only children had.

"Mattie, Mattie, what happen, girl?"

"Somebody run you over?"

"You get shoot? You got a bullet in you?"

"Mattie! Mattie! You going to dead?"

Hands, all around, grabbing. Concerned, but curious. Voices getting louder when she didn't answer. She halted in the center of the dirt yard, spinning around in a frantic effort to spot the taxi, thinking that maybe she could run for it and come back later, when the yard was empty and the shop closed, but it had already driven off.

She felt the heat of bodies pressing against her, their skin against hers, as they jostled for a better vantage point. Her mouth rounded like a fish's. They were using up her air; there was so little left for her. She opened her lungs, fighting for it.

His jacket fell around her shoulders, long enough to fall to mid thigh, shrouding the bloom of blood that spread across the front and back of her skirt like the signs of an unexpected period. He moved aggressively, setting his body between her and the children, deflecting their rude gaze.

"I'm here with you," he told her. His voice was low enough that only she could hear. "Don't be afraid."

She realized that she wasn't. Not anymore.

Faith

Faith stood at the main entrance to her home, between a pair of heavy, dark-stained mahogany doors that had been thrown open for the reception. Her arms were folded demurely before her, free of their gloves by now, fingers interlocking. Her head, cocked to one side, gave credence to the polite expression into which her features were schooled. Ossie Peterkin was a bore—a phenomenal one. Predictably, he was the last guest to leave, and was taking his own sweet time about it, too. For the last twenty minutes he had been waxing platitudinous about what a great loss to the business community—nay, the world—her husband's death was. About what a brilliant man he had been, what a fine, upstanding citizen, and how everyone who knew him was crushed, shocked, devastated. And if there was ever anything she needed, anything at all, she shouldn't hesitate to call upon him, because if there was one thing Ossie Peterkin understood, it was that young widows had needs, and as a gentleman, he was only too willing to be of service.

Faith nodded at intervals, forcing herself to concentrate on his elaborate, circuitous prose, praying that her eyes would not roll of their own volition. Peterkin knew Dominic from the cricket club, a group of wealthy men who gathered at the Queen's Park Oval not to play cricket, but to watch it, from the best seats in the pavillion, in cool, covered luxury. There, they ate lavish meals washed down by extravagant liquor, smoked cigars, shared jokes, and hammered out business deals in the hallowed club hallways, which no female was allowed to darken.

Peterkin was a powerful man, juggling a vice presidentship at a major insurance company and a chairmanship of one of the largest banks in the city. As such, he could prove useful, so Faith endured his foul exhalations and the sight of nostril hairs that curled down to meet his moustache. Eventually, though, he ran out of wind, wrapped it up, clasped her dry hand between his clammy ones, and made his arthritic way down her neatly paved drive, leaving her to a near-empty house in which she could mourn her husband in peace.

She stepped back inside, snapped her fingers at one of the caterer's lackeys, and pointed at the doors. The boy closed them without a word. The main hall and entertainment area smelled of food: onions from the canapés, and tuna—she'd *told* them not to use tuna, as it stayed on the breath and smelled like hell—from the puffs. One or two stuffed crab backs had survived the onslaught of the hordes, as had half a dozen shrimp cocktails, tails curled over the lips of their champagne glasses, smothered in deep red sauce. The caterer had a thing for seafood, even though Faith had *insisted* that poultry was so much more versatile and graceful. She shrugged.

She signed the invoices for the food and drink, dismissing the urge to haggle over the final cost. She was simply too tired to bother. In the corner of the room, the new maid, Teresa, hovered, waiting for instructions, too stupid to figure out for herself what to do next. Ever since Elba had retired, they just couldn't find anyone who had the brains or the inclination to get to working on her own. Even when she was still there, there had been trouble: from the moment her nephew took it into his head to marry the daughter of the house, Elba had gotten an attitude on her. She'd been near impossible to work with.

Faith pursed her lips at the memory. It wasn't that Jonah wasn't a nice boy; he was, and she supposed he made her daughter happy. It was just that Dominic had always been so full of ideas about people and their station in life—or lack thereof. He'd all but thrown Justice and Jonah together, even when there were young men around who had been far better connected and had come from families who were, well, their kind of people. Justice was young and couldn't truly be expected to understand the workings of her own heart, and she'd always had a crush on Jonah, even when she was just an infant, and he still a growing boy. She could just as easily have been steered in a more suitable direction, but Dominic had insisted. . . .

At least he had qualities that could be nurtured over time. He showed her the respect and deference to which she was entitled, as his mother-in-law, and usually acceded to her requests without a murmur. He'd loved Dominic; that had never been in doubt. Even to the point of assuming the ghastly responsibility of bathing and dressing her husband this morning, a custom that she could never understand, but one which country people—Jonah's people—seemed to find vital. It wasn't something she saw as necessary, not when you took into consideration the sum she was paying the funeral home to manage this whole business in the first place.

Teresa stood where she was, at the far end of the room, probably waiting for Faith to come over and relieve her of the anxiety of her own ignorance, but if she thought *Faith* was walking over to *her*, she was wrong. Faith folded her arms and waited her out. Eventually, it sank in, and the girl waddled over. She was not very attractive—thick-waisted, pudding-faced, and much too dark—but Dominic had liked her. Dominic had liked everybody.

"Mistress Evers?"

"Yes?" she answered, trying to disguise her triumph at winning their little battle of wills.

"What you want me to do now?"

Faith tried not to look exasperated. "I just had two hundred people in here, eating and drinking. Maybe you should clean up after them?"

The girl's face showed no sign of offense at her sarcasm. Perhaps she just wasn't bright enough to get it. "Yes, ma'am."

"And see if you can get the smell of tuna out of here before it sinks into my walls permanently, you hear? I can't abide the smell of stale fish."

Teresa nodded.

"Where's my daughter?"

"In the family room, Mistress Evers." Teresa pointed, just in case Faith should lose her way in her own home.

Without a word of thanks, Faith crossed the wide tiled floor and passed into the corridor leading to a more private wing of the house. The pervading smell of leftover fish was slowly replaced in her nostrils by more familiar scents: teak oil rubbed into the paneled walls, fresh polish on the parquet, and deeper, older woody smells from the African masks and statuettes with which Dominic had lined the walls. Dominic's art was at sharp odds with the house itself, which she had restored in keeping with its original old-world Spanish architecture.

He'd been an avid collector and had insisted on bringing home some horrific phallic statue or barbaric mask every time he traveled to Africa, Guyana, Haiti, or north along the Caribbean archipelago. She, personally, loathed them: they were so crude and primitive. She would have preferred something more civilized and, in fact, kept her own collection of china plates, porcelain knickknacks and Delft tea ware in her own private reading room. But Dominic had reached back into his past and celebrated not the heritage that had given him gemstone green eyes and skin the color of a young antelope, but the one that left a bit of thickness to his lips and the irrepressible kink in his hair that he had succeeded in passing on to their daughter.

For the life of her, she couldn't understand why. He was one of the lucky ones. Couldn't he see that? Instead of thanking his stars for the few slender strands of coding in his blood that had given him access to places and opportunities that so many would never have, he persisted in surrounding himself with reminders of distant and shadowy ancestors. Pity.

Faith stopped before an ugly grinning figurine that stood on a pedestal in an alcove like an evil, lurking spirit. It was one of the older ones and had been in their home at least twenty years. It had come from Ghana, or Mozambique, or some such wretched place. Dominic would have been able to quote its age and provenance without hesitation. She especially hated this one, partly because it was cruder than the rest, gouged out of wood that would have been better suited to a cooking fire, and partly because there was an aura about it that made the hair on the back of her neck tingle every time she passed it. She could never shake the suspicion that it had been infused with sentience by some chanting shaman . . . and the spirit that dwelled within it did not like her. But, as if by a linking of souls, Dominic had been as enamored of it as she was disdainful. It was always the first piece of art that he showed off to friends while taking them through his house, and in times of trouble he would actually take it to his den, set it on his desk, and sit and stare at it, as though seeking counsel from another realm.

Somewhere in her subconscious she had always comforted herself with the thought that if Dominic were ever not there—the word "dead" had never rested well with her—it would be the first to go. In fact, she had often begged him to get rid of it, to give it away, sell it, whatever, and put in its place a nice vase or pot, something less menacing. When they argued, she often threatened to throw it out the minute he turned his back—dump it in the bin like so much trash, or take it out into the garden and incinerate it among the fallen leaves—but her husband had known her threats had been empty and had taken no heed.

The memory of this intention made her pick the relic up off its pedestal. It was heavier than it looked and, inexplicably, warm. She brought it to her face, sniffed it lightly—it was polished frequently along with the others, but somehow smelled of ashes—and turned it around. The hollow eyes held hers, mocking, daring her to do with it what it knew she intended.

"It's over," she told it, keeping her voice steady with effort. It was only a matter of time now, and she didn't want it to think it had her beaten.

The little man said nothing.

Faith continued on her way, still holding the thing, to a room at the end of the hall with a high-arched entrance and bay windows that opened onto the setting sun. The pastel green of the walls, so pale that it was almost not green at all, and the lush ferns that hung from baskets and spread outward in large pots on the floor made it look and feel several degrees cooler than any other room in the house. The wide, spinning blades of the two overhead fans were Amerindian-made and came from Guyana. They consisted of flexible *terite* woven onto wooden frames and were in sharp contrast to the electric air-conditioning in all the other rooms. It was her favorite spot.

Justice was seated at the window, still in her funeral dress, bare feet tucked up under her, arms folded on the back of the seat, looking out onto the driveway like a forlorn maiden awaiting the return of her betrothed from out at sea. Irritation tugged at Faith's lips. Trust Justice to be so soft and patient.

As Faith neared her, Justice lifted her chin from her hands and looked up at her mother. "He's not back yet," she said. Her voice was small.

"I can see that." Faith stopped at the window, letting her eyes stray out onto the driveway in spite of herself. "But it doesn't mean you have to sit here and wait for him. When he gets back, you'll hear the car. Why don't you go upstairs and change out of that dress?"

Justice didn't budge. Instead, her gaze fell to the statuette Faith was still clutching. Her eyes rounded slightly, full of questions, but she said not a word.

"You know Jonah." The room was too quiet for too long; Faith felt she had to speak. "Never happy unless he's rescuing someone, or some thing. When he's finished doing his chivalry bit, he'll be back."

Justice's brows drew together. "Maybe that girl's seriously hurt. There was blood on her. I saw it. Maybe she's dying."

"She's not dying. It's probably just a scratch. She's probably just fine, judging from the way she took off out of the churchyard."

"Then, why's he staying so long?" There was a plaintive note to her voice. "Suppose something happened to *him* . . ."

Faith's tone was wry. "Maybe she found out who he is. Maybe right now she's got his back against the wall, talking compensation. You know how things go. There's only one reaction people have when they smell money: greed."

"That's not true—"

Faith cut across her. "It is true, and you'd do well to recognize it, both of you. It's beyond me how you and your husband manage to wander through your lives unaware of the truth. As a matter of fact, if I know Jonah, he's probably busy trying to talk the girl into taking *more* than she's asking. Always going soft in the head for a charity case. I could never fathom how someone with such a brain for business could be so bad with money."

Justice protested. "He's not bad with money. He's just . . . generous."

Faith tried not to snort. It wasn't worth the effort. She tried with Justice, honestly she did, but there was a little girl in there somewhere who still believed in all the virtues and who held it deep in her heart that the world was, in fact, a good place. She supposed that in a strange way it was evidence that she had mothered her right: protecting her from the evils that lurked beyond the walls of their secluded garden. But still, she feared for her. This girl simply did not possess the necessary tools for survival; it was up to Faith to provide the teeth and claws where Justice had none.

So rather than give words to the response that sprang to her mind, she patted her daughter awkwardly on the shoulder—touching had never come easy to her—and said, "Fine. Sit here if you like, and wait. If you need something to drink, there's orange juice in the kitchen. And some of those damned puffs. Let Teresa bring you something."

Justice made a face at the mention of food, and Faith gave her a sharp look. "Did you eat today?" It wasn't her imagination: her daughter was getting thinner. It was there in the curve of her collarbone, which protruded slightly just above her neckline. In the elbows, the knees. She waited for an answer, and when none came, she persisted. "What'd you eat today, Justice?"

Justice looked at her, uncomprehending. "What d'you mean?"

"Just that."

She let her eyes roll upward, trying to remember. "Um," she said after a while. "Nothing, I think."

"Why not?"

Justice's face said *stupid question.* "Because Papa's dead."

"And you want to join him? You think that makes sense? I'll call Teresa. She'll bring you—"

"I'm not eating because I *don't* want to join him! He was . . . Papa was . . ."

"A little overweight. That's got nothing to do with anything. People die, Justice. Your father just died."

"Of a heart attack. And he was fat. Not a little overweight. He was big. You yourself talked to him about it. And he didn't listen."

Faith was too tired for this. She struggled to hold on to her patience. "Thin people have heart problems, too. And you're thin enough as it is. And don't tell me it has anything to do with your father. You don't get this thin in three days. What are you doing? You and your scales, weighing out food. Who else d'you know that weighs out food? You and your powdered drinks. Justice . . ." She wanted to say, *You're beautiful enough as you are*, but she didn't know how. She wasn't big on compliments.

Justice turned again to the window. "I'll eat when Jonah comes." There was no room for argument.

Without saying anything further, Faith left her.

Upstairs, in the room she had shared with Dominic throughout their marriage, the silence was wider and deeper than anywhere else in the house. It was the kind of quiet that rang in her ears like a gong, that settled upon her hair and skin like a weight, as if this particular room were under twenty feet of water. Without setting down the statuette that she still clutched, Faith somehow managed to slip off her shiny black pumps and wriggle out of her dark silk pantyhose. The carpet, with its thick, buff-colored pile, was soft under her feet. The carpet had been her idea: Dominic had never been able to fathom the use of such dense carpeting in a tropical climate. But Faith had liked the feel of it, the luxury of it, and had compensated for the heat that it retained by keeping the room cooled to a constant sixty-seven degrees.

Their bed was broad enough that a couple could just as comfortably sleep on it sideways as lengthways. The bed head was old brass; the bedding new linen. The air smelled of cinnamon, as it always had, although Faith could never figure out exactly why, because she was not prone to using that scent anywhere in the house. As she drew near to the bed, she halted, fingers rising fast to her lips to still a soundless cry. Teresa. That stupid, stupid girl. She'd done her chores while they were away at the funeral, tidying the room as she always did, making up the bed and turning down the covers to allow her to slide easily inside. But either through force of habit or sheer idiocy—and Faith was more willing to believe the latter—she had turned down not one side of the bed, but two. Dominic on the left, her on the right, two neat flaps of linen folded back with the precision of origami. A bed made for a dead man.

Faith stood there with the wooden statuette clutched to her chest and her eyes fixed on the left side of the bed, too daunted by this vacant spot to move closer. Her shoulders ached, her head throbbed, and her mouth was dry. The past three nights, she had slept in that bed alone, bolstered only by Valium and brandy. She wasn't sure she had the courage to face it a fourth time, or a fifth, or sixth. . . .

She wasn't used to death: it hadn't visited her often. Her parents were still living, she was an only child, and she wasn't old enough to suffer the sensation of being stalked by death that resulted from watching your contemporaries being claimed one by one. Death was something she was unprepared for, an uninvited guest who had come calling in the still of night, finding her with nothing in the cupboards to lay out on the table, nothing in the fridge to offer it to drink.

She had heard or read of women who lost a husband and who thereafter claimed to sense his presence in the home. Some said they smelled him near; some felt him in their beds. Others had even more bizarre stories to tell: that they would step into a room and see him sitting in his favorite chair, just for a second, before he flickered and went out like a failing light bulb, or that they were roused from sleep to the sound of his car pulling into the garage late at night, or heard his key turning in the lock.

She'd experienced none of these things. Was it something that came later, or did these presences only visit some women but not others? Were these sounds in fact there, but she was unable to hear them? Her only sensation was emptiness, a great void, an aching chasm that went on forever. For her, these past nights had been filled with a nothingness huger than she could ever have imagined.

Nobody, not even those closest to her, would ever understand that. Nobody could understand the hurt. There were even those who believed that she *felt* no pain, as if the man she had married could just up and exit without notice, ignominiously sprawled on his back in an emptying opera hall, without leaving her shattered liked a glass falling from careless fingers. She was no fool. She'd seen and felt the curious glances, both at the church and here, in her own reception room. Those had been the glances of people who couldn't understand why the new widow showed no outward grief, why she had sat at the front pew, watching screws being put into her husband's coffin, and not shed a tear. Why no wail had passed her lips, why she had not leaped from her seat to throw herself upon the coffin, berating the unmoving thing inside for having left her without so much as a warning. That was the way it was done here. People loved drama and would have wanted nothing more than to see her composure crack, her dignity slip, long enough for her to make a great show of hurling herself into the open mouth of the grave, pleading out loud to be held back, before she joined her husband in the cold earth. That would have been theater. That would have satisfied the hordes.

But would anyone who had ever met her, or knew who she was and what she and her family stood for, really expect her to fall to the floor, make a display of herself, like a fishwife? She had given them none of that, and many had gone away disappointed. *Hadn't she loved him?* she had heard them think. *Hadn't she cared?* They didn't understand. Her decorum made her who she was. Her grace, her poise, her calm. That was who Dominic had married. If they believed that his death would have turned her into something less, they were wrong. And if they left the graveyard feeling denied of the sideshow for which they had come, well, to hell with them.

Drawing on her courage, she neared the bed, with the two neat flaps in its cover, one of them waiting to be filled in a way it never would again. Suddenly, she felt exhausted. Planning a funeral was tiring. Being strong, even more so. She moved around to Dominic's side of the bed and lifted her knee onto it, preparing to slide in, but could go no farther. She couldn't remember a single night in all twenty-five years of marriage in which she had ever slept on that side, not even when their sexual encounters brought their pillows and bed-clothes into disarray. Before Dominic was engulfed by sleep, she would always nudge him over, and he would always comply, allowing her her rightful position.

This evening, as much as she would want to—maybe sleeping there, in his spot, would engender one of these visions of a lost one that she had heard so much about—she could not. Her body held memories of its proscribed position and re-fused to violate its limits. She grimaced in frustration and got out of the bed again, moving around to the other side and slipping in, feeling defeated. The late afternoon light seeped through the open curtains, making the room too bright to sleep in, but she was too exhausted to get up and close them. A pillow over her eyes would be good enough. It would soon be dark.

It was only as she turned onto her side that she realized she was still holding on to Dominic's damned ugly African stat-uette. She looked down at it in her hands, eyebrows shooting up. "Still here?" she asked it in surprise.

It grinned its mocking grin, tongue as long as its exposed penis, eyes just holes in its head. It was laughing at her be-cause it knew she was too tired to make good on her threat to get rid of it tonight, but its victory would be short-lived. She would see to that. She set it down onto the pillow next to her, wondering to herself why she didn't just throw it onto the floor and be done with it, but unable to muster the energy to do so. Its bare, obscene genitals disturbed her, though, lying in her bed like that. There was something about that that just wasn't right. So she flipped it over onto its belly and settled down, arm across her eyes, blocking out the light, and tried to sleep.

Jonah, Mattie, and Auntie Lou

Jonah half followed, half led Mattie through the press of excited children, with one hand on her shoulder, twisting his body to shield her from their curious view. She appeared more frightened by them than she had been at the clinic, or even earlier, when she was extricating herself from the twisted wreck of her bike. He looked down at her. Her skin was ashy, and her eyes wide, their pupils dilated, like dark caves clearly visible under the sea. That chill of fear, the same ocean-undertow chill that had emanated from her since the accident, was still there. Less intense, and diluted by other things—caution, resentment, even curiosity—but still there. It bothered him that his presence was the source of most of this. Surely he disturbed her more than the children did with their rude questions!

Maybe she was going into some sort of delayed shock, he thought guiltily. For the hundredth time today, he cursed his own carelessness. His guilt and his sense of duty made him protective, and he had to dismiss the urge to lift her into his arms once again and hold her aloft of the crowd.

"Ten paces." He tried to comfort her. "No more than that. Look, the door's right there, see?"

She nodded almost meekly, the fire she had shown all day dimmed. Gently, he propelled her on. The doors that were thrown open were painted fire engine red—or had been,

many moons ago. Old gloss paint flaked off in places, showing several layers, each a bright, eye-catching color. A sign
above the door was elaborately hand-painted, if somewhat
faded, and depicted an assortment of sweetmeats. They had
been rendered by an artist who evidently had had no time for
perspective or proportion: red-and-white mint sticks towered
over Coca-Cola bottles; brown, irregular lumps that he
assumed depicted tamarind balls looked about the size of
basketballs. Bright polka dots were squeezed into every space
that was bereft of some type of tooth-rotting treat, and
rainbow-striped, uneven lettering credited ownership of the
establishment to someone called Auntie Lou. At the doorway, most of the children stopped, contenting themselves
with jostling for a good view, but respectful enough—or
wary enough of Jonah's bulk and forbidding expression—to
keep their distance.

The inside of the store was quieter, but not much cooler.
The decor consisted of three or four low wooden benches
against the walls, which allowed children to sit out of the sun
while they consumed their treats. Both the walls and the
benches were covered with graffiti: lovers' names etched
within hearts, tributes to popular athletes or film stars, chal-
lenges from one school to the next to come out and fight,
telephone numbers, and disparaging comments about other
children which, had they been written by one adult about another, would have amounted to libel.

The room was cut in half by a counter that ran from wall
to wall, and which was littered with clear glass gallon bottles
which had once held mustard or mayonnaise, but which now
put on display every imaginable type of sweet. Jonah stopped
short, distracted from his purpose by the sights and smells
around him. He had the giddying sensation of being thrust
backward into his own past, to a shed in his home village
that bulged, as this one did, with enough to delight any child.
Although he and his young cohorts had never had much to

spend there, they had still found themselves in the shed after school, and when any child had had money, he'd always been willing to pass his purchases around so that everyone got a nibble or a lick.

Jonah's gaze fell on a jar full of many-colored, sugary lumps. Paradise plums. When was the last time he'd felt one melting on his tongue? Surely not since he'd left his seaside home for the city. He could almost smell the wild, sweet essence that had been boiled into them in the cauldron.

"Jesus, child!" A loud, almost masculine voice tore him from his reverie, and Jonah started. A hinged flap of counter-top flipped up, and a waist-high door was blown open under the weight of the fattest woman he had ever seen. She squeezed herself through the door, wincing with the effort, and then with surprising speed was upon them. "Matilda, baby, what happened?" Then the woman's eyes were upon Jonah, half accusing, half scared. "What happened to her?"

Mattie spoke before he could. "Nothing, Auntie Lou. A little—"

"Nothing?" The woman snorted, pulling Jonah's jacket away from Mattie's shoulders to get a better look at the bloodstains on the front of her skirt. "What you call this? This is what you call nothing?" Without waiting for an answer, she ushered them both through the door into the business side of the parlor with a firmness that brooked no opposition. Then, remembering their audience, she leaned over the counter. "Out, out! Y'all don't have a house to go to? What y'all still hanging around here at this hour for?" Fat rolled under her arms as she shooed them away like wayward chickens.

"We always here at this hour, Auntie Lou," one plucky youngster pointed out. She was reluctant to budge from the doorway, not when there was so much action to see yet. "*You* the one always let us stay." She grinned like an imp.

"That don't matter," Auntie Lou boomed. "I don't wanna

hear that. Y'all hurry on home, especially you with that big mouth on you." She pointed at the girl who had answered her. "Who tell you you could back-chat grown people? You think I coulda talk back to my elders when I was your age?" She sucked her teeth. "G'wan home now, you hear? Don't make me have to come round there after you."

The children laughed, obviously used to her veering moods, but scampered anyway.

"And close that door behind you, Miss Mouth. You hear me?"

The girl hurried back and pulled the door shut before leaving with her chortling schoolmates. That done with, Louisa turned toward them again.

This time, it was Jonah who spoke first. "She had an accident, ma'am. In the churchyard this morning. We—" He broke off, realizing that he was about to say, "We collided," but that was cowardice. "I hit her," he said.

The dark face grew darker, but before Louisa could speak, Mattie cut in. "I rode in front him, Auntie."

"No, I should have seen . . . I wasn't paying attention . . ."

"I don't wanna hear nothing 'bout who hit who. Y'all young people always with your speed." She frowned at Jonah, and he winced under her reproach. "You young men drive y'all cars like y'all don't realize it's a lethal weapon. Like y'all always got to be somewhere fast. And you . . ." She had Mattie by the arm and was leading her away. "I told you take a taxi. I didn't tell you take a taxi? But no. You think you too big to listen. You never listen to nothing nobody tell you, until it's too late."

Mattie's eyelids drooped slightly, and Auntie Lou's tirade halted in midstream. "Baby. Come, pet." She forced Mattie's head against her massive breast and began to lead her away, making Mattie's gait so awkward that Jonah smiled, in spite of himself.

Before the two women could disappear through the doorway, he called out, "I'll be leaving . . ."

"Stay."

The single command held him fast. After the door closed before him, he stood with his hands in his pockets, afraid to sit, straining to sense what was going on back there. Most likely a bath and bed for Mattie. Then the old lady would come out, and he would have to face her alone. Whatever reproof she would have for him, he deserved it, and he would accept it like a man. Still, she made him nervous.

He stared down at his shoes, trying to slow his racing mind. Shoes bought for a funeral—one that he'd missed. He thought of Justice and had to scrunch his eyes up against the image of her. What had he done? Left his wife to bury her father alone. Well, not alone: Faith was there, but she would be cold comfort.

He glanced at the door and wished he could just slip out. He'd shirked one responsibility to fulfill another, but now the call of his wife was greater than the call of duty. He could quietly go; he'd be back soon enough, maybe tomorrow or the day after. There would be business to settle: the question of the bike and the injury he'd caused. He had no intention of denying liability for either. But now, all he wanted was Justice. He was tired, and he realized that he needed as much to be consoled as to console.

But no. He turned his back to the door so that he would not be tempted. When a man was faced with hard choices, duty had to win out. Duty was what lay at the frontier between boyhood and manhood: that was something Dominic had taught him. He'd see Justice soon. In an hour, or perhaps a little more. And when he did, God, how he needed her. Fine prickles ran over his skin at the thought of how deep he would sink into her to find solace. The anticipation alone made his anxiety ebb. Comfort would come for both of them.

"The son-in-law, yeah?"

The voice startled him. He spun around, blinking. Time had passed. The large woman was back in the room, and he had not even heard her enter. "Ma'am?"

"You Dominic's son-in-law. The one married his daughter. Justice." She wasn't asking.

Jonah was surprised, and it showed on his face.

She laughed. "What, you think because I old I stupid? I know things 'bout your family you yourself don't know."

She was probably right. He'd certainly learned enough about them today. Her rasping laugh took him by surprise. He hadn't expected her to be anywhere near pleasant to him, not considering the damage he'd done to Mattie. He kept a wary eye on her as she approached.

"Reyes, right?"

"Jonah, yes."

"Everybody calls me Auntie Lou." She held her hand out. He took it. "Miss Lou." He couldn't call her Auntie. It wouldn't be right.

A grin split her face. "Nice to see them fancy clothes don't stop you from being a country boy. Tell me where you grew up again? Maracas?"

"Las Cuevas."

She nodded. "Good people."

He felt both proud and bashful. He stood there, face flushed, not knowing what else to say. Eventually, "How's Mattie?"

"Sleeping."

He couldn't say anything.

She tried to comfort him. "It's not as bad as it looks. Don't worry up your head too much. She small, but she strong. Like her mother. Not a nice way to spend a birthday, though."

His brows flew up. "It's her birthday?"

Louisa nodded. "Twenty-four. Got a cake sitting in the fridge, waiting. You got to keep them things in the fridge, these days. This place crawling with ants. They all over the place, everywhere you turn. Don't know what to do with them anymore." She shook her head and trailed off, frowning at the bother the ants brought her.

Jonah wondered if he could possibly have felt any worse. Not only had he run the girl down on the day her father was buried, but on her birthday, too. If it hadn't been for him, she'd have been eating her grandmother's cake right about now. "I wish I'd known," he said regretfully.

She looked philosophical. "What you woulda done? Bought her a present? When the Lord choose to set his plans in motion, he don't pick no special day. Nothing you can do to stop that now."

The fact that she was right didn't make him feel any better. He tried to find another way to help. "She has a prescription. If you give it to me, I can run out and fill it."

She gave him that same look Mattie had in the taxi. Pride affronted. "I can take care of that. Never you mind."

"But it's my responsibility—"

She cocked her head to one side. "Young man, you ain't got a wife home grieving for her father?"

Having someone else remind him of his failings embarrassed him. "Yes, ma'am."

"Then, what you waiting for? Go on home."

He didn't argue. He preceded her to the other side of the counter. He had one hand on the doorknob when she stopped him.

"Dominic was a private man, you know."

"I understand that. Now more than ever."

"He wasn't the kind of man who liked his business knocking dog all over town. Him being dead now don't change that. He still wouldn'ta liked it."

He knew exactly what she was saying, but that couldn't be right. Did she expect him to keep quiet about all this? Was she really telling him in one breath to go home to his wife, while asking him in the other to keep from her that she had a sister? He protested. "Miss Lou, Dominic was my family, too. My wife has a sister—"

"My daughter's child. My *dead* daughter."

"Justice should know. I can't hide this. It's not right—"

"What's not right is starting up a whole heap of trouble you can't stop. Troubling his family with things he never wanted them to know. What, you think if you tell them, they gonna thank you? You think your wife gonna be happy? Dominic's wife? All they'll feel is lied to. All they gonna feel is hurt. That what you want?"

"What I want is . . ." He stopped. What did he want? He tried to remember what had rushed through him this morning at the moment he'd seen Mattie's eyes. Shock, definitely. Puzzlement. And later, when the reality of Dominic's lie, a lie that had run on like a never-ending joke for decades, had hit home, there had been hurt. His idol's clay feet had crumbled into dust. If he went home with this uncanny story, how long would the dust take to settle?

Dominic had been all the father he'd ever needed, but the blood tie was Justice's, not his. If Jonah had been hurt by the news, how would she fare? How would she feel if on the day she'd put him into the ground, she learned that on all those Wednesday nights she'd waited up late to greet her father, he was embracing her with the scent of another woman still clinging to his skin? And then there was Faith, with all her fears of gossip, and her adamant belief that appearances were everything. For such a scandal to fall into her garden. . . .

Louisa's eyes glinted as she read understanding on Jonah's face. "You see now, boy?"

Jonah nodded mutely.

"The trouble you could cause, it don't serve no purpose. You don't always have to tell the whole truth. Sometimes you better served just staying quiet."

Jonah opened the door and stepped out into the front yard before he said anything, and when he did, there was no need to give Louisa his promise. It was already there. "You'll let me know how Mattie's doing?"

"Course."

"Can I pass by to see if she's okay? I owe her a bike."

There was still that wrong to be put right. He looked hopeful.

Louisa clucked her tongue, but didn't answer.

The glass on the western side of the house looked like sheets of beaten copper as sun dipped behind the trees. All was quiet. Faith's guests must have left a long time before. As he walked up the main drive with the sound of the taxi fading in the distance, Jonah couldn't stop himself from looking up at the window of the family room, which opened onto the garden. It was empty. Many afternoons, when he was due home from work, Justice would sit there and wait for the first glimpse of him as he turned into the drive. True, it wasn't necessary, and embarrassed him a little: waiting at the window was something a cat did, or a dog. But if he were honest, he would have to admit that seeing her face behind the frosted glass could make any number of worries go away.

He slipped the key into the lock, taking care as he pushed on the front door to do so gently. One of the twin doors had a tendency to creak, and in the dense silence it would echo down the hall. But almost in deference to the house of mourning, the door opened without a sound.

His nostrils filled with the sharp scent of artificial lemons and wax. "Hello?"

Teresa, bent over before the large table in the drawing room, looked up, polishing cloth in hand. "Mister Jonah, you come home." She passed the back of her hand across her forehead.

Jonah came to where she crouched. "Teresa, what're you doing?"

She threw him a look of thinly masked exasperation. "Polishing the table."

"I know, but why?"

"Ms. Evers say the room smelling of fish. So she tell me clean it."

He tried not to smile. Faith could be fussy—when it came to the hard work of others. Teresa had been on her feet when they had left for the funeral this morning and most likely hadn't had the chance to take a break. Usually, he didn't have much to do with the house staff: that task fell to Faith, and to Dominic if Faith wasn't around. But with Dominic gone, he was the master of the house.

"That's enough, Teresa. You've got to be tired. Why don't you go home? You can finish in the morning."

She gave him a blank look, unaccustomed as she was to receiving instructions from him. A few uneasy seconds passed, and then Teresa bent her head and resumed polishing.

Jonah was taken aback. He tried again, tilting his head to one side to catch a glimpse of her face. "Teresa? Go home."

She rubbed hard at an imaginary blemish on the glossy tabletop and then halted. With the hand that held the polishing rag resting on her hip she spoke, slowly and patiently. "Mister Jonah, I know you trying to be nice and all, but you know what? Mistress Evers tell me to clean, so I cleaning. You understand?"

"And *I'm* telling you to—"

She bent her head and focused on the table, her fingertips dashing along the shiny surface. He was glad she couldn't see the chagrin on his face. "That's all right, Mister Jonah. I almost done."

He left without pushing it further.

Upstairs, none of the lights were on. Flicking a switch dispersed the shadows, but to Jonah, the gloom was still heavy. He passed the door to the bedroom Faith had shared with her husband, treading quietly. The next room was his and Justice's. This was not an arrangement that had ever suited Jonah. It embarrassed him to share a bedroom wall with his in-laws: there was something uneasy about making love to a woman when her parents slept a few yards away.

But theirs was the room in which Justice had slept all the

nights of her life, and nothing could sway her from staying. It was like an old shoe, she'd protested whenever the talk came up about inhabiting the guest wing or even building a home of their own. It just seemed to fit. Jonah learned to swallow his protests and to make love in silence, trusting in the construction of the separating wall to spare him embarrassment.

He stood outside their room, ear to the door. Inside, he could hear nothing. He had to quell a vague sense of disappointment. He twisted on the scrolled brass handle and leaned his weight on the door—to find it didn't budge. Puzzled, he looked down and jiggled on the handle. Locked.

"Justice?" Their door was never locked, not unless they both were inside. There was a flapping of wings in his gut. He knew she'd be upset, worried, maybe. He had, after all, missed her father's funeral. But angry enough to lock the door? "Tish, please." His lips were against the dark wood.

There was a stirring inside, a rustle. He tried again. "Baby. Little girl. Please, I'm sorry. Let me in, so I can see you. You really want me to talk to you like this, through a door?"

The wings in his stomach turned to claws as he waited. The rustling in the room stopped. She was listening. "You saw what happened. That girl. You were there. You saw me hit her. For the love of God, Tish, you saw the blood. What you expected me to do?"

Still nothing, but he could sense her resolve soften. "You think I didn't want to be there with you? I was supposed to bear him down the aisle. Front right, remember? You think I'd have given up that chance if I didn't have to? At least you got to say goodbye. At least—"

The bolt slid back, but she didn't open the door. He did, gently, because she was right in its path. He wanted to open his arms to her and rush forward to be forgiven, but as he saw her, he halted.

The glow of the dying sun filled their room, washing the

bed, the twin bedside tables, and the two brocaded armchairs with a tinge of peach. The pink walls—the only color Justice would allow them to be—had the warmth of human skin. But Justice, she looked as if she were standing in her own personal moonbeam. Her silver-whiteness fought against the fading light and was winning. Her pallor extended to the cotton and lace of her dressing gown, and her dark hair looked limp and untended, even though she, like her mother, had had it done especially for the funeral, just twelve hours ago.

Jonah extended his hand to try to dust away the blue shadows under her eyes, but they were still there after his thumb had passed. "Tish?" He felt as if he'd been away a year and returned home to a shocking change in her.

"You could've been dead!"

He frowned, trying to understand. "What?"

"You were gone for hours and hours! You left me there, alone in the church with *Mama*, and then here with all those awful people. Sucking up to her and going on and on about Papa. And all I could think about was you out there, maybe dead or something!"

He stepped closer, wanting to touch her again, but afraid to. She was like a hairline crack in a dam wall. If he touched her too hard, and something shifted, what would happen? He spoke carefully. "Dead how?"

"On the road!" She waved her arms above her head, chastisement for his inability to understand the obvious. "You ran away. *Ran!* Out in the street, with all those cars. After some . . ." She stopped, and her arms fell to her sides. With disconcerting speed, her voice became calm, reasonable. "How is she?"

He struggled to keep pace with her shift in thinking. "How is . . . You mean Mattie?"

"That her name?"

"Yes."

"She alive?"

"Alive, yes. It wasn't a bad injury. She had a gash on her

thigh. I took her to the clinic to get it stitched. And then I took her home. That's why I was gone so long."

"Stitches, huh?" Justice was smiling, interested. "How many?"

"Um . . ." He tried to remember. "Five, maybe. About that."

"And her head?"

"Her head?"

"Did she hit it?"

"She bumped it, but the X rays were fine." Maybe it would be a good idea to get Justice to lie down. He slid a hand down to her waist and tried gently to nudge her toward the bed. "Let's lie down for a while, Tish."

Justice didn't budge. "Wasn't it an ugly dress she was wearing? It was ugly, wasn't it? She looked like a big grape. And so fat down below. That bottom . . ." Her laugh was like a shard of glass. "I don't understand how some women just don't know how to take care of themselves—"

"Tish, come, baby. Come lie down with me." He loosened the knot on his tie and dragged it up over his head without completely untying it, then began on the buttons on his shirt. For the first time, Justice noticed the blood and slapped a hand over her mouth. Before she could panic, Jonah hastened to comfort her. "It's okay. I'm not hurt. It's just a stain. I had to lift Mattie up to get her to the doctor."

"So it's her blood?"

"Yes."

"Oh." She looked satisfied that that made it all right. As if Mattie's blood spilling was fine with her. She touched her hair distractedly, hand moving inch by inch along her scalp, like someone searching for a hairpin, frowning, lost in her thoughts again.

Jonah stripped the shirt off and left it where it fell, then a few seconds later, dropped his navy pants on top of it. He was grimy, hot, and uncomfortable, and needed a bath, but needed to hold Justice even more. He tried again to guide her to the bed, and this time, she complied. Before she could climb in, he scooped her up into his arms, noticing fleetingly how insubstantial she felt compared to Mattie this morning. He laid her down quickly, scared. What did she weigh now? A hundred?

Justice spoke. "So, was she really coming to Papa's funeral, dressed like that? Did you see her hat? Old-lady hat, with a *net!* Or was she just passing by?"

Jonah swallowed hard and settled down next to Mattie's sister. "She was coming to the funeral."

"No! Really? Did she know him?"

"Yes."

"How? Was she a cleaner from the office or something? A waitress at the club?"

This wasn't right. Holding his silence wasn't right. Justice should know. Jonah wasn't a good liar; Rosalie had raised him to tell the truth even when the price you had to pay for it was more than a lie would be worth. His wife had a sister. Shouldn't she know?

Justice was still guessing. "Lunch counter lady? Trainee? Cousin?" She corrected herself with a chuckle that sounded disconcertingly like Faith's. "No, not a cousin. Not even second or third. She couldn't be, not dark as she is . . ."

He remembered what Mattie had said about her mother, how Dominic had never married her because she just wasn't right for his circle. Too dark for their palm-lined street in St. Clair. His own light skin chastised him. Maybe Aunt Louisa was right. Justice wouldn't understand. When the truth could rock a very fragile boat, was it really okay to lie? He settled for nondisclosure. "Not a cousin. Not a trainee or a . . . waitress. She just knew him from way back. That's all." He clamped his teeth together to stop himself from saying any more.

Justice shrugged, dismissing the issue as unimportant. Jonah rolled over onto his side, facing her, sliding a hand down along a hip that was barely wider than her waist. He brought his head closer to nuzzle her cheek. Her hair smelled of fruit and herbs, essential oils. Girl smells.

"What're you doing?"

In his palm, her breast was the size of a lemon. The nipple soft, almost flat. "Kissing my wife." He slipped a leg over both of hers.

Her hand came up between them, flat against his chest. "You smell." She made a face.

"I've been out all day," he said reasonably. "It's to be expected."

"No. You smell like..." She sniffed at him, and then wrinkled her nose. "Blood. And dust. Street dust. Ugh."

He could get up and get cleaned, but his body didn't want to be apart from hers. Not now. He'd had a horrible day: too long, too hard, and filled with too many shocks. He needed her. He relinquished her breast and slid his hand down to hook his thumb into the elastic of her panties. She always wore plain cotton, high-waisted ones, printed with strawberries and butterflies. He called them her Raggedy-Ann knickers. "The blood smell is all in your head. Because you saw my shirt. It's not on me; you can't—"

She shoved him with surprising force. "No, no, Jonah. You smell. It's... Don't touch me."

He gave in, rolled out of bed, and stood beside her. "Okay, sweetheart. I'll take a shower. Wait for me. I won't be long." He took a last lingering look at her. "Okay?"

Her hands crossed over her chest, and she held a breast in each hand as if she were protecting fledgling doves. Hers was a child's pout. Her gaze dropped to the bulge of his erection, visible through his shorts. "Oh, ugh!"

He looked down at himself, bemused. "Ugh?"

"Papa's dead. How could you?"

Embarrassed, he could feel his erection dwindle. "I know he's dead, Justice. I didn't mean any disrespect. I just had a bad day, and I want my wife. I need you. It's been..." He stopped. How long had it been? Two weeks? More? Justice hadn't been inclined lately and always had a good excuse. Fatigue. The flu. Something.

She went on, oblivious. "And what about Mama? She's right next door. In an empty bed. What about her?"

The mention of his mother-in-law put paid to his erection for good, but it did nothing to reduce the frustration welling up inside him. "What *about* her?"

"She lost her husband. She's got nobody. My mother's all alone, and you want to—" She bit her lip.

"Fuck?" He tried not to sound harsh, but the combination of her condemnation and the ache in his balls made his voice more grating than he'd intended.

It was a word Justice never used herself and hated to hear coming from other people. She put her hands over her ears. "You don't have to talk of it that way."

Jonah repented. "Sorry, baby." He knelt on the bed, leaning toward her, but she scooted over to the far edge.

"Don't."

Resignedly, he got up again and cast about the room for a towel. "I'll go take a shower. Okay?"

She didn't answer. Instead, she studied the lilies of the valley embossed into the bedspread, twisting her fingers into her hair again.

In the bathroom doorway, he tried one last time. "When I come back, can we just lie together? Would that be all right?"

Justice didn't look around. The hair twisting gained speed. "If you like," she said. She sighed.

Blood Pye and Mattie

"I tired tell you I don't want no three-footed rat inside my house."

Mattie's grandmother looked like she was fixing to be a bitch today, but Blood Pye was in a good mood. He'd had a fair day at the tracks and had come away a few hundred richer. He showed her his teeth and hefted Threes higher on his shoulder. "And *I* tired tell *you*, this ain't no rat. Is a mongoose."

Louisa sniffed. She was wedged into the doorway like a piece of chocolate cake crammed into a mailbox slot. "Call it what you want. It look like a big-ass rat to me." She glared at Threes, who didn't look worried over the exchange at all. "It probably full of ticks and fleas and nimbles and all sort of things."

Blood Pye gave her a scornful look. Didn't she know a man wasn't a man if he didn't treat his animals right? "I bathe Threes once a week, every Saturday God bring. He ain't got no ticks. No nimbles, neither. Him and all my cocks, they ain't got no insects." What the cocks had was far more lethal: there had been three more dead just this morning, but he didn't owe her that information. "Besides," he added, "Threes is a harmless li'l thing. He don't bother nobody."

He tried to peep past her into the living room to see if

Mattie was there, but Louisa shifted, blocking his view. "It bother me just looking at it!"

"I can go in?" he asked. He tried to be polite, because getting mean wouldn't make any sense.

She huffed and pretended not to hear him.

"Mattie-oy!" Blood Pye cupped his hand to his mouth and bawled out for his girl.

An answering shout came from upstairs. "Pye! That you?"

"Is me, girl. You letting me in or what?"

There was a brief pause, and then he could tell by her voice that she was nearer, perhaps at the top of the stairs. "So come in if you want to come in. What keeping you?"

He smiled at the old lady, just as sweet as before. "Louisa?" He never called her Auntie, like every other idiot that came into the parlor did. That annoyed her, and maybe that was what made it such fun. "You letting me pass? I believe your granddaughter invite me in." He held her gaze steadily, the smile getting just a little harder around the edges, as his mouth was getting tired. They had both been here before, and she always let him in eventually. He couldn't understand why she didn't just stand clear of the door when she saw him stepping into the yard and be done with it.

He hummed an old calypso about an unsuitable young man courting a girl above his station, forcing the sound out through his teeth and enjoying the irony of the lyrics that swam in his head. After a few moments, Louisa stepped aside, eyes bugging. "All y'all youngsters think y'all so damn smart. Like y'all know everything, more than us who done lived our life already. But you know what the old hog say to the little piglet? One day, one day, *congo-tay*. One day, you gonna know. You gonna get old just like me, and you gonna look back—"

He wasn't in the mood to hear it. He hurried through the doorway, hanging on to Threes lest she take a swipe at him with a broom or something. "You try to have a nice day now,

Lou-Lou," he said, his words sweeter than anything she made in her shop.

Louisa sucked her teeth.

Mattie was waiting for him on the landing. She looked good in some sort of housedress thing made of shiny material with watermelons printed all over it. A slice of melon fell right on the tip of each breast, and he wondered briefly if the person who had made the dress had planned it that way. He was surprised at how glad he was to see her. He wasn't usually that emotional over his women, but her eyes were green, green, green, and bright and smiling.

The first thing she said to him belied the grin on her face. "So you finally turn up, eh? I coulda been dying . . ."

Mattie was always bitching about the time it took for him to come see her, like she thought he was supposed to be there every day or something. He was used enough to her complaint to know not to pay it much mind. "I been busy, babes. You know how it is."

"Yeah, but I been in an accident. You didn't even—"

He bent over and kissed her, and that shut her up. She kissed him back; but then Threes chuffed in her ear, and she flinched. "You bring that thing? You know how my grandmother don't like it."

He gave her the same smile he'd given Louisa. "He'll be quiet. Don't worry." He led the way to her room. "Just let's set him in a corner. He'll go to sleep. He'll be quiet; watch and see."

Mattie looked doubtful, but followed him into her bedroom and shut the door. That was a good sign. She sat on the edge of the bed, pulling her housedress down to cover her knees.

He liked her bedroom. It was always clean and cool, and welcoming, even though the mirrors that lined the walls were a little too weird for him. Wherever he went in the room, he could spot himself, sometimes whole, like in her big mirror, and sometimes fragmented, taken apart by any of the small ones and reflected in another, bouncing his image back and forth between them like schoolchildren playing piggy-in-the-middle. It was eerie; they somehow made him feel unwhole. He could never understand why there were so many. Why would anyone need to see themselves every minute of the day? But that was women all over. Vain.

He looked down at Mattie, sitting on the bed, waiting for him to join her, and grinned, trying to appease, even before she could begin to complain. Three days had passed since her accident, and he hadn't come to see her. Sometimes you just couldn't get around to things you needed to get around to. *He* understood that, but women didn't. He wasn't in the mood to put up with any whining, so he headed her off at the pass with an apology. "Sorry I didn't come to see you earlier. I was tied up real, real bad." He wasn't lying: there had been horse races going on here and in England. Big money to be won—or lost.

"That wasn't no way to spend your birthday, though," he went on. "A funeral and an accident." She looked reflective, so he rushed to speak again. He wasn't about to let the light go out of her face. "I know it late, but I bring you a present anyway." He fished in his pocket. Women's things were so damn tiny, always getting lost. He brought out a small box that he'd wrapped himself and handed it clumsily over.

He was rewarded with a smile. She ripped the package open, and Blood Pye leaned forward to see her take the small ladybug pin out of the cardboard box. It was a nice trinket; it looked almost expensive.

"Pye! It's . . . so pretty!" She rubbed the tip of her finger across the red lacquer and closed her eyes. She ran her tongue over her lips like she was tasting something sweet.

He glanced at his watch, quickly, while her eyes were still closed. He enjoyed Mattie's company, but he was a busy man. But Mattie was the kind of woman who expected you to get all the niceties out of the way first. "You hurt bad?" he asked. He'd expected to see her all bruised up and looking like hell.

"Just a cut. Nothing big." She cradled the bug pin in her hand like it was alive.

"Where?"

She slipped up the hem of her dress, revealing a large, flat bandage. "Here." She was smiling more than somebody in pain had a right to.

Threes leaped off his shoulder and scuttled under the bed. Blood Pye dropped to his knees and pressed his lips against her skin, just above the bandage. "Better now?"

"Not yet." She slid her hand down across his shaved scalp.

She smelled of a cross between baby powder and antiseptic. The fabric of the bandage was rough against his cheek as he let his kisses roam higher, until his mouth was flat against her crotch. She was as plump down there as she was all around her middle: for a small girl, her ass and thighs just kind of took you by surprise. Glorious. Like climbing into the driver's seat of a zippy little sports car and discovering that the upholstery was thicker and more comfortable than anything you had at home in front of your TV. He slapped her bottom playfully, and the flesh was so firm it didn't even ripple.

She fell backward against her bed with a sigh. Her nails scratched at his nape, and he tilted his head back slightly to increase the pressure of the contact. "My grandmother don't like us doing this up here," she murmured. She took her hand away from his head long enough to pull at the sash around her waist. It fell away with one tug. "She catch us, she throwing you out, and you never getting back in."

He was used to this game; she played it often. She liked to know he was willing to risk expulsion for her. "Your grandmother don't like me, period. But she can't hear nothing. She out in front."

"She could come back upstairs for something," Mattie argued, but her housedress was off and on the floor.

He was so excited by the dark shadow behind her curtain-lace panties that he almost forgot to play the game. He popped his belt buckle with one hand, levering himself up over her with the other. "All the more reason for you to be real quiet."

"Real quiet? How quiet you think we can be? She ain't deaf, you know. And she ain't stupid. Maybe we better not."

He was done arguing. He could take so much of her teasing, and then no more. So instead of answering, he kissed her, letting his moustache tickle her upper lip, letting his tongue trail against her front teeth until she was done arguing, too. Her hand down the front of his pants made him drunker than a night out at the club.

In sharp contrast to his shaved scalp, the hair on his crotch was thick, black, and crisp. It crackled as she touched him. Excitement and anticipation collided as he felt her sharp nails scrape his skin. He leaned over her, getting into position.

"Where them rubber things you got?"

He froze, and then groaned. "God, baby. Gimme a break."

"What kind of break you want? I ain't watching you all day, all night. I don't know where you go and what you get up to half the time. You think I'm stupid? You think I don't know you?"

"I keep telling you: I ain't with nobody else." Not a hell of a lot, at least, he reminded himself. A little dip in another ocean never hurt anybody. "Why you can't trust me?"

She ignored him and went on. "Besides, when you ain't out drinking and checking them girls you like to hang out with, you messing with them chickens. You think I want any of your stinkin' chicken germs all over me?"

The mention of his cocks, and the quiet plague that was killing them, almost made him go soft. He passed his hand over his eyes to steady the blood that rushed there. "Mattie, baby, don't let's talk about that, okay? I only come here to pass some time with my woman. You can't just leave it at that?" He tried to smile again.

"I'll leave it at that. Just get it on before things start drying up over here, okay?"

He moved quickly, pulling the foil packet from his wallet, hating the *snick-snick* sound of the rubber as he forced it down over himself. What pissed him off the most was that Mattie never made a secret of the fact that her insistence on his using it was not a matter of personal conviction or philosophy: it was all about him, and what he did—or what she thought he did—when she wasn't around. And he took that personally. He'd longed to ask her if she would be as dogmatic with other men; but the idea of her with anyone else made his stomach roll, so he could never give voice to the question.

"You ready?"

He moved over her again, grumbling. "They never make these goddamn things big enough anyway. Like getting choked to death . . ."

She laughed, but not at him. Her knees fell open, and he was between them, and he forgot to be disgruntled. Her closed hand, still holding the ladybug, curled around his neck. She was tight; she always was. How anybody could have an ass and thighs like she did and still be so narrow and tight was beyond him. Her bandage brushed against his leg.

"Ouch! Be careful, Pye. Watch my leg. I got stitches, you know. You hurt me and it's over. Hear?"

He was sinking fast. She was so, so sweet. "I'll be careful," he managed to say. He shifted his weight.

The gentle rocking of the bed roused the mongoose, who skittered out from under it for a better view, front paws up on the edge, sniffing. Blood Pye slid a hand under Mattie's back and tilted her to one side so that Threes would be out of her line of vision, but he wasn't quick enough. Her spine stiffened, and her muscles convulsed against his prick, ejecting him. She slid up higher against the bed, eyes on Threes.

"Don't tell me that thing watching us! You always let him do that. I told you, Pye, I don't want no animal watching me while I—"

He laid a finger across her lips. "Mattie, Mattie, please. He ain't staring at you. He just come up for air. That's all. He gonna go back under the bed in a minute. Don't stop me, please. You got me all heat up . . ." He nudged Threes with his foot.

"He didn't come up for no air. He come up to watch. Why you always gotta bring him?"

" 'Cause he's my friend."

"And me?"

"You my *girl*friend." He wished there was more he could say; she seemed to be waiting on something. He scoured his mind for something that would pour oil on her waters, anything that would have her soft and sweet and pressed against him again. There was nothing he wanted more than to be back in that warm, snug nest. He crawled back over her and probed between her legs, but, as slick and wet as she was, she was a locked door.

"It won't work." She looked regretful, as though there was nothing in her power to *make* it work. "I gone cold."

He groaned. He looked down at himself: he was still harder than a kick in the head. There was a pain that started in his balls and ended somewhere deep in his gut. He slipped his hand down between her legs, coaxing her, trailing her own moisture upward to her belly, voice soft and urging. "Come on. Try. Work with me. Mattie, baby . . ." Above her head, he could see the reflection of his face, tense and sweating. Anxious.

Then her body softened against his hand, opening under his fingers. He felt a quick thrill of triumph, and he pressed against her, feeling welcoming warmth where a few moments ago there was resistance. But at the point of contact, before he could slide fully in, the pain in his balls and belly turned into a lance of fire that sliced up, and up, and up, until color and light pounded at the back of his eyes. Then the fire-lance dulled, the lights went out, leaving just lingering halos in the darkness of his head, and his body went limp against her breast.

"Shit." She was the one to speak first.

"Sorry." Goddamn. He felt like a fool. Going off half-cocked like a schoolboy.

"S'all right," she told him, but that was what women thought they had to say, even if they were pissed at you, or, worse, laughing inside. He was afraid to open his eyes to see which it was. He felt a gust of air rush out of her nostrils, against his neck, and then her breasts bobbed against his chest. He looked at her, incredulous. She *was* laughing.

"Look, it just happened . . . ," he began.

"I'm not . . ." Her belly twitched with mirth. "I'm not laughing at you. I'm laughing at *him*." She extricated an arm that had been sandwiched between them and pointed at Threes, who was still down at the edge of the bed, up on his hind leg, forepaws on the mattress, staring intently. "You think he know what you just did? You let your friend watch you do it; you think he gonna go back and tell your chickens you false start with me today? Next time you walk into the cock pen, they all gonna be dissing you!" She let out a peal of laughter.

Blood Pye had to struggle to smile, trying not to feel too embarrassed. Sometimes you had to just take it on the chin. Besides, Mattie wasn't being nasty, not like some skanky girls you could come across, who could make you feel like less than a man with just one contemptuous look.

He settled down next to her, glad that she made no move to cover her own nakedness. If she stayed that way, and let him look, he'd be ready again in no time.

"So, what they gonna give you?" he asked after a while.

"Who?"

"This sonofabitch that hit you with his car. He's your daddy's son, right?"

"In law. He married to Charity/Justice/Whatever. My sister."

She knew damn well what her sister's name was. Didn't he have to listen to her long-ass stories about the old man's family, and his big house, and how the world they lived in was so strange and foreign and distant that they seemed to live across a border, in a land she had no visa to enter? His own daddy had lots of kids; most of them he never met, and didn't care to, so part of him could never fathom the longing in her voice to touch that man's other life, if only for a moment. When she got into her talkative moods, she'd drop her voice and whisper bitterly about what it was like being a secret—not having one, *being* one—and that sometimes she felt that she would be better off buried away like an incriminating love letter from an old indiscretion, hidden behind books that no one ever read. When she talked about it that way, he was half-sure he understood.

He lifted himself on one elbow to look into her face. "And what he gonna give you?"

"For what?"

"For running you over. He shoulda watched where he was going. Messed up your leg and everything."

She shrugged. "Nothing. I don't know. I never asked for anything."

"What you mean, you never asked for anything? He owe you, girl. Look at your leg! He shoulda been paying attention."

"Me, too." She inched down the bed and threw her legs off, making to get up. He stopped her.

"Don't go. We talking. You don't realize how much money you could be into? Ain't they got money? And what about inheritance? You're his daughter; you got to be getting something."

She shrugged. "He's only been dead a few days. What, you think money just fall into your lap when people die? Besides, I don't want no money. He didn't give me anything while he was alive, except dribbles and bits. Christmas presents, and money for my birthday. Chinese food every Wednesday night, before he went upstairs with my mother. What make you think he left anything for me?"

Now, she couldn't really mean that. "Don't be stupid, girl. Who you think you are, Saint Matilda? Nobody can't be so unselfish all the time. Not when it got so much money up for grabs. Watch me in my face and tell me you never wonder for a second how much he coulda left for you."

She dipped her head. "Well, maybe. No way to tell." She pulled her housedress closed, covering up those beautiful breasts and pinned it securely with the lady bug. There would be no second wind for him today. He dismissed the idea regretfully.

With a martyred sigh, he tugged the rubber off, knotted it, and slipped it into his pocket, even though there was a waste-basket within throwing distance. He'd heard enough horror stories from his friends about girls who waited until you were gone to fish your rubber out of the bin and do God knew what with it, only to stick you nine months later with paternity. Not that Mattie was the type to do that, especially since she was the one to make him wear them in the first place, but he'd been hanging on the block long enough to know that whenever you left a woman's house, you left with your little fellas.

Still and all, they weren't talking about sex anymore; they were talking about money, and that beat sex any day. He pulled his jeans back on and said, "No way to tell? They got something called a will . . ."

She flashed her eyes at him. "I know what a will is."

"And you saying that rich man who see you every week ain't gonna have nothing left over for you after he dead? Come on. All you got to do is wait 'til they read it. Then they got to give you your share, whether they like it or not. And rich people always studying how to get richer; they gonna read that will any day now. You just wait."

She looked embarrassed to admit that she had actually
been thinking about the money. Sometimes Mattie acted as
though money was a *bad* thing. "Well, I suppose. But whatever he left me don't matter. How much don't matter. I never
going to get anything near to what he'd have left his other
daughter, seeing as how he gave her his last name, instead of
me. But all I want to see is my name on paper. If he put me
down on a piece of paper for his whole family to see, and for
everybody to know he was willing to admit I was his, then,
how much he left me ain't important."

"You crazy? You don't know what you saying. Stand up
for what's yours, girl! If he leave some petty *caca-poule* for
you, you just got to complain. They got ways to do that."

Some people just didn't understand. Some people didn't
know how to recognize an opportunity and seize it. Before he
could tell her so, Threes got bored with staring them down
and waddled up to him, clawing at his pants leg, wanting to
be lifted up onto his shoulder. He scooped him up and
nudged him into position. If only everybody could be so
straightforward and direct. You knew what you wanted, you
asked for it, and most of the time, you got it—even if it sometimes took a little encouragement.

Scratching the mongoose's head, he remembered her dig
about the chickens. He could have told her that if things kept
on the way they were going, there wouldn't be any chickens
left to laugh at him. The change he'd won on the horses
today would buy him a little time, maybe a few days at best,
but after that, he'd be no better off than when he started.

"Hey." He put his hand on her shoulder and made soothing strokes down her back. "I want you to think about something."

"I'm not going over there," she said at once.

"Shh." He brought his finger to his lips. Women had to be
gentled, coaxed, just like young chickens. "I ain't asking you
to do nothing. I just want you to think about it. Don't throw

the thought out of your mind yet. Let it sit there a while, and you can go back to it in a bit and think about it some more."

"What you want me to think about?"

"All the things you could do if you got a little of what your daddy had. What's rightfully yours." He toyed with the ladybug pin on her chest, not wanting to overdo it by trying to hold her, but knowing that contact was essential for his words to be absorbed. "You don't have to say yes or no or maybe. You just have to think about it. You can promise me that?"

Her gaze was distant, past his shoulder, not focused anywhere, but falling somewhere on the back wall of the room. He joined her in her silence; to speak now could shatter her trance and undo all he had done. She wasn't sold over: he hadn't expected her to be.

But she was listening. And that was enough.

Mattie and Jonah

Mattie touched the wound on her thigh, none too gently. The dull pain with which it responded was a comfort. Pain meant you were still flesh; solid flesh, not a mirage. The buzzing in her ears and the throbbing in her body that from time to time warned her that she was slipping away into that state she feared had become steadily more intense ever since her father had died. She remembered feeling the first few stabs of it that Sunday morning, when she'd rifled through the newspapers to learn that he'd gone.

Dominic had been the one to remind her, by his presence, by his being, that she was real. She'd been *his* secret, and, as much as he'd loved her, his shame. He'd kept her under wraps, checking on her from time to time like a man peeping under the mattress just to reassure himself that his nest egg had not been stolen.

At her father's insistence, she'd hidden in broad daylight, living her life as any child did: going to school, playing in the schoolyard with friends, even having birthday parties, although he never attended them. Working in the parlor after her mother had died, being seen by and interacting with all those who streamed in and out to make their purchases. But as far as Dominic's family knew, Mattie did not exist, and from Thursday to Tuesday, she didn't exist for her father, either.

She often wondered if, had she found the courage to taxi over to his house in St. Clair and ring the bell, she would have been met with any acknowledgement from him. If her father had come to the door, to find her standing there, would he have seen her—or admit that he had—or would he have looked right through her and pretended to himself that the bell had tripped off due to some electrical fluke? Compliance with his enforced code of silence, by herself, her mother, and her mother's mother, had allowed him to go on with his unblemished, enviable life, and let him be a pillar of his church, and let the people of his community admire and look up to him and his perfect family. Her silence had ensured his untarnished character. Her nonexistence had made his own existence more concrete.

Her grandmother knew who she was, and so did her man, but they were not Dominic's people; they lived on the wrong side of his veil of secrets. It was the old story about the tree falling in the forest. She knew in her heart that if no one were there to hear it fall, it would make no noise. So now that her father was no longer here, and lacked the power to confirm or deny her very being, what was she? *Was* she?

She propped her elbows on the front counter of the parlor and rested her chin on her hands, brooding. It was after ten, and the recess crowd had scurried back off to their nearby schools, even the stragglers who stole every possible moment away from class. The shop would be quiet for another two hours, before the lunchtime crowd turned up. Even with the front door open, it was sweltering. Typical dry season weather: Easter was looming, and the heat unrelenting. Some of the sweets in their big jars were growing sticky, and Mattie hoped she'd get them sold soon, before they melted right away.

She set a coin on its side and spun it, watching it whirl and skip along the Formica top, and when it fell over, she set it spinning again. It hit a bump, a small irregularity in the worn surface, and that was enough to set it off its tangent, skating over the edge and onto the floor. Sucking her teeth, she bent over to look for it.

Nothing. It had rolled out of sight. She dropped to her knees, searching under the cupboards, squinting into the dimness.

There were footfalls just inside the doorway, and then a voice. "Hello? Anybody here?"

Mattie stiffened. Still absorbed by her musings, she was slow to return to reality, and for a moment she panicked. Then she remembered that the customer could hardly be expected to see her down behind the counter, so she popped to her feet, abandoning the lost coin.

The man was standing with his back turned slightly to her, trying to look past the shop and into the living room doorway. "Hello?" he called again.

"Here!" she said breathlessly, and slapped her hand on the countertop. The loud crack echoed like a falling tree, and he heard it and spun round. She knew him immediately. Jonah Reyes. "Here," she said again.

"Mattie." He looked pleased.

"You can see me?" She half expected him to say no.

He frowned, puzzled. "Can I...?" Then he nodded, slowly. "Yes. Yes, I can see you."

You a damn fool, she chastised herself. *Asking stupid questions.* With great effort, she grounded herself firmly in reality. "What you want?"

"Nothing," he said quickly, and then corrected himself. "I mean, I don't want anything from you. I just came to give you something."

She watched him suspiciously. "What you want to give me?"

He looked pleased with himself, as if he had pulled off a coup. "Come outside and see." He held out his hand.

Instead of looking down at it, she focused on his face. "You can't give me in here?"

He looked thoughtful. "Maybe. I suppose I could. But it's nicer outside. More fun outside."

She was scornful. "When I got up this morning, I wasn't thinking about 'fun.' I was thinking about minding my store."

He looked around them ostentatiously. "It's not exactly thronging with customers. Come on. Step outside, just for a second. Then you can come back in if you like." He still hadn't let his hand fall back to his side. It remained open, palm up, beckoning.

Reluctant, but curious, she lifted the barrier between herself and the customers' side of the store, walked through it, and let the lid fall. His grin grew even wider, the eyes behind his thin glasses full of anticipation. What surprise could he possibly have for her that would get him so excited?

The answer lay on the other side of the door. Propped up against the wall was a sleek, shiny bike. In spite of herself, Mattie stooped over to look at it. The seat and frame were the color of strawberry-flavored lipstick, and the chrome trim was so shiny, she could see her own reflection. The bell distorted the image of her face, making it ripple out of proportion. She leaned closer, touching her reflection, half expecting it to be warm and yielding, like flesh.

"Ten speeds," he said, gleeful. "And a basket in the back, for you to put things in. And a holder for your water. Nicer than the one you had, isn't it? Faster."

"And what's it for?"

"Because I wrecked yours. This is for you. To replace your old one. And for your birthday, too. You like it?"

She frowned. "How'd you know it was my birthday that day?" Then she tapped her forehead lightly in realization. The question was a waste of good air. Auntie Lou. Always ready to chat about anything with a stranger.

He looked embarrassed. "I'm just sorry I didn't know at the time. If I had . . ." He looked helpless.

Her lips moved wryly. "What? You wouldn't have hit me?"

Blood flooded his face, so out of pity she let the subject drop and inched around the bike, bent over to inspect it up close. The chrome wheel guards bounced the orange of her dress right back at her. It *was* a nice bike, and offering it to her was a decent gesture; there was nothing that said he had to. She looked up to smile at him, and as she did so, she jumped. He'd been bending over, too, not watching the bike, but watching *her* watch the bike. No, not looking at her, but looking *into* her. The dark eyes were focused, unwavering, questing.

His gaze penetrated, and if she could have twisted out of his visual grasp, she would have; but she was riveted there, pierced by his wordless questions. A few days before, she had not existed for this man. Then, with the screeching of brakes and the crunching of metal, she'd been thrown into his line of vision, moving from nothingness into being. Now someone else from Dominic's circle knew who and what she was. Jonah Reyes was the listener in her forest. With this realization, the threatening tingle in her body dulled, receding from a persistent throb into a hum that all but blended into the background.

She got to her feet. "Thanks," she managed to tell him. She let him think she was thanking him for the bike.

"You want to ride it?" He indicated the road outside with a jerk of his head.

"What, now?"

"Yes. I'll go with you. We can take it for a spin. That way, if you don't like it, we can get a new one."

Her laugh was incredulous, but not unkind. "You plan on trotting along beside me?"

"I plan on *riding* along beside you. On my bike. I got one just like yours, only green. And bigger. It's in the back of my van. Come show me around your neighborhood. I haven't ridden in years. Not since I was a boy. I used to like to ride for miles, up out to the coast sometimes. Maracas and Las Cuevas, to visit my mother. I'd really like to be back in the saddle again. What you say?"

The caprice of the wealthy, she thought. He was able to get up and decide he wanted to take a ride in the middle of the day, just like that. Didn't he have a living to earn? "My father's business," she asked him, "it just sits there losing money while you go riding? Weren't you his second in command? Aren't you the boss now?"

He spun the pedal with his toe. "It's not losing money. It's doing okay. I just took a few hours off to come see you. Didn't Dominic ever do that, on a whim?"

"No."

"Will you come with me anyway?"

She pointed at the store behind her. "Maybe you don't need to be around where you work every minute of the day, but some of us got to do just that. We don't work, we don't eat. And I got a store to mind."

The thought didn't seem to have struck him before. "Where's your grandmother?"

"Out."

"Just you here, then?"

"Yeah. And the business don't run with the store closed."

His hand went to his back pocket. "How much do you take in in an hour?"

Mattie gaped. He wasn't serious. He wasn't offering to buy her time, like some stray *jammette* off the street. "Tell me you not offering what I think you are," she grunted. She shoved on the bike, and it toppled over in his direction. He wasn't fast enough to catch it, and the bell made a dinging sound as it smacked into the hard dirt. "Tell me you're not thinking you can just hand me money and make it okay. Look, I don't need your money, and I don't need your damn bike. Take it back to the store; see if you'll get a refund."

With one hand, he tried to right the bike, and with the

other, he tried to stop her from turning and storming back into the house. "Sorry. Oh, God, Mattie, I'm sorry. That was stupid. I didn't mean it that way."

"How'd you mean it?"

"I just want so badly for you to have this bike."

"Why, so you won't have to feel guilty?"

"No." He thought about it for a few moments. "At least, not entirely. I feel bad about what happened. And I want to make it right. But I want you to have the bike to make *you* feel better, not just to make *me* feel better."

"So, lean it up against the wall and walk away."

He leaned it against the wall, but made no move to go anywhere. "But I want to be with you when you ride it. I want to watch you enjoy it."

Was he for real? Did he plan on sitting back, pleased with himself, watching her enjoy his gift like some beneficent elf? "You don't know me. You don't know anything about me. You only met me once. Why you care whether I enjoy it or not? What's it to you?"

He was patient as he explained, half to himself as well as to her. "Because you're . . . family."

She swallowed hard. Family. Dominic's family, and so his. Did he really believe that sharing a bloodline with his wife made her one of them? Her father had always made it clear to her that blood ties were incidental. Now this man was speaking to her as if she were a part of his world. *I belong; therefore I am. You accept me; therefore I exist.*

Oh, temptation.

She turned her head to the store entrance. Inside, all was quiet. "Kids don't come out until lunchtime," she said haltingly. "Besides, it's Lent. Half the children don't get any sweet money: they're supposed to be fasting." She hoped her reasoning would quell her own doubts. "Slower than usual, anyhow you look at it."

"Bad for the business of indulgence, Lent." He looked sympathetic.

"Yes."

He looked at his watch. "More than enough time to try the bikes out," he said.

She patted herself down for her keys and, without another word, pulled the front door closed, locked it, and began wheeling the bike out of the yard.

"You don't want to change first?" he called after her. "You're not dressed for riding."

She was perfectly capable of riding in a skirt, but she didn't bother to reassure him of that. He sounded like her grandmother. Instead, she took in his leather shoes, knife-pleated pants, long-sleeved shirt, and tie, and retorted, "You neither."

He followed close on her heels. She didn't wait for him to haul his bike out of the back of the van—Dominic's van, she noticed, the one he used on weekends—but slung a leg over her own and sailed off. She was at the end of the street before he caught up with her.

He let her lead the way. She chose the high road, crossing over into less densely populated terrain, climbing steadily upward, away from the schools and shopping district. Farther up, a large, sprawling monastery cut into the face of the forested hillside like a thick scar. It would be quiet there, and cool, and if there were a route that would test the mettle of a bike, this would be it.

Neither of them was winded, but neither chose to speak, either. They rode neck and neck, striving to pull ahead, each one's pride refusing to be bested. But even as the climb grew harder, the contest settled into something more amicable. Company rather than competition. Mattie stole a sideways glance at him. Perspiration flecked his brow and upper lip, soaked into his shirt at the armpits, and yet there was serenity on his face, perhaps pleasure at sailing free on an open road on this hot weekday morning.

She broke the silence. "Here." She skidded to a stop on a grassy verge and leaped off before he could voice an opinion.

He stopped next to her, but remained on his bike. "The monastery's just two turns ahead. The view's better from there. It's just a minute away."

From where she sat she could see all the way to the southern end of the island, where the valley smoothed out to plains and then rose again into a jagged mountain range. Most of the lowland was blanketed in haze. She shrugged. "I've seen the view up there. The view's fine here, too." She gave him a taunting smile. "What you want to go all the way to the end for? To pray? Dip your finger in holy water and ask for special favors? You one of them good Catholic boys?"

He gave in to her decision to stop without further protest and set his bike down next to hers, squatting beside her before speaking. "I don't know about the 'good' part."

"Something special make you bad?"

"No. But nothing special makes me good, either."

"Aren't we all like that?"

"Most of us, I guess. Hard getting used to the idea, though. You go along hoping it's not true, that some people really are perfect. Then one little bad thing changes everything."

She knew he was thinking of Dominic. There had been so much disappointment in his eyes the day he'd discovered her, and from the look of him, she was sure he was still turning the revelation over and over in his mind. That irritated her. Why did he so insist that Dominic be what he wanted him to be? Did he expect everyone to conform to his idea of them? "He wasn't a god, you know," she pointed out.

"I know that. That's silly."

"Just because it's silly don't mean you don't think it. Or wish it. And why's he got to be one anyway? It's not like he was your real father. Not like he made you. You married into the family. The stakes aren't all that high."

"They are high. And he *was* my real father. He was more my father than the man that lay with my mother. He took me in, and he didn't have to. He treated me like a son, and he didn't have to. I was just the maid's nephew, but he never made me feel like there was anything wrong with that."

Mattie was surprised. This pretty city boy with the fine leather shoes, the maid's nephew? She didn't remember Dominic ever having said anything about that!

"I knew more about him than I did about my own wife," he was saying. "When I got there, she was just a baby, wanting to play dress-up, inviting me to pretend tea parties. But he wanted to talk with me, really talk. About whatever was in the newspapers that day, or about whatever book I was reading. For twenty years, he talked about everything. Except you."

"And he let the maid's nephew marry his daughter?" She wrinkled her nose in disbelief. This was the man who had refused to marry a candy-store girl, even though she was the only woman he'd ever loved, because that sort of thing just wasn't done. Were the rules any less stringent for his precious daughter?

"He wasn't like that. He loved me."

She didn't bother to argue. What Dominic was and wasn't like slipped and sloshed with the tide. "And you loved him."

"Yes."

"And her."

"Yes, of course. She's my wife." His voice was confident, but his hand flew to his wedding band, checking to ensure it was still there.

"Which came first?"

"What?" He frowned.

"You love the daughter because you loved the man, or you loved the man because you loved the daughter?" Mattie watched him closely, trying to read his face. Her question startled him, and she expected outrage, hot denials, or a reminder that it was none of her business. But instead, he looked stunned, his brows shooting up over the rim of his glasses. She'd never met this woman with whom she shared her father's genes, and could not guess at how loveable she was, but she had known Dominic all her life and knew how easy it was for him to draw people to him. To make them love him.

Jonah plucked at the grass by his knee, holding a blade between his fingers, and watching it flap agitatedly in the wind. He let it go, and it was snatched away and swept up into the air. He plucked another and held it tight. "I love my wife," he said eventually.

She could have left well enough alone, but here was a man who had the keys to that forbidden door, and for as long as he was around, the door would be just ajar enough for her to peer through it. "And my sister," she asked. "She thinks our father is a god, too?"

He brought the blade of grass level with his eyes, following the pattern of veins along its side. "Justice loved him."

"And was she shocked and horrified to find out about me? Did knowing make her lose her faith?" She tried to keep her teeth from grinding as she forced out the words. *Shocking*. A terrible thing it was, to know that you *shocked* people just by being.

He laid the blade of grass carefully down, as if he didn't want it to get lost among the others, in case he needed to pick it up again. "She doesn't know."

"You didn't tell her?"

He shook his head.

"Why not?" She'd been sure he'd gone back home, on the day of the funeral, to break the news. He didn't look like one for secrets.

His eyes were on hers. "Because you didn't want me to. On the day I met you, you were hiding. That awful hat, to hide your eyes. Remember? And then you ran. Don't tell me you were going to walk up the aisle and introduce yourself to Faith. You started it. The secrecy. And then, when I was leaving your house, your grandmother asked me not to say anything."

"But whether I wanted it or not, and no matter what Auntie Lou said, you were going to talk anyway."

He nodded.

"So what stopped you?"

He frowned into the distance at the hazy curtain that shrouded the valley below, focusing hard. "Justice was always fragile. She's young—"

"Same age as me. She's a grown-up."

"Yes, yes, I know. But there's something about her that's different. There's always been a little child in her that never went away. And lately, I've been thinking that she's not well. She's thinner and thinner, almost every time I look at her. And pale."

"Flu?"

"No. Something else. She goes somewhere in her mind, and I can't follow."

"What's that got to do with me?"

"I just thought that . . . if I told her . . ." He struggled with his answer. "No offense, but this just isn't the right time. She's still grieving. It all happened so suddenly, and she was there when he died. It would be a shock."

"And when would the right time be?"

Guilt flooded his face, and Mattie knew that time might never come. "Justice tends to be slow to heal," he told her. "It might be a while until she's ready to hear something like that."

"A long while," Mattie said dryly. So that was the way it was going to be. Someone else had decided that she could peep through that door, but not enter. Someone else had decided that there were very good reasons for her to remain half hidden in the shadows, little more than a shadow herself. "What if I say she's ready?" she surprised herself by asking.

He was immediately tense. "What's that supposed to mean?"

"What if I'm tired of hiding? What if I'm tired of spending my whole life pretending I'm not here, just so that somebody else can feel better? What happened between my mother and father is no big deal. Men have mistresses. It happens every day. Now both of them are dead, so there's no secret to protect anymore. What if I decide it's time for everyone to stop being ashamed of me?"

"Maybe Dominic was ashamed. *I'm* just concerned."

"Not concerned for *me*. How come I'm family enough for you, but not for anyone else in your house? Suppose I decide enough's enough? Suppose I walk up your drive and bang on the door until your wife or my father's wife comes to answer it, and I lift my head so they can see his eyes on me? Would that be such a terrible thing?"

"And what would that achieve?"

"It would give me what's rightfully mine."

He watched her shrewdly, understanding coming. "And what would that be, money? Don't worry . . ." He got up and dusted off the seat of his pants, righting his bike and holding it steady with one hand. "I know there's a will, and the time will come to read it. Soon. Maybe you're mentioned. Even if you're not, I handle the business now." He looked proud just to be able to say it. "I'll make sure you get a reasonable—"

She shut him up with a thump on the shoulder. Even back on her feet again, that was as high as she could reach. "What you take me for?" she shouted into his face, although she knew damn well he could hear her perfectly. "I told you last time, I don't want your money. You think you can just hand money over, like it means nothing to you, and everything will be all right?"

"I'm not handing anything over. You're the one talking about what's rightfully yours. If you're shaking me down, at least be honest about it. Don't throw it all back on me!"

"I'm not shaking you down. It's not about money. How many times I have to tell you that?" She thought about Blood Pye guiltily. He might have been correct, at least a little, about some of Dominic's money being rightfully hers. But money was something you spent too soon and usually had nothing to show for it afterward. There were things in life worth more than any amount of money could pay for. This young pretty boy, who was so anxious to step into Dominic's shoes, would never understand that.

He was still standing too close, hands on his hips, belligerent and defensive, waiting for an answer. She replied fast, not giving herself enough time to think, lest she grow cowardly and back out. "It's not about money. I was never talking about money. I'm talking about bursting in on their comfort and wrecking their idea of their perfect world. I want to leave footprints in their flower beds and then track the dirt in through the front door. I want your wife and mother-in-law to see me!" She thumped her chest. "*See me!* And *know!* Understand?"

His ire rose to match hers. "You weren't singing that song a week ago. I had to chase you over half of Woodbrook just to get you to a doctor! A week ago the last thing you wanted was for them to *see you*. What happened?"

"Nothing happened. Nothing's changed. I just got tired of everyone, everybody, telling me to lay low and not make any trouble. I had all my life to get good at that. Duck and cover whenever there was a threat of discovery. I remember shopping in a store one day, before Christmas, a long time ago. My mother took me to look for a new dress to wear to church on Christmas morning. And I saw my father, just the back of his head, from across the aisle. He had a little girl hanging onto one arm and a woman on the other. My mother snatched me up and ran in the other direction, to the back exit, and started kicking at the back door, trying to get out. The guard thought we were stealing the dress, 'cause she had it in her hand. And my father never even noticed. With all that racket going on, my mother and the guard shouting at each other, and her still trying to force her way through the back, he just finished shopping and left. Because commotion didn't have a place in his perfect life.

"And we left without the dress. Christmas morning came,

and I had to wear the dress I got the year before. It was too tight. I couldn't sit straight, or turn, or bend over. But that didn't matter to my mother because Dominic's secret was *safe*." She sprayed the last word up into his face, but he didn't flinch. She could feel the bands of the dress pinching her even now. "So what if I decide that I've had enough? Suppose I say it's over? Would you deny me that?"

"It's not in my power to give or deny. I just think that now is not the right moment. My mother-in-law is grieving for her husband. My wife is . . . not well. I'm begging you—"

"You, beg?" She laughed. "I'm the beggar here. You're making me the beggar here."

"No, no!" He tried to brush her assertion away with his hands. "It's not like that. All I want is time. Please. I'm asking you to give me some time."

"So you become the keeper of the secret?"

"If you see it that way."

"And you become the one to tell me if it's okay or when it's okay to let it out, right?"

"All I can do is ask."

She needed to be cruel. She needed to inflict on him the hurt she was feeling. "So tell me; how long you been waiting to be Dominic? You spend all your life watching him, looking up to him, copying the way he walked and the way he talked? You hung on to every word so you can say them back to yourself when you're alone? Somewhere inside of you, you were happy when he died, right? So his space would be vacant, and you could fill it."

His hand flew to his stomach, as if she had kicked him there. "When he died, everything crashed. My hands were on his chest. My mouth was on his, trying to give him my breath. I felt his soul slip from his body. I wanted mine to slip away, too, and follow his. I lost everything. So don't tell me about—"

"You still have your wife," she countered. "And Dominic's wife, looking for you to be the man of the house."

"Faith doesn't need me to be anything for her."

"And the business," she went on, forcing her fist into the wound she'd ripped into him. "And the cars. Funny thing is, the only thing you don't have, that you'll never have, is his last name."

When he cringed, she saw that she'd hit home. She stepped closer to him, so that there was barely a space between her body and his. Her temerity surprised her. Her awareness of his warmth, as she stood on tiptoe to bring her lips close to his ear, surprised her even more. "Well," she whispered, so that even the wind was deaf to her, "looks like you and I are in the same boat, doesn't it?"

He bent nearer, the better to hear. His hand came up to touch the side of her head, and he let his fingers move across her twists, experimentally, feeling out their thickness. "Looks like it," he said after a while. His voice was muffled by her hair.

He was part ally, part jailor. Part prisoner himself, locked away in one of the many cells Dominic had constructed for the people in his life, to keep them just where it would benefit him most. She almost felt sorry for him. Loving Dominic had trapped them both, as surely as flies on flypaper.

A car whizzed past on its way to the Mount. Pilgrims seeking a sanctuary in which to pray. *To everyone his own,* Mattie thought. Her altar, hers and Jonah's, was made up of memories of one man's life.

"What's next?" he asked softly.

Her proximity to her sister's husband made her ache in a way she had not anticipated. She squeezed her eyes shut, afraid to look at him, in case she saw the same ache mirrored there. She thrust her hands behind her back, hand over wrist, hand over wrist, holding them fast so that the urge to touch him, even briefly, would not overcome her. But neither backed away; they stood jaw to jaw, mouth to ear, so that a murmur could pass from one to the other unintercepted even by any spirit that might have wandered down from the monastery. As she was so much shorter than he, she had to remain on tiptoe to achieve this, and her calf muscles quivered with the strain.

He sensed the effort it took for her to keep her balance, and his arm whipped around her, encountering her intertwined hands, into the small of her back, firm and gentle, giving her support. When she was unable to answer, he asked again. "Mattie? What do we do next?"

"I'll swap you," she bartered like a market vendor. "Story for story. You tell me about growing up with him in that big house. About how a maid's nephew became his son. I'll tell you about the living room behind the sweet shop. Playing cards and eating take-away food. What my mother was like, and what he was like when he was with my mother." His hand was so warm over hers. "Deal?"

She waited. She could feel the muscles of his jaw working against her cheek. If she tipped forward even an inch, she would be able to feel the movement of his chest that went with the rasp of his breath against her ear.

Bad idea, she thought. If they came together again, to talk about Dominic, to go over and over his life as the faithful read and reread accounts of the lives of the saints, they would be like addicts feeding each other's habit. Shooting each other up with the drug they both craved, even though they knew it to be poison. She wanted to withdraw her crazy suggestion and let Dominic rest. Let them each pry themselves away from that sticky flypaper on their own. But she waited for his answer anyway, hoping that maybe he would be the one to say no and to tell her it was a stupid thought.

"Tomorrow, in the afternoon, when your shop's quiet again," he said. "Here." He pointed. "You'll remember this tree? I'll meet you under it. Then we'll talk."

She dropped down from tiptoe and felt a cramping in her legs, but it was a moment before his arm came away from her waist. She opened her eyes after all and looked up at him.

He inhaled sharply between his teeth. "Your eyes . . . they're so much like . . ."

"Hers," she finished for him. Her guilt at striking such an unholy deal with her sister's husband was not as great as she'd have expected. She broke their contact and instead laid her hands on the cool metal of her bike. She glanced into the small rearview mirror mounted on the handlebar and saw that her reflection was startlingly clear, each detail almost surreal. More tangible than she herself was. She wheeled onto the edge of the road and waited for him to mount his own bike.

Then she shot off, lengths ahead of him, the downhill ride much easier than their climb had been. He made no attempt to chase her, or to keep up, and that stung. It was late, and the sweet shop had been unattended for far too long; but business passed through her mind for only a fleeting moment. Instead, as she rode, she sifted through her memories, seeking out gems, of Wednesday evenings that stood out in her mind for fun or pathos. When she found a good one, she filed it away, rehearsing it in her mind, making sure she forgot nothing, or that the distortion of time had not skewed the details.

Tomorrow, she would become a storyteller.

Justice

Justice laid the glass penguin down next to the swan and dropped the soft chamois she was holding into her lap. Her menagerie took up most of the space on her dressing table: her make-up was all shoved to one side, and as for Jonah, well, he had to keep his own things in the bathroom. There were actually two penguins: an upright adult and a small reclining chick. These she kept far away from the big, bloated sea lion, because if she remembered right, sea lions fed on penguin chicks. Didn't they?

Among her collection was a family of Siamese cats, poodles tied together with gold thread around the neck, owls, dolphins, a whale, a speeding greyhound, a mother duck tailed by six ducklings, a snail, and a spider with emerald eyes. Each one had been a gift from her father, and each had been bought just for her in some distant country, whenever Papa traveled. She'd gotten her first, a laughing pig, when she'd been just five or six. Within days she'd dropped it to the floor, and its head had smashed like an egg. She remembered the screams tearing out of her as the pig lay dead on the floor. The only person home at the time had been Elba, Jonah's aunt, who had come in, panicked, and scooped her up, searching for whatever injury could have made a little girl cry so much. Even after Elba had cleaned up the shattered pieces of crystal, Justice continued to cry, and kept on wailing until her father came home. He'd scoured the streets until he found another piglet, not exactly the same, he'd told her, but a pig was a pig.

Justice had refused to touch it. A pig *wasn't* a pig. The one her father had given her had died because she'd dropped it, and nothing anybody could do would change that. After several nights of being unable to sleep while the interloper sat on her table and grinned its piggy grin at her, she'd sneaked it out into the garden and poked it down a hole with a stick. If anybody noticed the pig missing, they never mentioned it.

Once, after they were married, Jonah had made the mistake of buying her a glass panda, when he'd traveled abroad in her father's stead. She'd smiled at the time and tried to act pleased, but he'd sensed her coolness and begged for an explanation. There was none that she could give. Didn't he understand that the glass animal zoo was something between herself and her father? Couldn't he see that this was a special place he couldn't go? In the end, she moved the panda onto a bookshelf, far from the other animals, and tried to forget it was there.

Before she could resume dusting, the door opened behind her, and she looked around to see her husband toss his briefcase onto a chair and begin plucking at his tie. "Sweetheart," he said.

She didn't get up. He walked over and crouched next to her, kissing her on the forehead. "What did you do today?" he asked.

What did she do? She tried to recall. "Nothing," she mumbled finally. "You?"

Something flickered over his face, like jalousies being snapped shut in a distant window. "I went riding. After work."

"Again?" For a week, maybe more, ever since he'd taken up with that new bike of his, he'd come in an hour or so later than usual, shirt damp from exertion, face flushed from exercise.

"Again. It's good for me." He shot her a look. "Do you mind?"

She wondered if she minded or not. She hadn't sat in the window waiting for him since the day they had buried Papa. At first, because getting downstairs to the window took too much energy out of her, and lately, because his hours had become so unpredictable that there wasn't much point. She tried to frame an answer, but he didn't wait for one. Instead, he fussed with her hair, picking fluff out of it, and let his eyes run down her body. She was wearing nothing but a silk shift that slipped over the head and fell to the knee, covering her nakedness underneath. She hadn't felt like getting dressed when she'd gotten out of bed this morning, so she hadn't bothered to.

When he lifted his eyes to hers again, there was concern there. "Tish?"

"Yes?" She focused on his mouth, trying to concentrate on what he was saying. All she could see was within a small circle centered on his face, and around that, everything was fuzzy and gray. As he spoke, his teeth and lips formed elaborate shapes.

"You had a bath today?"

"I haven't got anywhere to go." She laughed lightly. "I haven't left the room. Why would I need a bath?"

"It doesn't matter if you go anywhere," he told her. "You can have a bath all the same. And wash your hair. It's so pretty when it's clean and shiny. And you'll feel better."

"I feel fine."

"All the same." Still, this quiet, patient, gentle voice. "You can still have one. I'll help you, if you like." Gently, he tilted her chin so that she could see the bathroom door. It was way, way across the room. It would take forever to get there. "Come," he told her. He got to his feet and tugged her up. "Sit with me while I let the bath fill."

She followed him willingly. Jonah had always looked out for her, even when she was a little girl. He'd been a big brother to her, but without the big brother pranks like spiders in the hair and shoves off the swing. Always gentle, protective, and kind. So much of Papa in him.

She sat on the toilet and watched as he fiddled with the fixtures over the tub. When she was very small, Papa had been the one to help her with her bath, either him or Elba. Mama hadn't been one for that sort of thing; she always complained that Justice splashed so much that when it was all over, *she* was the one that needed drying. But Papa hadn't minded the splashing. It always made him laugh. Sometimes he'd splash back, drenching the bathroom walls, water even reaching as far as the sink. Then he'd wrap her up in a towel and sweep her off to bed and call Elba up to take care of the mess.

Jonah poured pink liquid under the water's stream and then tested the temperature. "It's nice and hot. It's just the way you like it, Tish." The room smelled of strawberries. He waited for her to strip off and climb in, but when she made no move to do so, he motioned for her to hold her arms up and slid the shift over her head. He stopped in midmotion and goggled.

She stood, arms still in the air, above her head like a ballerina's, and turned for him, slowly. "Nice, huh?" She looked down at herself. She could see past her small breasts to the concave curve of her belly, deepening out of her line of vision, and then her hip bones, jutting like natural outcroppings on a smooth cliff face. "I'm smaller than Mama is now," she informed him. "Her dresses would just swallow me up. I'm going to have to go shopping soon, to get new clothes. But not too fast, in a little while. Otherwise, it would be a waste of time. A few weeks from now, they won't fit, either."

"God, Justice," her husband said. He touched her abdomen lightly, seeming afraid that pressure would hurt. "What are you doing to yourself?"

"Dieting." The irritation in her voice was manifest. Always asking the same questions, over and over, like a simple-minded little boy. Men were so foolish sometimes. They understood so little of the ways of women. "I've told you. A thousand times, I've told you."

"That's not dieting. That's—"

"What? What is it?"

"It's crazy. It's madness. Look at yourself. Have you seen yourself?"

Some days, she did nothing all day but stand in front of the mirror, dressed or not, and make slow turns, admiring her hard work. Feeling good about her success. *Of course* she'd seen herself. Her body was a work in progress, and she was doing a damn fine job. "Yes, I see myself. And what I see, I like."

"But, baby, please. You're much too thin. How much thinner you want to be?"

"Slim, not thin," she corrected. "Thin is for beggars and starving children." How much slimmer did she want to be? That was another stupid question. Slim had no limit, just as elegance had no outer edge. She was sorry Papa wasn't around to see her as she was now, smaller than his wife for the first time since she was thirteen. But Mama was there. Mama knew now that there was one thing her daughter did better than she could. How wonderful that was!

He looked about to contradict her, but after a pause, said, "Your water's getting cold." He held out his hand like a gentleman offering to help a lady dismount from a horse. She took it and let him settle her into the bath. It *was* just the way she liked it. In some ways, he was so good at knowing what she wanted, but in others, he hadn't a clue. She closed her eyes. She could sense and hear him close by, feel the bath sponge squeezing water into her hair, and then gentle hands lathered up shampoo. He kept scooping up the rivulets of suds that ran down her forehead, to prevent them from flowing into her eyes. She tilted her head to help him.

When he was finished shampooing, he began on her body, using the same big sponge. Even on her breasts, his touch was light and gentle, like that of a nurse. Ever since the day of the funeral, he'd made no attempt to make love with her, and she'd made no attempt to initiate it or to question his forbearance.

Actually, she was glad he hadn't tried, as she didn't think she had the energy to deal with the argument that would follow her refusal. It would somehow feel weird, she and Jonah doing that, now that Papa was gone. When he was still alive she'd taken special pleasure in reaching for Jonah while her father and mother slept next door. There was something calming about knowing that Papa was nearby. There was an energy that came off him, like warmth off the sun, which penetrated the wall between the two bedrooms as if there were no barrier there.

If she scrunched up her eyes hard enough and concentrated, Jonah's voice would become Papa's, and his touch, and even his scent. This was the boy her father had raised, who had wanted so desperately to be just like him that he adopted every gesture, every turn of phrase, his morality, and his politics. The wedding ring Jonah had placed on her finger was like a metal connection jammed into a wall socket, causing electricity to leap across a divide it had no business crossing. By marrying the man who was her father's "son," but not her brother, she could be both daughter and lover and still know in her heart that there was no guilt to be felt for the liaison. It had been sanctified and blessed by God, hadn't it? A priest had joined their hands, and they had legal documents to prove that she had every right to be in this man's bed. And even though Jonah's loving was only a conduit leading her straight to the man she really loved, who lay asleep in the other room next to her mother, it was all right and good. There had been no sinful joining of flesh, no moral crime that would have caused the angels to cry out their outrage to the sky.

And although Papa had loved her back, more than he did any living creature, he had never known her secret. There had never been a shred of evidence in her eyes when she'd smiled at him, or in her hugs, or in her chaste little kisses. Her special love for him had been her private, high-walled garden.

But now he was gone, and with him, the desire that singed her. The electricity that had coursed between them no longer arced through the wall; the distance between her and the grave was one even that could not bridge. With Papa's death had gone her need for her husband. Now, for her, he was sexless, neuter. Or maybe *she* was; it didn't matter. She pressed against him for warmth at night, as a sister would in her older brother's bed during a storm, giving no signal that she wanted more than that, and to his credit, he made no further attempt to seek it.

When he was done bathing her, Jonah asked her to stand up. She did, letting the water course down her body and back into the tub. She waited patiently for him to get her a towel, but instead of doing so, he leaned over, taking her in his arms, lifting her high against him without effort. She gasped. "Don't fight me." He sat on the toilet and held her against him. His cotton shirt sucked up the water, becoming darker wherever her body made contact. His lap was soaked. He didn't notice, or else he didn't care. Instead, he pressed her head into his shoulder and steadied her with one hand. "I just want to hold on to you for a bit. Is that okay?"

Rather than answer, she suffered his touch patiently, closing her eyes so that she didn't have to look into his. It was a while before she realized he was talking, making idle conversation about nothing. It took so much energy to listen that after she had determined that he wasn't expecting her to respond, she gave up the effort and let her mind drift, hearing the sound of his voice rising and falling, and the metered pauses and inflections, but making no attempt to decipher their meaning.

"You trying to give her a cold?"

That wasn't Jonah's voice. Justice's eyes opened. Mama

was standing in the doorway. She was holding the ugly African statue she'd taken to carrying around, grasping it in her hand like a club. "You should be ashamed of yourself. Making my daughter sit around wet like that. Exposed. While you paw her. What the hell has gotten into you, boy?" Jonah's body snapped taut under her. "What're you doing here?" he asked.

Mama gave him one of her hard looks. "I live here." Jonah grunted. "You know what I mean. What are you doing in our bathroom, Faith? Don't my wife and I have a right to privacy?"

Mama's gaze traveled from Jonah's face to the wet marks on his shirt, and then to Justice's naked body. There were so many emotions on her face, and each one was nameless. Justice felt her mother's eyes touch her like fingers, moving from her cheekbones to her chin, to the hollows at her throat and the angles of her shoulders, pausing for a while at her small breasts, then past them, tapping along the clear line of her sternum. Her hip bones like parentheses framing the fine hairs on her crotch. She sucked her belly in, imagining it touching her spine, smiling up at her mother with pride, and more.

Mama didn't bother to answer Jonah. She didn't look at him a second time. Instead, she walked deeper into the room and spoke directly to Justice. "You planning to sit there, wet, all day? You actually *trying* to catch pneumonia?"

Justice felt her mother's hand encircle her upper arm, jerking her onto her feet. Jonah uttered a protest, his arm still around her waist, trying to keep her on his lap; but reluctant to hurt her by struggling, he let her go, and the momentum propelled her forward. Mama shoved her through the door into the bedroom. "Get dried and get dressed. I don't plan on having a second funeral, understand?"

Her towel was in the bathroom, and Mama was blocking the door; so Justice patted herself dry with a bedspread and began searching for something to wear. She'd rather put her housedress back on again, but Mama wouldn't like that. She'd been wearing the same one all week.

Behind her, she heard Jonah say, "Faith, I asked you a question."

Mama's voice was neutral, uninterested. "What question was that, Jonah?"

"Whether my wife and I are allowed any—"

"Privacy? I heard you. I wasn't sure you really expected an answer."

"It's a straightforward question." Jonah still hadn't risen from his seat on the toilet.

"Listen, Jonah. Let me explain something to you. This is my home."

"Mine, too."

Mama went on as though he had said nothing. "I walk through its rooms as I please. You should know that by now."

Justice looked around, still naked, to see her mother agitatedly thumping the statue against her legs, holding it by its feet. Jonah got up, and as he was taller, she had to tilt her head way back to look at him. There was anger on his face and in his voice.

"You'd never have done that if Dominic was still here," he told her.

"Dominic isn't. And besides, I had no idea you were home already. You've been coming home so late these days, I really wasn't expecting you. And I wasn't looking for you; I came to speak to my daughter. And she doesn't mind if I don't knock, do you, Justice?"

Her mother and her husband both turned to her, Mama expectant, not questioning her support, and Jonah silently pleading for her not to embarrass him. Justice hated confrontation, hated the tension and the unspoken words that could hurt so much more than the ones that found voice. She hung her head and didn't answer.

Instead of waiting for a reply, Mama turned to Jonah

again, who was struggling to master his perplexed expression. Neither his height nor his proximity intimidated her. When she spoke next, she used the voice she usually kept in store for uppity sales people and servants who didn't know their place. "I think it's time you understood something, Jonah: being the only male *in* the house doesn't make you the man *of* the house. This is my house, and *I* am the one in charge. Whatever route you took to get here, and whatever influence you had over my husband to allow you to worm your way out of the servants' quarters and into my daughter's bed, died when he did—"

"Mama!" Justice was aghast. She should say something, do something to stop this; but Mama had her warrior face on, and when she did, someone was going to get slashed. It could be Jonah or it could be her, and although she hated to see the hurt and anger and embarrassment that were rushing into his face and mottling his skin, he was the one in the line of fire now, not her, and trying to help him would only deflect Mama's wounding words, not stop them. She scurried to the farthest corner of the room and fumbled with her clothing, trying to drag it on in the vain hope that Mama would be satisfied that there would be no pneumonia in the offing and leave.

Jonah was grasping the countertop as if it would keep him from tearing at her, and Justice read tension in his body, a tensing and coiling that told her it was all he could do not to retaliate, or defend himself; but Mama went on, unaware of the danger, or unafraid of it. "You're dealing with me now, Jonah. I'm the one that's left. And believe me, your influence does not extend this far. You don't sit on my furniture and eat at my table and sleep in this bed"—she pointed through the doorway to the big four-poster Justice had slept in all her life—"because you have a godfather to run interference for you. You do all that because I allow it. And when my husband's lawyer reads his will on Tuesday, I have no doubt that he will have been very generous to you. But that won't change a thing. You will always be what you are: a grubby little beach brat that manages to look presentable because my husband cleaned you up and taught you how to speak properly and use a knife and fork. I don't run the business, not because I can't, but because I couldn't be bothered. You run his business because you happen to have a brain in your head, and my husband taught you well. But that's as far as it goes. I am proprietor, Director, and CEO, and you will always work for me. So do yourself a favor and don't push your luck, is that clear?"

Before Jonah could answer, she spun, with Papa's black statuette across her breast like a soldier shouldering arms, and left the room.

Faith and the Statuette

By the time she made it to her private study, Faith was trembling. Part of her felt a little guilty at having flown off the handle at Jonah like that—he'd looked so stunned, it was almost comical—but the greater part of her was enraged. Really, what had he been thinking? Had he taken a good look at Justice? She was thin enough to catch a chill in a warm wind.

What was the child doing? Her and her dieting. Of course, she'd always taught her daughter that a lady should look after herself, and not let her body run to ruin like a thick-hipped country woman, but this was pushing it. Justice was never meant to be that slender; she'd inherited more of her father's genes than her mother's, and Dominic had always been stocky. She liked her daughter better with more flesh on her bones anyway. She'd have to talk to her, or maybe call a doctor in. That was it. If Justice got any worse, she was calling a doctor.

Faith set the wretched statuette down on an ornamental wooden shelf, already crowded with pieces of art that were more to her own taste. The crude black wood looked odd among her Wedgwood and Delftware. She couldn't for the life of her figure out what she was still doing with it and, for that matter, why she was actually walking around with it wherever she went, caring for it like a changeling baby.

By now, it should have been ashes in her back garden. How many times had she promised it that this was to be its fate? But each day she'd put off the cremation until the next, and each day she found she didn't have the strength—or had grown a little more reluctant. Perhaps the thing was exerting some sort of influence, penetrating her subconscious in an effort to stay its own execution.

But that would be stupid: in order for it to do so, it would have to be sentient, and heaven knew, she wasn't crazy enough to believe *that*—although you never could tell with these damn African artifacts. For all she knew, her entire house could be peopled by a host of vulgar spirits, each resident in one godawful black statue or the other.

"Thanks, Dominic," she murmured. God, but it was hot today. Easter weather. Not even the scent of rain on the horizon. The air was dry and close, and she was thirsty. She wrenched open the door to her study and shouted into the hallway. "Teresa!"

The stubby maid materialized, having been haunting that wing of the house all afternoon, waiting to be called. "Mistress Evers?"

Faith thought fast. Orange juice? Not likely. Not after the kind of afternoon she'd had. "Scotch. Now."

Teresa disappeared and returned with a glass full of the blessed yellow liquid, holding it in both hands. Faith tried not to twist her lips. The girl had used an eight-ounce glass, not a tumbler, and had poured it so full she had to hold her hand steady not to spill a drop. And just because she hadn't specified ice, the stupid girl hadn't bothered to put any. Did they drink their scotch warm where she came from? The thought almost made her smile. What was she thinking? Teresa's people probably couldn't afford scotch in the first place.

She kicked the door shut in Teresa's waiting face and resumed her position before the statue, taking a swig of the burning liquid. She was almost sure that a fraction of a second before she focused on it, it wiped a mocking grin off its face. She took several more deep gulps, folded her arms, and steeled her will.

"Only a matter of time," she warned it. Warm scotch wasn't all that bad, she decided, and took another swallow. "You think the execution has been cancelled, but you're wrong. All you got was a stay."

Talking to the damn little man felt like the most natural thing in the world. She wasn't the first: many a time she'd walked in on her husband doing just that. In times of stress, he used to take it off its pedestal and set it on his desk and actually speak to it . . . *speak* to it . . . and wait for a reply. He claimed it had helped him think. A down-market oracle.

The last of the scotch burned her chest, but after the burn, a soothing. "Go on, beg for mercy," she told him. "Beg, and maybe I'll let you see another day. If not, I'm sure there's some kerosene in the garage. Matches in the kitchen. And your ashes, you want them buried or tossed on the wind? Maybe under the rosebushes? You'd probably help them grow." She chuckled at her own wit.

Was it getting hotter, or was it the fire in her throat? She wished she'd had the foresight to tell Teresa to bring her the whole bottle and considered calling her over once more, but she didn't relish the idea of having to look into those patient, cowlike eyes again. Instead, she patted the sprinkling of perspiration on her brow and fanned herself with her hand, trying hard to focus on the dark spot among the china blue.

"No breasts," the statue said.

"What?"

"Did you see your daughter? No breasts. They dried up. Got sucked in and eaten by her own body. Like an octopus eating its own arms. A waste."

She set the empty glass carefully down on the floor. Shock and vindication ran through her. So, the thing *was* alive! She'd been right all along. And whatever African jumbie had been sheltering in the chunk of wood had chosen to speak. In

English, no less. Maybe he would appreciate being spoken to in his native tongue. "Ooga-booga!" she shouted, waving her arms above her head. She laughed.

"You mock me?" he roared. The Delftware rattled.

Faith jumped back, startled. "No! I'm ... sorry." She hoped she sounded sincere: if he could speak, he could cast curses. Better not to get him angry. Magic was a dangerous thing.

But at least *somebody* was saying *something*. That was remarkable enough, after the silence that had fallen upon the house since the last acquaintance had dropped by to offer condolences. This was the beginning of that hard part. This was where the theory of widowhood translated into practice. The house had become such a hushed, sad place, she was willing to talk to just about anyone, even if it meant she was losing her mind.

But if it came to that, what would they talk about? What did you say to a man-spirit no longer than your forearm? How much did he know? How much did he see? She remembered the last place she'd taken him, and the rude remark he'd made about Justice, and blushed on her daughter's behalf.

"I let you look at my daughter naked," she chastised him, but kept her tone moderate, so he wouldn't be annoyed. "You should have looked away."

"The eyes of the spirit never close." The voice was a rumble, coming up out of a crack in the earth. "Every day I see her, I wonder ... What is this sickness? Is it an illness of body or soul? She was such a fat little thing ..."

"Justice was never *fat!*"

He ignored her. "I remember her as a child, trotting through the hall in her slippers. Needy. Scared to be alone. Daddy's girl, and when Daddy wasn't there, always wanting to be near Jonah. Her big brother."

"Husband." She wondered if she sounded bitter.

It laughed. "For now."

"What's that mean?"

The statuette said nothing. His hollow eyes, gouged out by a wood-carver's knife, were full of knowledge and light.

Faith stuck her face nearer to him, trying to pierce the light, or read through it. "What's that mean? Tell me, or—"

"Or what? Matches? Kerosene? Haven't you got enough fires of your own to put out?"

"Like?"

"Like the one in your daughter's bed. Like the one in yours. I can smell the smoke. When you set me down next to you before you sleep, on my own pillow—"

"Never again," she snapped. "That was a mistake. Tonight, I sleep alone."

"Tonight, I sleep with you. And tomorrow night, and the next, because you can't bear it. To be alone and alone and alone. Tonight I get to watch you burn, on one half of a very big bed."

"That's unkind!" How could he be so cruel? Didn't he know what it was like? To roll over in bed after twenty-five years and find nobody there?

"Life's unkind, Faith."

"I never told you you could use my name!"

"Sorry, Faith."

There was moisture on her cheeks, like condensate on the outside of a chilled glass. It was humiliating, having someone else—some*thing* else—know of her pain. He was right. She burned, every second. In her heart, and between her legs. And to think that this grotesque little man had lain silently in bed and watched her on the nights she'd sought to mute her sorrow by slipping her hand down under the sheets, between her thighs, to bring herself the consolation that Dominic would never be able to bring her again. Had he laughed at her adolescent stupidity, or had he been aroused, taking vicarious pleasure from her own pathetic self-gratification?

Her eyes went unbidden to the oversized, jutting black penis at his own crotch. The artist who had created him had

had an inflated opinion of the organ's capabilities. Surely no human man was built like that! The statue saw her glance and murmured softly, "Hurts, doesn't it? Hunger."

He hadn't said it unkindly, but it still stung. "Shut up."

"When the ache starts in your breasts. Bigger than your daughter's now, your breasts. For a change. She used to have some luscious, round ones."

"Do not talk about my daughter anymore! I forbid it!" She wasn't sure if she was outraged by the audacity of the creature or jealous of his shift in attention.

"And then the ache spreads. Down. *There*." His attention was entirely on her again, and Faith calmed a little.

"How would you know? You're wood. And not very *good* wood . . ."

A soft chuckle. "I know. I see what you see. I feel what you feel. I'm closer to you than you can ever hold me."

The wetness on her cheeks was dripping off her chin now. She hunched over to wipe her face with the hem of her skirt, an ill-bred gesture if there ever was one, but the only person looking wouldn't mind, she was sure. When she could speak again, her voice shook. "And does it end?"

"Does what end?"

"The ache. The heat."

The statue thought for such a long time that she became afraid that it had gone silent again. She snatched it up and shook it. The wood-flesh was warm. "I asked you a question!" she screamed. "Answer me!"

"Let me tell you this. . . ," he began, and then there was a banging on the door. The firelight went out of his eyes.

Heart thumping, Faith reeled to the door and threw it open, to see Teresa standing there, her eyes round like a cow's. "Mistress Evers? I hear you shouting. You hurt yourself?"

Unbelievable. The girl had cut in on the most intimate conversation of her life. "What?"

Teresa tried not to stare at the statue clutched in her hands. "I was just wondering . . ."

Faith knew without having to be told that her conversation with the black spirit was over. The membrane that joined them had been rent apart by this ninny. "You cleaned up this room yet?"

Teresa gulped. "No, ma'am."

"So what're you waiting for?"

Teresa hung her head and slipped inside. "I'll start it right away, Mistress . . ."

Faith snatched the empty glass up off the floor and all but threw it at her. "Do it. And do it properly. But before you start, get me some more scotch. And try to be civilized; put some ice in it this time. I'll be in my room."

She left Teresa staring, bewildered, at her receding back.

Blood Pye

"They say it come out of England," Half-Way yelled.
Even out in the yard, the music was so loud that Blood
Pye had to cup his hand over one ear and strain to catch what
his friend was saying. The older man's nickname had been
given to him years before, out of good-natured ribbing for
the way he had begun going gray: entirely on one side of his
head, as if a draftsman had taken pencil and ruler and drawn
a perfect line down the center. Although the hair was as thick
as a carpet, one side gleamed like steel wool, while the other
was matte black. The coloring extended to his eyebrows,
moustache, and the hair on his chest and arms. All in all, he
looked like a man who had fallen asleep lying on his side in
the sun and had suffered some strange radiation. Blood Pye
had tried over the years to convince him that the best way to
deal with the bizarre phenomenon was to shave it all off, but
Half-Way had always refused. His wife liked it that way, he
insisted.

"I hear them cocks up there just falling over dead, dead,
like nobody business," Half-Way said.

Blood Pye sucked on the end of his hemp cigarette and
contemplated the glow that intensified on the tip of it. He
could have done with something stronger; as a matter of fact,
he had a couple of spliffs in his back pocket, but it made
more sense to start small, working his way up from the hemp

rather than the other way around. The smoke filled his mouth, sweet on his tongue and seductive in his mind, like a woman's kiss. Mattie didn't like him smoking; not weed, anyway. She said she could smell it on him, even hours after he'd finished his last joint. But right now, he needed it. Unlike a woman, weed was reliable: when life was turning to shit all around you, you knew it would be there, always willing, always able to soothe your troubled spirit.

"Not England," he contradicted his friend. "That ain't no white people disease. I been in this business long time, man, and I telling you, this thing come up off the mainland. Venezuela. Is a big place down there; endless jungle and rivers and shit. They got germs down there that could crawl up your legs and eat your dick before you could say Jack Robinson. You take two steps and your balls drop off. This thing what killing my birds—"

"Shh." Half-Way put a finger to his lips.

Blood Pye shut himself up by popping the cigarette back into his mouth again. The Hiding Place Bar wasn't as full as it could have been, even on a Friday, but there were still enough people about to hear what he was saying, especially since the noise forced them to shout. And Blood Pye was a breeder: the last thing he needed was for word to get around that there was trouble in his camp, something dark and dangerous that was leaving a trail of death wherever it passed.

There was a cockfight on tonight. Not a major one, more of a local thing than an international event, with just a few breeders pitting their birds against each other's. For the first time since he was seventeen or so, and his father had deemed him old enough and good enough to fight his own birds rather than tag along to help out, Blood Pye had brought no contenders. He'd made up a hollow lie to the punters who usually bet on his birds, telling them some bullshit about a training regime that required his cocks to rest a few weeks. He wasn't sure that the lie had rung true, but that was not the worrying thing. What bothered him was that he wasn't the only one who hadn't brought birds tonight. Half-Way was a gaunt man in his fifties who loved his birds like children, giving them the run of his house and, much to his wife's perpetual despair, even letting the best ones sleep in two of his three bedrooms. So, when he'd also walked into the compound of the Hiding Place empty-handed and stuttered something about taking a break for a week, maybe two, Pye had felt his blood chill.

Half-Way had trained birds with Pye's father and had known him since he was a boy. There were things that the men understood and things that didn't have to be said. It hadn't taken him long to invite the older man outside for a smoke, away from curious ears, to find that other cocks were dying, too.

So, in the relative privacy of the backyard, each man had confessed his secret to the other, and each had found that the other had no solution, no plan to stem the loss. Just this morning, Half-Way had woken up to find a pure-black stud with fifteen victories to its name lying on its back with its claws clenched, already swarming with black biting ants. "Couldn't even bury him decent," Half-Way had lamented. "The only way to kill that sickness is fire. And he ain't the last. I bet you anything, by the time I get home tonight, two, three more gone."

They stood next to each other on the hard-packed earth, with their backs to the hibiscus hedge that bordered the yard, arms folded across their chests, each one unconsciously mimicking the other in the position and tension of his body. Light ash fell on his long-sleeved white shirt, and Pye clicked his tongue as he dusted himself off. Unlike most of the men there tonight, he was dressed, as always, in a plain linen shirt and black tie, even though he rolled his sleeves up as a concession to the heat. Cockfighting was a gentleman's sport, and he always ensured that he dressed like one.

After a long and thoughtful silence, he finished his hemp, flicked the butt into the bushes without putting it out, and

reached for his weed. If he ever needed it, it was now. He lit
one and passed it to Half-Way before lighting his own. "So
what we gonna do about it?"

Half-Way scratched his head. He grimaced, showing yellowed teeth. Before he could speak, a voice above the noise
called their names.

"What y'all doing out here so long? Like my liquor ain't
good enough for you no more?" Ramesh, the owner of the
Hiding Place, limped over, grinning a twisted grin that never
seemed quite sincere. As he reached the two men, he stopped,
looking up into their faces, eyes glistening in the weak overhead lights. He barely came up to Pye's breastbone, having
stopped growing around the age of ten. His hands and feet
were those of a child, and one leg was shorter than the other,
hence his limp.

He was an East Indian from Barrackpore, sugarcane country, who owned three bars and made no attempt to hide the
fact that he had a wife running each of them on his behalf.
How the police had never taken him in for polygamy was
anybody's guess, but Blood Pye was quite sure it had to do
with Ramesh's frequent, unabashed declarations that everyone had their price.

"Your liquor just fine," Blood Pye assured him. Ramesh
was a powerful man in the gambling world, and his reach extended beyond cockfighting to embrace cards, numbers games,
and anything that ran, flew, or fought. As a matter of fact,
Pye owed Ramesh a couple of grand after a few bad bets, and
the man had been kind enough to forbear on calling in the
debt until he could see his way clear to paying it back. He
even consented to keep his interest rates down to a generous
thirty percent, so Pye would do well not to offend. "You got
the best drinks in town, as a matter of fact," he flattered.
"We just . . ." He floundered.

"Just taking a smoke, Ramesh," Half-Way finished for
him, words smooth and voice even.

Ramesh slapped Half-Way on the arm, a bit too heartily,

almost knocking the spliff out of his hand. "And what, you see any 'No Smoking' signs in my bar? Come on, the fight going sweet downstairs. Some good birds in the *gayelle* tonight, and more to come. What, you think just because y'all ain't got no birds fighting tonight, you don't have to watch?"

Blood Pye tensed. Something didn't sit right. Usually Ramesh didn't give a shit whether you hung around inside or out, as long as you bought lots of drinks and bet heavily on the birds. He sure as hell didn't go around from customer to customer urging them to move from one place to the next.

Ramesh's smile was taut, a diagonal slash across his face. "And it ain't like neither of you to walk in here with your two hands swinging. Both of y'all ain't brought no birds tonight. Something wrong or what?"

He knew. Or suspected. Something was rotten in the bird business, and the man smelled it. This time, it was Pye's turn to be smooth. "Nothing ain't wrong. We just got this new training thing going on, Half-Way and me. While we doing it, the birds got to take a break. When we done, and we bring them in, you'll see. All them other breeders gonna be bawling for murder when we take our cocks out of the basket. You gonna see blood like you never see before." He slapped the dwarf amicably on the shoulder, but lightly, for fear of knocking him over. "You just wait."

Ramesh watched him hard, small black eyes shrewd, but after a few tense moments, he passed his stubby hand over his slicked-back hair and gestured. "No problem. When y'all ready to fight again, you know just where to come. In the meantime, come downstairs and have a drink, and watch a fight." Then, a look only for Blood Pye. "You could place some bets, Pye. God alone know you could do with a win right now."

Blood Pye didn't like the way Ramesh referred to his string of bad luck with money, but when a man was down, even a dog would pee on him. As soon as he got back on his feet, he'd show the bastard; but until then, he was beholden, and it would be best to keep a civil tongue. He tried to keep his face neutral as he and Half-Way followed behind, through the back doors and into the bar. Above ground, it looked like any other watering hole, with men hunched over the counter trying to sweet-talk the waitresses, old metal chairs scattered among equally dilapidated tables, and a few people playing rummy and all-fours around them. This was the part of the bar presented to the public, the uninitiated who came only to drink, but at the back there was a flight of stairs that dropped sharply downward and through a door that looked as though it led only to a small cellar.

Ramesh threw open the door, and the sound that hit them was not the music being belted out upstairs on a scratchy turntable, but a roar of excitement, of men shouting, egging on the birds engaged in battle at the center of the large underground room. A shallow, round pit, the *gayelle*, lay at the center, ringed by a wall that was barely knee-high. A poultry scale hung on one wall, with a metal funnel into which the cocks could be thrust for the weighing-in, and next to that, a blackboard with the night's lineup scrawled in chalk: weight, price, and the breeder's name.

A few familiar breeders stood around, either holding cages protectively against their chests or keeping an eye on the ones propped up near their feet. Inside them, cocks fidgeted, itching for their turn in the ring. When the crowd shifted, Blood Pye caught a glimpse of a large russet ball launching in the air, talons extended. Even from this distance he could see the dark shape of the spurs attached to its heels. Like himself, this cock's owner used tortoiseshell honed to a sharp edge; it cut clean, and the wounds healed fast. He knew the bird well; in fact, just a few months before he'd come up against it and lost. This one was a wheeler, a bird that danced in the ring like a boxer, around and around its opponent, avoiding attacks but offering few advances, until the other bird grew tired. Then, and only then, was it ready to strike; and when it did, it had the advantage of greater energy, and it usually won.

Pye's nostrils were filled with sawdust and rum, and the sweeter scent of balm and expensive cognac. Breeders drank the rum; the cognac was saved for massaging the cocks after a battle, to soothe their muscles and to keep their wounds clean. His heart beat faster, as it did every time he walked into a game room, every time he smelled that unbelievable scent of excitement and power. Nothing he smoked or drank could ever do that for him. Nothing he ever did with a woman could. As a matter of fact, he was hard in his pants right now, as he often was when a battle was on.

The only things missing to make the thrill complete were his own birds. He wondered why the hell he had come, but that was a question that didn't merit an answer. He was here because here was where he felt alive. He was here because there was nowhere else in the world that he could go and listen to his soul sing, and when it sang it made one single high note like a chord being plucked on some divine guitar, going on and on and on.

He passed a hand over his smoothly shaved head, weary in spite of his excitement. Half-Way was close at his elbow, the only person here who knew what he was feeling, because he was feeling it, too.

In his ear, Half-Way spoke. "What you gonna do, Pye? What *we* gonna do?"

"Fix it," Pye told him. "Fix the problem. Fast."

"How?"

Pye kept his eyes on the ring, watching as the judge stopped the fight. The white cock was wedged against the side of the *gayelle,* still feisty, but too weary to strike back. Nine seconds, ten, and then the game was over. Real men didn't fight their birds to the death. That was like hamstringing a racehorse or ruining a painting. The cock had fought, and it had lost. A good vet and its owner's patient care would get it back in the ring again in a few weeks. When the victor was declared and congratulations and curses passed among winners and losers, Pye turned to his friend. His eyes were black, intense. "We get help. I know of a man, a vet from Barbados, who could help. We could bring him in and set this right."

Half-Way curled his lip. "And where we getting the money from? Half my birds dead, and ain't no way I'm gonna try to sell nobody none of the others. I got a reputation to uphold. You, too. And your ass deeper in debt than mine. Where we getting this money to bring in your vet? You got a shitload of it buried under a mango tree? Somebody dead and leave you a whole lot of bread?"

Pye smiled for the first time tonight. Half-Way had no idea how close he had come to the mark. "Not me. I ain't know nobody with that kind of money who dead, but somebody who belong to me do. I'm seeing her tomorrow. And she the kind of girl who gonna want to help her man out. Don't worry. I'll get the money. Soon. Okay?"

Mattie and Jonah

***

What Mattie liked most about her meetings with Jonah was the stories. They met each afternoon after work, when sane people stayed indoors and out of the heat, in the shadow of the monastery, under the spreading Samaan tree they had come to think of as theirs. Each came riding, Jonah looking especially ridiculous in his business clothes, with his tie flapping in the breeze as he tackled the steeper slopes, and she sometimes forgetting to pull off her apron when she sneaked out of the sweet shop. And although every afternoon they began by sailing side by side along the road that looped in wide arcs around the mountain, they always ended up winded, at the base of the tree, catching their breath before the stories began.

At first, as promised, they had talked about Dominic. Swapping tales like children exchanging bubble gum cards in the schoolyard. She talked about the Dominic Jonah had never known, the one who ate fried chicken with his hands and put his bare feet up on the sofa and cursed when he played gin. He described in minute detail the huge house and garden within the high walls in St. Clair, the cocktail dinners at which guests turned up in dark-tinted cars and left their drivers waiting outside. About Dominic's study, with the big brass globe and walls of books, and the games he played with the young boy who had been so eager to grow into the man he had become.

Each one's curiosity fed the other's. At the point where their personal histories collided, they communed over the bread and wine of anecdotes and laughter. She brought the few photographs she had of herself, Claudine, and Dominic. Jonah brought his own family photographs, and among them, his wedding photos. She sat on the ground with the large fabric-covered album opened on her lap and touched the face of the woman at his side, resplendent in white gauze that frothed around her like sea foam. The face was soft, round, younger than the age Mattie knew her to be. A sweet plumpness about her, a girlishness that knew no hardship, no cares written in the eyes they shared with their father.

"My sister."

"Yes. Justice."

"You knew her all her life, then."

"She was like a little sister to me. Dominic made me walk her to school every day, even when she was very young, and go back to get her in the afternoons. Even when I wanted to stay behind after class for football or cricket, I'd have to go across town to get her, take her home, and run back to school. I think I must have missed the start of every game I ever played."

"Not so much a sister that you didn't want to marry her." She watched him for a reaction, knowing she was pushing into a private space between a man and his wife.

He didn't even flinch. "We grew into each other. She was always there when I needed her, and I was always there for her. Justice isn't like everyone else. She . . ." He stopped and frowned.

Mattie waited.

"She needs someone strong." He took the photo album gently from her and held it open on his own lap, touching the celluloid face much as she had a few moments before.

"And that's you."

"Yes. Me. When she was a teenager and there were boys she liked, I remember grilling them, picking and choosing for her, deciding who she could and couldn't see. She hated me for it, especially when Dominic washed his hands of the whole business and left those decisions up to me. He trusted my judgment. From the time she was sixteen to the time she was about eighteen, we probably didn't have a civil conversation, but that was okay because as much as she hated my interference, I knew I was looking out for her. Eventually, she got used to it, and even came to me for advice and help.

"Then I noticed there was something different in the way she was looking at me. She was looking at me like she did when she was five or six and I was her hero. But she wasn't five; she was nineteen and still knew barely a thing about men, but was excited about what she was learning. She decided I was to be her teacher. And that scared me. It felt . . . not right. She was supposed to be my sister. It was all I had ever known her to be. But then, after a while, it just made sense. Like I said, we grew into each other."

" 'Growing into' don't mean love," Mattie pointed out. She waited for him to tell her to mind her own business.

"The love's there," he insisted. She wondered why he looked so sad when he said it. "I know her better than anyone."

"And she knows you?"

Jonah shut the album and let it rest on the grass next to him, leaned back against the trunk of their tree, and shut his eyes. She waited so long for an answer that she became afraid that he had fallen asleep, but the erratic rhythm of his breathing told her this was not so. After a while, when no answer came, she gave up waiting and shifted along the grass until she, too, had her back against the broad, rough trunk. Between them his hand lay flat on the album, with the plain gold band, her sister's ring, wrapped around his finger.

Instinct told her to stretch her own hand out upon his, to comfort, or to remind him she was there. Prudence told her otherwise.

After the first few meetings, their conversations grew broader. Sometimes they did nothing but sit in the grass and read the paper and *tut-tut* about what a terrible place the world had become. Other times, they talked not about Dominic but about themselves. On these occasions, Mattie spoke less than she listened; Jonah's life held her in thrall. She loved to listen to his stories about the beaches at Las Cuevas on the rocky north coast, and about the boy who used to slip away from the straggly line of houses overlooking the bay with the other boys and run barefoot onto the damp sand as sandflies clung to them, sucking on warm blood until they either fell off, satiated, or were slapped away, leaving drying red smears.

They would dart in and out among the boats, fancying themselves helpful, hanging on to the green seine, although the ropes cut at their palms, until the catch was spilled onto the sand. And while the men set about tossing still-struggling kingfish, carite, grouper, and shark into huge barrels of ice on the backs of trucks waiting to speed through the mountains to market, young Jonah and his friends squabbled with stray dogs over what was left.

They hopped through the waves at the shoreline like sandpipers, scooping up handfuls of shiny silver joshua no longer than their fingers, tugging their shirtfronts up into makeshift carriers and pressing their bounty against their chests as they ran home.

By the time Jonah made it in through the front door, his mother, Rosalie, would be up, bathed, dressed, and fussing. She always slapped him sharply in the back of the head twice, once for leaving the house without telling her, and once for messing with those filthy-mouthed no-account 'rabs he continually warned him about, who had no future other than a life mired in the sand, and who would do their best to drag him down to their level, when everyone knew he was destined for greater things.

That said, she would relieve him of his bundle, run the little fish quickly under water and rub them down with lime and salt, and then fry them dry in a deep iron saucepan until they crackled. Then they sat together at the low table in the kitchen, and with his knees pressed against his mother's, he would fill his belly with hard hops bread and hot joshua: head, bones, guts, all.

"She must be proud of you," Mattie said once, when he was done talking.

"She is," Jonah said.

"And you? This where you saw yourself?"

He laughed. "Maybe later, after she sent me off to the city. Back then, I never wanted to grow up to be anything other than a fish."

"A merman, you mean." Her eyes were on him, trying to see him as he would be, his torso slick, hips narrowing to a long tail that sliced through water. What kind of tail did mermen have? A marlin's? A shark's?

But he shook his head vigorously. "Not a merman, a fish through and through. So I wouldn't have to depend upon lungs and air. Or these." He patted his legs.

She knew what it was like to want to be something else more than anything in the world, knowing in your heart that wishing and hoping didn't make it so. "Never found a way to do it, eh?" she sympathized.

His smile was rueful. "Not for lack of trying."

Jonah was late. Mattie's frequent, anxious glances at her watch weren't doing much to inch the long hand along. Even under the shelter of the huge tree, whose branches stretched out and hung down to create a cool, dark cave, she felt exposed. With the island's Catholics deep into Lent, traffic had increased, as the faithful swarmed the monastery seeking refuge and rosaries, solace and holy water. The quiet road had become a busy thoroughfare. Car after car strained to make the incline, stirring up dust and dead leaves behind them. The occupants threw her curious glances. She turned her back on the road.

He had always been as eager to meet her as she was to meet him, and like Dominic, he was a stickler for time. Jonah wasn't a man to be late because his timing was off; he was late because something had gone wrong. She tried not to think of the ghastly possibilities: a car having stopped too quickly or not quickly enough, a child running into the road after a ball. She had an image of her father dying without warning on the floor of the opera house, wondering if lightning struck in the same place twice, but she dismissed the thought. Jonah was strong and healthy. Could it be something to do with his wife?

His wife. Maybe his absence today was not through mishap but through conscience. Maybe, like her, he had sensed the shift in their conversations, the subtle mutation of their purpose from piecing together parts of Dominic's puzzle to searching out fragments of their own. She came now not to talk about her father, but to listen to Jonah. Even when he had nothing to say, but sat in silence beside her, she was content. There was a calm there that flowed out of him and into her, an oasis in the midst of her tumultuous day. A nobility and guilelessness that was at odds with the hard, critical world in which he lived.

This nobility had very likely begun to rebel against this shared space in which they enclosed themselves, the silence that let them touch each other without the contact of flesh. When the afternoon grew late and they parted ways, he returned home to his wife and whatever unspoken sadness lay behind those walls, a sadness that she sensed as surely as if she herself roamed that old house like a restless spirit, watching and listening.

The idea made her guilty, but angry in her guilt. Her sister had always laid legitimate claim to their father, and she,

Mattie, had made do with the crumbs that fell from her table. This time around, Justice's claim to Jonah was as real as the gold band he wore, and yet Mattie found herself coveting the peace he brought with him, and all he could give her, even for their short hour every afternoon. He saw her the way Dominic had seen her, knowing exactly who she was and where she had come from, and that alone was worth everything. Surely her sister would not begrudge her these few innocent moments?

Innocent it was, she reminded herself. Although out of the corner of her eye she had admired the crispness of his hair—what her grandmother liked to call "good hair"—the shape of his profile, the skin that glowed like copper in the sun, the height of him, and the breadth of him, she was sure she never looked at all these things as a woman did a man. She never sensed him as a woman sensed a man. What she felt was clean and pure, separate from and above all that. Wasn't it?

Besides, she *had* a man. Blood Pye was everything Jonah wasn't: brash and loud and lusty. He took what he wanted and gave her as much respect as he was capable of doing. He could never see his way clear to giving her anything close to a commitment, though. She knew he strayed, and when he did, he did so blithely, moving from girl to girl like an insect spreading sticky pollen. That, as irksome as it was, would never change, and for the time being, at least they could dawdle through life, enjoying each other's company. Meeting with Jonah didn't violate that. The restless nights she spent in anticipation of seeing Jonah again didn't infringe on what she had with Pye. The darkness and the light had their own set times in the sky.

Mattie looked at her watch again. Their hour was up, and he hadn't come. She knew it would be sensible to get up off the ground, swat the grass off her skirt, and make for home, but instead of obeying her command, her body chose to linger. A short while longer, perhaps. Five minutes, or ten. Ten minutes, and if she didn't see him, she'd be gone.

Dust again, rising up into the air, and the sound of an engine. Even though she was yards away from the roadside, Mattie flinched instinctively. But the car did not go past; tires screamed, and it stopped. She spun in the direction of the sound. It was Jonah, not on his green bike, but leaping out of the same silver car he had been driving that day they had crashed into each other's life. The front bumper was as smooth as though nothing had ever happened to it.

She tried to quell the surging happiness that rose up inside her as he skated down the incline. He wasn't dressed for riding. He wore a suit the color of flint, jacket still buttoned, and his tie was tucked neatly in and fastened with a silver pin, rather than flapping about as he usually left it. He didn't have to come much closer for her to see the consternation on his face.

She met him in the middle. "What?"

"I'm sorry." He was out of breath, but not from the short run. "I kept you waiting. Mattie, I'm—"

"What happened? Tell me!"

He looked at her, hard, trying to read her face much as he had that first day. He tried to disengage her hand from his jacket and moved toward the tree. "Come, Mattie."

She resisted. "Why?"

"Come and sit."

She didn't like the pity in his eyes. If there was something he had to say, let him say it now, here. "I don't want to sit," she told him.

"Please." He still held her hand, but didn't try to pull it.

She followed him to the tree and watched with passing amazement as he sat in the grass without any regard for the costly suit. As had become his habit, he plucked a blade of grass from between his knees and stared at it. "I've just come from the lawyer's office," he began.

"And?"

"And he read your father's will."

Her legs were as reluctant to keep her standing now as

they had been to get her up minutes before. Her knees gave, and she dropped beside him. "Was my sister there?"

"Yes."

"And my father's wife?"

"Yes, of course."

The will. That was fast: only a month or so since his death. She'd never been to a will reading, or known anyone who'd had one, but she'd have thought that people waited a decent interval, maybe after the forty-days mass. But she guessed that rich people were different. Family might be one thing, but money was another.

As Jonah didn't speak, Mattie let his silence take her to an imaginary room in the city, with the lawyer on one side of a frightening desk and Dominic's family on the other. Faith Evers all hairspray and linen, eyes sharp, ears straining to hear every word. *What's mine now?* Dominic's daughter, younger by months than Mattie was, but like Jacob having stolen Esau's birthright to become heir apparent. Sitting close to her husband, in the circle of his arm.

And the lawyer, making his way down the list: money, houses, cars. This charity and that. Would her name have cropped up before or after the charities? If she squeezed her eyes really tight, she could see her name on the lawyer's papers, black on white. Her father had written her name down, for the second time in her life. She let her fingers slip to the gold bangle on her wrist, the one engraved by her father for her birthday three years ago: "Matilda, love, Daddy." Even her Christmas and birthday gifts had always arrived without cards or tags. Now, her name in his will, an acknowledgement that she was his, and that she was here in this form, in this place and time, because of him.

She wondered what Dominic had left her. Maybe his chess game, carved out of dark and light jade, which he sometimes secreted from the house and took to her on Wednesday afternoons, when he had decided she was old enough to learn to play. Dominic had told her that any person who could master chess could dictate his own destiny; the shrewdness, the planning, and the visioning were the same. Mattie had loved that set. No two pieces, not even the pawns, were exactly alike, as they had all been done by hand. Had her father remembered her love of the game, or had he chosen to leave her money? Would there be a check, or some kind of fund? She wasn't sure how these things worked.

Not that it mattered. Dominic's money was something she had never craved. She couldn't remember ever waking up a single day in her life knowing that there was nothing in the kitchen to eat, and as far as she was concerned, that made her as wealthy as she ever needed to be. Whatever he'd left her was nothing compared to the gift of having her name said out loud in front of people who had spent her entire life ignorant of her existence. Finally, her father had said to everyone, "This child is mine."

His wife and daughter had been shocked, certainly, and hurt, most likely, but that was a price they would have to pay. With that shock and hurt would come awareness.

She held her arm up, the one on which she wore the bangle, and watched the light as it played on the gold and among the fine hairs on her skin. She made a fist, clenched and unclenched her hand, feeling the nails scratch her palm. She wondered if after this she would still need all those mirrors at home.

She let her arm fall into her lap and looked at Jonah. He was still not looking at her, head bent. "Were they very upset?"

He turned his overcast eyes to her. "What d'you mean?"

"When they found out about me. Who I am, and what I am. Were they upset when they heard my name?"

He looked stricken, incredulous. Time slowed and became a yawning gap between them, giving her ample opportunity to realize what a fool she was. Before he could open his mouth to speak, she knew the reason for the pity in his eyes. *No, no, no.*

"There was nothing—" he began.

"No."

"—about you."

"Stop it, Jonah!" She clapped her hands over her ears. She moved to rise, but he anticipated her and was on his feet before she was, pulling her against him.

"I'm sorry."

Her stomach roiled. She wheeled out of his grasp, sure she would spill vomit laced with disappointment onto his shiny black shoes; but her stomach was empty, and her mouth remained dry.

Denial. Long after he was cold and buried, her father had denied her existence, a liar to the last. Why? Had he sought to protect his family, or was he, even when it would no longer matter, striving to protect his public face, the one with a wife and child and a hundred clubs and charities, rather than the private man with a mistress and daughter holed up in a side street miles from anyone who knew him? Had Dominic been that vain? Had he been so concerned with who he was and who people imagined him to be that even his corpse could not withstand the gossip?

"Mattie, there are things that we can do," Jonah was saying. "A will can be challenged. I know lawyers. I know people. Let me help."

Jonah disappointed her. He didn't understand. After all the afternoons they had spent together here, talking, giving each other glimpses of their souls, did he really not understand? She grasped her bike and set it upright, throwing her leg over. She glanced into the small mirror on the handlebar and realized her reflection wasn't there. In the chrome plating along the chassis, only the sun was visible. With Dominic's denial, her fragile self had shattered, like a mirror falling to the ground.

She pushed off, leaning forward to gather the momentum to make it up the grassy incline. Behind her, Jonah called her name. At the roadside, she hesitated. She could go downward, back to Curepe and home, but there would be walls there, surrounding her; and she was sure that if she walked into a room now, her agitation alone would cause the air to be sucked out of it, and everything in it, including herself, would be crushed.

She headed up toward the monastery, legs pumping. A hundred years of monks and chapels, supplications and benedictions, would wrap the mountain in a blanket of peace, would it not? Enough peace to draw on. Behind her, the murmur of an engine, like vibrations in a cat's throat. Jonah. As fast as she was going, she was no match for him, and yet he did not try to best her; he simply followed.

She pressed on, past the yellowed monastery walls and through the courtyard, then beyond them, as far as the road would take her. Then under her wheels there was grass, and Jonah could no longer follow. But a look over her shoulder told her he was on foot, long legs pounding, pursuing her as he had that first day at her father's funeral. She was a gazelle, and he a leopard: focused, relentless, persistent. Not even tiring.

The forest behind the monastery was run through with footpaths. It was a favorite of nature lovers, bird watchers, and butterfly hunters, and each path led to some delightful place: river, valley, clearing, thicket. The uneven ground barely suited a bike, and with every rut she hit, the impact jarred her to the teeth. Even when the path she had chosen narrowed, she pressed on, struggling to maintain traction in the taller grass. When the wheels began spinning, she was unable to guide herself. She found herself being propelled forward, weaving crazily. Right ahead, the path came to a sudden stop near a cluster of grugru trees: tall palms armored the length of their trunks with black spines as long as her thumb. She stuck a foot out in an attempt to slow the bike and avoid impact; but Jonah's hands were around her waist, and she was being plucked from the bike and gathered up against his chest.

The bike careened into the grugru trees, crunching into the porcupine's spines at their base, and then fell over. Mattie could feel Jonah's chest rising and falling against her back, warm air on her neck. "Put me down!"

He disobeyed, holding her in his arms and moving away from the thorny patch. Her angry struggles were no match for his strength, but she persisted, even when his hard arms tightened. "I want to get my bike back. Let me go!"

"I'll get it for you. In a moment." He set her feet on the ground, but didn't take his arms from around her. She had to twist her body at an awkward angle and turn her head to look at his face. "I'm sorry, Mattie."

"Why? You didn't do nothing." His "sorry" wouldn't help her. He didn't understand anyway. He never would.

"You know what I mean. I can help you. I told you, there are ways. You're his child, and he owes you. I can help you get what's yours."

She laughed. "You mean you'll help me take away what belongs to your own family? What the hell kind of man are you?"

"You're my family, too. What belongs to us belongs to you."

"Dominic didn't think so."

"Dominic was wrong."

She managed to slide her arms up and elbow him in the chest, but was free only when he decided abruptly to let go. She staggered, but regained her balance and spun to face him. "You're such a fool, Jonah. You don't know anything. You think you know me?"

"I know a few things. I want to know more."

"You don't know enough. You think I want his money? What makes you think I want my father's money? Just because it's important to you, and your wife and that woman, don't make it important to everybody."

"But he had so much. He had enough to do whatever he

wanted and go wherever he pleased. And you have . . ." He swallowed.

"Nothing? Shows how much you know. You're a fool. I got things you can't even see. And none of the things I got cost money. You think just because your ass come from some shack by the beach, that makes you a simple man? That makes you just like me? Let me tell you: you changed more than you think. You ain't the country boy you like to pretend to be. Dominic worked hard on you. He spent half his life making you over into his own image and likeness. You were his ball of clay. You ain't nothing other than what he chose to make you. And now what he made you into can't even see why his money don't mean nothing to me."

"Why, then? Tell me."

"You wouldn't understand."

"Help me understand."

She held up her braceleted wrist before his eyes. "You see this?"

He nodded.

"This is the only proof I have that my father knew how to spell my name. He never wrote it down. He never sent me a letter or a card. Maybe he thought that if he did, it would make me so solid that I wouldn't disappear if he wanted. I was only real for him once a week, when he chose to make me real. The rest of the week, all I could do was wait and wait, until the next time he walked in and said, 'Hello, Mattie,' and I'd know for sure that that was not the week I turned invisible."

"You didn't need Dominic to make you real," Jonah countered. "You *are* real. Your grandmother knew you were real, and your mother."

She shook her head vigorously. "They only saw me because they loved me. I never knew if he did, because he never told me. And for him to love me was all I ever wanted. He was God for me. So tall and so smart. So strong. And what he did to me, he did double to my mother. Nothing ever hap-

pened for my mother unless he said it did. Nothing ever *was*
until he spoke it. For two decades I watched her, alive only
when he was there. And when he was gone, she faded. She
couldn't cast a shadow unless he was the light. She couldn't
even die until he came to say goodbye."

When Jonah put his arms around her again, she didn't
fight to break free. "And did you disappear, too? When he
wasn't around?"

"At least my mother cast a shadow. The light passed right
through me. I was like a jellyfish. I passed over sand, and all
you could see was the sand."

"*I* see you, Mattie." His hands slipped slowly from her
shoulders, along her arms, until they stopped at either side of
her waist. "I feel you. You're warm. You're real."

"Because you . . . *know*."

"No, because you *are*. You don't need me to prove that to
you."

Where his hands rested, her body felt bruised. She put her
hands over his. The ring on his left was cooler than his flesh.
She wanted him to know she wasn't the only one Dominic
had branded. "You're not him, you know. You can walk and
talk like him and run his company for him. But you can't be
him."

He looked down at himself with a bemused expression. "I
realize that . . . now."

"And if you didn't have to be him, who would you be?"

Puzzlement, and near panic. "I have no idea."

They stood like that, a whisper apart, he looking into her
eyes, searching for his own reflection, she searching for hers.
And whereas the mirror of her own bike had yielded nothing,
in his eyes she saw her own face clearly. The vision brought
her solace. After a while, she said, "Are we lost, then?"

He shook his head. "You're not if I know where you are.
I'm not, if you know where I am."

"And what if you go away?"

"I'm not going anywhere."

"But Dominic—"

"Forget Dominic. This is different. This is us. You know, the ancients used to keep the souls of the people they loved in clay pots, and they carried those pots with them wherever they went. When the tribe moved. When they went to war. So the living would always be able to keep the dead safe, and the dead would always be able to guide the living."

She laughed again, but not as mockingly as before. "So I give you a piece of my soul?"

"In return for a piece of mine. Fair exchange is no robbery."

"And how you plan to do this? You get some obeah-woman to put my soul in a pot? Jonah—"

The pressure of his mouth on hers cut her off in midsentence. He moved so swiftly that she didn't even have the time to protest, or decide whether she would have protested, had she the time to do so. The kiss was neither light, nor gentle, nor exploring, but forceful and insistent, propelled by dammed-up need. His teeth were hard and sharp, and he made no effort to shield her from the damage that they might do; but the pain was a welcome distraction, much as a bashed finger distracts from a stubbed toe.

She opened her mouth to allow the tip of his tongue entry. It was sharp and probing, sweet, and its invasion sent stabs the length of her body. Needing more than this single point of contact, she pressed against him, and he engulfed her, welcoming her into the harbor of his arms. Under the light fabric of his suit, his muscles were taut. He had grown hard fast; as she was so much shorter than he, his erection pressed against her belly, almost at the base of her rib cage. She wished she were taller, so she could feel the probing against the heat that was building up between her legs.

He sensed her want, grasped her bottom in both hands and lifted her without effort, pulling her against him just right, and that first contact made her gasp. As her mouth opened in surprise, he opened his wider, too. Each was a snake trying to engulf the other. And then, like a far-off earth tremor that one sensed rather than felt, the tingling began. First, in her pubis, which she ground against his in an increasingly urgent attempt to take, take, take, then up to her quivering belly. Up again, through her center, past her heart and into her throat, which constricted instinctively to protect her, to keep confined the part of her she was willing to give him.

She sensed the same tremor in him, like a heat rising purposefully from his crotch to his belly to his lungs, a living thing determined to get out. Then, light in her mouth, white energy, forcing past her lips to meet his own light on its way into her. The transfer had begun.

With an impatient grunt, he set her on her feet again, and her body screamed in protest at the separation. Everything wanted him: her skin, her lips, her hard nipples. And that light! She wanted to take more of his into herself, and give him more of hers. She shot her hand up behind his head and tried to force his mouth against hers again, like a homing pigeon returning to its coop after a long flight to find the windows closed, yet determined to enter at all costs.

He resisted, but only briefly enough to tear off his jacket and spread it out at their feet. "Come."

She let him lay her down upon the fabric. It was barely large enough to keep her head, torso and hips off the ground; she had to draw her knees up to spare the backs of her legs contact with the bristly grass. Even kneeling above her, he looked tall. As she struggled with the knot of his tie, she kept her gaze on his face. He was intense, somber, and unsmiling. Her courage almost failed her. "It's okay," he told her. "This is about trust." For the first time, he cupped her small breast, and her pulse leaped.

"All right." Just as she would have to trust him with the part of her he would be leaving with when they were done, so, too, would she have to trust him now. She closed her eyes and made her body relax, trying to imagine every vertebra touching the ground, like a necklace of beads laid out in a straight line.

In this time, and in this place, there would be no stripping down, as much as she wanted to see him naked and splendid. But at least she could undo the buttons on his shirt, and did so, pushing it open to gaze on his chest. She could almost see the minute reverberations of his heart as it beat within his ribs. His skin was bright, glowing several shades lighter than her own, and not being able to see them both against each other in stark contrast made her further regret that they both could not be completely naked.

She yelped in surprise as he thrust his hands under her skirt to pull her panties down. He caught sight of the small wound she'd received on her thigh when he'd collided with her that day. It was half-healed, with the stitches gone, and puckered like a pouty lip. He ran his thumb along it, feeling its roughness. "Hurts?"

"No." The sensation went beyond pain to the realm of pleasure, the way it felt when one's tongue could not resist worrying a loose tooth.

He covered the *V* of her crotch with his palm. "So warm," he murmured, and rocked forward to kiss her. With his hand a positive electrode at one end of her, and his lips a negative one at the other, the circuit was closed, and the current flowed: from her and into him, and back again. They remained locked until the electric charge building up made the trees around them hum.

They began to move more quickly, not just because of their exposure and the risk it carried, but because their urgent need for each other had grown beyond endurance. She wasn't sure who undid his belt and fly, but when it was done he positioned himself between her legs. She reached down to grasp him, and he was both hard as iron and soft as kid leather. Blood surged to her lips at the thought of what he might taste like, but the heat in her belly was much too urgent to allow her to pause, even briefly, to find out.

He pressed against her slippery flesh, steadying himself with a hand on the ground at her side, and as he slid home, she thought of Blood Pye. Not with guilt, but with irony: between them, she had always insisted on a thin barrier of rubber. And yet here she was, partly clothed on the forest floor, skin to skin with a man she'd not known a month. It was about trust, he'd told her. She squeezed her eyes shut.

So much sensation! She ground her hips against his, hemming him in with her heels against his haunches, not allowing him to withdraw too far, lest he pop out accidentally and their connection be broken. Even when his thrusts grew more agitated, he kept his mouth locked on hers, sacrificing leverage for contact. She didn't need leverage; the contact, and the light he still poured into her, were enough.

Under her fingers, the muscles in the small of his back shuddered. Too soon, too soon! She wanted more, and more still. Let them stay here until the fall of night, she thought, and if anyone stumbled upon them, let them be damned.

"Mattie, Mattie, keep me safe," he exhaled, and his body went still.

"I will," she promised.

Instead of slipping from her, he lay on her breast. He was heavy, but she would rather bear his weight than have him move away. His head lay in the crook of her neck, and she cradled it, feeling the crispness of his hair. His chest rose and fell against hers as he struggled for air. She relished the feeling of his essence spilling into her: it filled the void left by what she had given him.

After he regained his peace, he rolled off her, but stayed close to her side. "It's sealed, then," he sighed.

"Yes."

Their music was the rustling of the grass. Between the heat of the afternoon and the heat of their encounter, his skin was sticky against hers. He let her nestle into the curve of his armpit, with her head against his chest, and through the wall of muscle and bone she could hear the thudding of his heart.

He didn't speak again until the erratic rhythm settled back into the regular thump of a bass drum. "We should get up," he said then. "Anyone can walk past. Hikers, bikers ..."

"I know," she agreed. She made no effort to move.

He was the one with the strength to get to his knees, helping her back into her panties and then pulling her skirt down before adjusting his own clothing. She lay with her knees drawn up and her legs closed protectively, both hands over her pubis like a little girl hiding a naughty secret, shy now that their blood had cooled. She didn't take her eyes off him, trying to read his face and see which way the tide of his emotions would turn. Would guilt come next? If it did, would it make him surly, belligerent, resentful, or sad?

While he was joined with her, he hadn't taken his glasses off, but now he did, cleaning them carefully with the silk of his tie. When he was done he held them aloft, staring at the sun through them, squinting. Then he put them back on and peered at her as if they gave him the power to see beyond her external being to a deeper place. Still kneeling, he reached out and touched her hand. "You okay?"

She didn't want to say "yes" out of good manners alone, so she lobbed the question back at him. "You?"

"I'm not ..." He ran his tongue along his lower lip, tasting his words before he spoke them. "I don't wish I hadn't."

"And what about my ... your wife?"

He thought hard, brow wrinkled, like someone straining to compute a difficult math question. Eventually, he answered, "It's complicated. Not what you want to hear, but it's all I can say right now."

"Not feeling guilty?"

"Not now. Not yet. Later, maybe. I don't know."

He hadn't taken his hand away from hers. In her confusion, his touch soothed.

"You done this before?" she asked.

"No!"

She flinched at the vehemence of his answer. She tried to placate him. "I wasn't judging you. It's not my place. I just wanted to know . . ."

"Know what?"

"What this is . . . you and me."

He pulled on her hand until she was sitting up. His face was close to hers. "What this is doesn't even have a name. I didn't ask for it. I wasn't expecting it. But we both needed it."

"And now?" If only he could make up her mind for her, give her an answer about what they had just shared that had nothing to do with Dominic or Justice or Blood Pye or the nothingness she sometimes saw in her mirror. An answer that had everything to do with him and her. Under him, her flesh had become indissoluble, and when she had stretched herself out for him, that had been all she had sought. But he'd given her more, or at least, let her glimpse more of what she could have, if he were hers.

In those intense moments of skin on skin, the companionship she had sought from him day after day under the Samaan tree had grown—exploded—into a greater want. He'd left her with a hunger for his mind, to engulf and possess. Her body would just be a conduit for such possession, but if this was all that was available to her, she would take it. Heat blossomed again in her breasts and her groin at the idea. She suffered through anxious seconds waiting for his answer.

"And now . . ." He looked almost sad. He rose, and pulled her up. "Now we have to get back. It's late. You left the store locked up, and the children—"

"Fuck the store!" Her hand shot up around his neck, taking them both by surprise, pulling him down to her lips.

He didn't resist her kiss, but was the first to break it. "Mattie, don't spoil this."

"Don't spoil what? What am I spoiling, Jonah?" The idea of leaving this quiet clearing, where only the trees bore witness to their encounter, scared her. Outside, there would be buildings and roads and cars and noise. Other people. His responsibilities, and hers. She wasn't ready.

"Don't let this turn sour. We made a pact. We sealed it, you and me . . ." He gestured at the ground. "Right here. That I'd look out for you, and you'd look out for me. If we leave in anger, we break it before we begin. You have to give me time. What we did—" He closed his eyes, and a shiver ran through him. She wondered if it was regret or remembered pleasure. "What we did changed my life. As a man, and as a husband. And I need time to work it through. Will you give me that?"

She was floundering at sea, and a log that had drifted within her grasp had been snatched away by a wave. Time? What did that mean? An hour? A day? A month?

"Will you?" he persisted.

"And tomorrow?" she countered. "What about tomorrow?"

"What *about* tomorrow?"

"You'll meet me under the tree? Like always?" His hesitation hurt, so she rushed on. "Not for . . . this. Just to talk. Or not talk. Bring a book, and sit by me. Read. Just to be there. Next to me."

His shoulders sagged, and suddenly he looked tired. Instead of answering, he turned and waded gingerly through the higher grass at the side, to the place where her bike lay entangled among the thorns, concentrating on getting it free. She watched him, shocked at how each movement of his body held her riveted. How could one afternoon, one collision of bodies, leave her overwhelmed by so much need?

When he brought the bike back, it was as if she had never asked the question. "I'll roll it out for you," he told her. "This path isn't right for riding. Walk with me."

They walked with the bike between them like a picket fence, short enough to see over, but a barrier nonetheless. Mattie knew better than to ask again, but silently begged him to say something, anything that would indicate that what happened between them was a beginning and not an end, but instead her ears were filled with the rustle of grass beneath their feet and the quickening of life around them as they left the forest and were once again on more traveled ground.

At his car, he released his grip on the bike and patted himself down for his keys. His jacket, slung over one arm, slipped to the ground, and she bent to retrieve it. It was stained and covered with bits of grass and dried leaves. She shook it out, snapping it like a toreador's cape, more interested in sparing him the discomfort of being discovered than her sister the pain of discovery.

"I'll come tomorrow." His words made something in her leap.

"Just to talk," she assured him, although her body and soul thirsted for more. She sensed his bewilderment, and even his surprise, at his decision. If she pushed him now, all would be lost. "We'll just talk, like before."

"Of course," he agreed. "Wait for me."

She sat beside the road long after he was out of sight.

Justice and Jonah

Justice hopped out onto the flagstones in front of the house while Mama went to park. She stood there, waiting, shading her eyes against the afternoon sun. The trip to the lawyer's office to hear Papa's will read was the first time she'd left the house since the funeral. Although common sense told her this was barely a month ago, it seemed longer.

Her confinement had not been unpleasant. The long, cool days she'd spent in the house had been a comfort. The first few days, she'd sat in her favorite chair by the window, and then, when the sunshine and the sight of the garden became too much, she'd been cocooned in her room, pulling down the blinds and lying in the dark, willing the hours to pass slowly, so that the moment when Jonah returned from work and threw open the windows would be delayed.

"I'd have thought your husband would've found his way back home by now." Mama's voice made her jump. She tossed the car keys up and caught them, her small hands clad in the white lambskin gloves she wore when she drove. Both women turned toward the drive, half expecting silver metal to flash at the entrance.

"Maybe he went back to work," Justice said disinterestedly.

Mama sniffed. "Your father made him a rich man today. You'd think the least he could do was see you home, instead of speeding out of there like a pigeon out of hell. Maybe he thought what he got wasn't enough. Maybe—"

"Jonah isn't like that," Justice surprised herself by saying. She hadn't spent a whole lot of time lately thinking about what Jonah was or wasn't like.

Mama nailed her with a stare. The noise she made was part laugh, part sneer. "Child, you have so much to learn. As a matter of fact, I almost hope you never learn it. I spent half my life building a shell around you . . . *being* a shell around you. If at the end of the day you wind up facing the world defenseless, like some naked bird, well . . ." She looked deep in thought for a moment, then said, "I suppose I'd have no one to blame but myself." The contemplative tone was replaced by her usual clipped, decisive one. "Let's go inside." As she turned, her heels made a hollow noise on the tiled path.

When Justice made no move to follow, Mama threw her an impatient look. "What're you waiting for? Come."

As she always did when Mama challenged her, Justice dropped her chin. With Mama, you did as she said. She felt her body sway unbidden, rocking in Mama's direction, so used was it to unquestioning compliance that it moved without her command. Yet something made her want to linger awhile, even though to be outdoors felt weird, almost unnatural. The air smelled different, and the garden lay waiting for her, like a quiet revelation. Unable to voice her rebellion, she shook her head.

Thirty seconds, and then Mama walked on, throwing the front door open so hard that it banged into the wall, and slamming it behind her.

Justice slipped off her shoes, as even the echo of her own footsteps intruded. From the tiles onto the gravel, and the rounded stones hurt her feet. Maybe her skin had become thinner over the months. Even the clasp of her bra and the button at the waist of her skirt had been making their presence felt lately, leaving bruises that she'd twist and contort her body in order to gaze upon them in mirrors.

She took pleasure in each soft bruise. They reminded her of *The Princess and the Pea,* one of the stories she used to beg Papa to read to her over and over as a child. When he read it, he'd always begun, "Once upon a time there was a princess, a tiny little thing, just like you . . ." Fascinating, she'd always thought, how delicate a girl would have to be to be bruised by something so small, so smooth. How loved she'd be, refined and set apart by royal blood. She tried to think of the gravel underfoot as a sea of fresh green peas, each one leaving its mark on her. Each one proving her lineage.

At the lily beds, she stopped. This corner of the garden was hers, given to her by her father. It was set apart by a low hedge and a wrought-iron gate that came barely to midthigh. The rest of the garden was cared for by the gardeners, but they were forbidden to enter this private space. It was hers and Papa's alone. Together, they had filled it with Easter lilies: stark white and bright orange. Now was their season for blooming. She'd never allowed them to be cut, even to fill Mama's hand-blown glass vases in the family room. For her, cutting was murder. Although lilies were there one day and withered away the next, whether cut or on the bush, bringing flowers inside was like laying out corpses for viewing.

Today, though, the question of cutting was moot. The blistering April sun had joined forces with her own neglect— when last had she even remembered that the lilies were there?—and reduced their vibrant bobbing heads to shriveled heaps of dusty straw.

Death. Justice swallowed, bracing for the chill that always ran through her at the thought of the word, or when the sight of it made it real. She wanted to back away and flee to her room, not look too hard at the graveyard her garden had become. Send Mama down to clean it up and make it all go away. But this time, a voice called, small and seductive, bringing her to her knees before the mound of dry dirt.

Death. It smiled coyly, then winked audaciously. She frowned. Had the stalker turned seducer? When? How?

Tentatively, she grasped a handful of the rotted flowers and brought them to her face, sniffing the scent of so much beauty laid low. Astounding. Its pungency did not terrify, but instead delighted her. She felt daring, flirting with the enemy. The dried flowers rustled under her fingers like a raw silk underskirt. She remembered the two old ladies touching Papa in his casket, something she herself was afraid to do. Was this what death felt like to the touch?

But Papa had gone quickly. Maybe, for him, it had been different. For the lilies, death had not come all at once. For plants it was a slow process, as thirst and heat suffered first the flowers, then the leaves, before it worked its way down the stalk. This made her wonder: were the bulbs, buried in their secret place, dead, too, or was the plant playing possum, sacrificing all that stood above ground so that it could take every last drop of life-sustaining water into its heart, holding it as a pearl diver in the depths held his breath?

She clawed at the earth, digging the lily bulb out of its dark grave. It was hard and cool, skin as papery as a crone's, but Justice could sense the spark of life within. Disappointment rose where relief at its survival should have.

Survival meant that when the rains came, the lily would be denied the luxury of sleep and the solace of silent contemplation, forced to spring again. What energy that would take! What effort! To suffer the forced cheeriness of the sun and the bullying of the rain. To be obliged to put on a party dress of petals, and to smile and smile, and have others smile back at you, when all you wanted to do was turn and face the wall.

She tilted her head to the sky, searching out someone to answer her. "Was I wrong all along?" She wasn't sure if she was speaking out loud or if her words resonated only in her head.

No voice spoke from the point where the blue sky faded into white, but confirmation blossomed in her heart. Her triumph at her revelation was like the shout of angels. This death that she feared was not a tragedy, but a kindness. She thought of the afternoons she spent waiting in the window for Papa, or her husband, to come home, concocting in her seething imagination a thousand disasters, and laughed hoarsely.

The "tragedy" that had befallen Papa had in fact been the throwing open of prison gates. He lay now in a quiet place, like the lily bulbs, but unlike the poor lilies, there was in him no spark left of this curse called life.

Justice looked at the bulb in her hand. The wretched thing would be better off if she spared it the misery of resurrection. She tried to break it open like a nut, cutting into the seam with her nails, but they were brittle from her fasting and split with the effort.

Undaunted, she brought it to her mouth and gnawed. In seconds, the mercy killing was complete. And whereas for her, food and drink had become wormwood and bile, the hard seed tasted fresh and clean, coated with dirt though it was. Justice placed a chunk of the butchered bulb on her tongue, marveling at its taste, closing her eyes against the pleasure that assailed her. Bright green heart and parchment brown skin, life and death in her mouth.

"Justice!" Before she could eat another piece, rough hands snatched them from her, scattering them among the shriveled carcasses of the lilies. She felt herself being dragged to her feet and spun around to face her husband.

"What the hell are you doing?" Aghast, he slapped lightly at the dust on her hands and pulled a handkerchief to swab away at her mouth. She resisted, but he held her fast.

He looked at the brown smear on the white square of cloth in his hand and then gaped at her as he would at a strange new animal. "Darling?"

Bastard. He'd burst in on her sweetness, cut in on her conversation with God. How dare he? She bucked wildly to free herself from his grasp. "Don't"—the grit between her teeth crunched in her ears—"touch me! Let me go, Jonah!" He released her immediately, but she did not run.

Shock and concern brought the weight of ten years to his face. "Justice, talk to me. Let me help you."

"I don't need help. I'm fine. I'm happy." She folded her arms across her unprotected breasts.

He countered with, "Fine? Justice, baby, you're not fine. Every day I come home and find a fainter shadow of you. You're dying. You doing this on purpose? You *want* to die?"

Her first smile in ages split her face. Until today, that thought had been far from enticing. Before today, that awesome dragon had been waiting to consume her, but now it undulated seductively, promising an exultant, eternal dance. Her eyes fluttered shut in anticipation.

"Let me help," she heard him say. "I can help you. There are people we can see, together, who'll make you all right."

She felt sorry for him. He was still stranded in this world, still a party to the death-fear that had held her crippled until the revelation had come. He was a heathen: she knew God. Like warm blood oozing from an internal wound, a new kind of love welled up in her. Not the counterfeit love that had brought her to their marriage bed—Papa's love by proxy— but something benevolent and holy. The kind an apostle of the only true, secret faith held for the lost. She reached up and touched his cheek. It was smooth: he was meticulous about shaving.

"Don't worry for me, Jonah. I'm happy. This is what I want."

His mouth fell open. "This is not what you want. This can't be what you want. Justice, you're sick. You're very sick. I don't know how I stood by and let you come to this. First, that infernal diet, and then I thought you were missing your father. But it's gone way beyond that now. I look at you, and I don't know who I'm looking at. If only I'd done . . . something."

"Why?" Her smile was beatific. "Why should you have done something?"

"Because you're my wife. My love. I should have . . . I owed you . . ." He was fumbling for words. His next words were more to himself than to her. "And now, today . . ." He took off his glasses and squeezed his eyes tight, running his fingers across them as if the light had become too much.

"What, today?" She asked with idle curiosity.

His body looked too heavy for him to support it on his own; so she held out her arms, and he let her hold him close. His chest lifted and fell erratically, and his arms came around her. His shirt felt grubby; strange, because he was always so careful with his clothing. The crisp cologne he preferred to wear had faded, subsumed by acrid sweat that had a top note of anxiety—and something else. Justice inhaled deeply, her senses heightened by her moments of revelation before his interruption.

And there it was, filling her nostrils, musky and distinct, separate from all the other smells he was made up of: the scent of another woman. Startled, she looked up at him, her mouth falling open. Jonah and a woman? She would never have thought it in his nature; he was as faithful as a dog, going about their marriage with the earnestness that could only come from not having grown up in a marital home himself. He was the kind of man who believed that marriage was serious business.

Yet the evidence of his straying was not only clinging to his skin like a warm aura, but there in the guilt and fear in his eyes, as he desperately tried to read her face, to see if, indeed, she had guessed, and how much she had guessed.

Poor thing. Instead of wifely outrage, she felt only sympathy for this man who stood in her dead garden and waited for the hammer to fall on the pin, blowing his life away. Fearing the end of something that was already over.

When the realization came to him that she knew, that he had not been imagining the glimmer of understanding in her eyes, he began to stutter. "I didn't . . . I didn't mean this. I didn't expect . . ."

She stepped away, more interested in the fact that she felt no offense at his breach of their vows than she was in his explanations. "Save it, Jonah." She was weary. Her bed was calling.

He followed her to the house. "Justice, enough. Don't walk away. If you value what we have, stay and listen. There's more to this than what happened today."

"I'm tired." Inside, Teresa, the young maid, was puttering about the main hall. She lifted her head at their entrance, her quick eyes deducing that they were fighting, and then let her head fall again, pretending not to hear.

"Too tired to work with me on this? Too tired to save what we have left?"

"What do we have left?" she challenged.

"I love you," he said. He was close on her tail as she climbed the stairs, her limbs aching.

Loved her? Maybe. Or thought he did. Still believing in the delusion they had shared these past few years. At her bedroom, she stopped, blocking the entrance with her body. "This isn't real. Why'd you keep on believing that this is real?"

"What's not real?" On his face was a look of pure puzzlement.

Before she could answer, the door to the next room opened, and Mama was standing in the hallway, watching them both. Justice went on anyway. "We made this up. We let Papa make us think that we had something. He set you to protect me when I was a little girl, told you that you had to watch out for me, walk me to school and walk me back. And when I got older, he made you think I still needed you . . ."

"*I* need *you*," he countered. "And nobody made me think that."

"What's going on here?" Mama's voice was shrill.

Jonah's head whipped in her direction. "Faith, if you don't mind . . ."

Mama's smile was cold. "If I don't mind what, Jonah?"

"I'm talking to Justice. This is private." He looked as if common decency alone prevented him from shoving Mama back into her room and slamming the door shut behind her. "For the love of God, can't you leave us alone?"

Mama never stopped smiling. "She's my daughter."

"She's my *wife!*"

Justice kept on talking. "I wasn't the one you wanted to be near. Not at first. You wanted to be Papa's son, but you couldn't, so you were happy to be his son-in-law. To live in this house, see him every day, have an office next to his. He worked his obeah on you just like he worked it on everybody else. There were three people in this marriage, Jonah. It was never about us; it was about *him* and us."

"And now?"

"He's dead."

"I know that!" He looked as tired as she felt.

"So what's left?"

"Us. You and me."

Mama interrupted. "Justice, maybe you should get some rest. You had a long day."

"Faith, I'm warning you!" Justice had never seen her husband look so angry.

Mama lifted her head and stared him down, eyes like stones. "What? What are you warning me of? You going to let the gutter you were born in rise up in you and attack me? You had the run of the house while my husband was alive, and you acted like you were to the manor born. But the rules have changed. This is my house now. We don't raise our voices here."

Mama was looking at Jonah with the same look she kept for the gardener and the paperboy, and Justice couldn't bear it. In spite of everything, he was a decent man and didn't deserve to be on the receiving end of Mama's darts. Before she could stop herself, she blurted, "Don't talk to him like that!"

Mama turned her eyes away from him and stared. Justice couldn't remember ever having said "don't" to her mother. She had to struggle against the urge to clap her hand over her mouth to keep anything else from popping out.

"What?" Mama's voice was dangerous.

"Don't talk to him like that. He's not the yard boy."

"I know what he is." A glance flew from Justice's face to Jonah's and back again.

Jonah exploded. "I am not staying here and listening to this. Justice, we have to talk. Come with me. Let's go—"

"Where?"

"Doesn't matter. Away. We can save what we have."

"Justice, go to bed," Mama said.

Jonah opened his hand, holding it out. "Just a short drive, love. We can save this."

"She's sick," Mama screamed. "Can't you see she's sick? No, all you can think about is what *you* want. Justice, go to bed."

Everything was shifting, colors swirling, making her seasick. She thought of the lily bulb and envied it the silence of the earth.

"You don't have to do anything. I'll drive us to the beach; you can sleep on the way. We can sit and hold hands. We don't have to talk at all. Just let me be with you. Tish, please."

"Bed, Justice."

Justice was sure she would throw up any minute, and all she would bring up from her empty stomach would be bile. She felt ashamed for turning her back on Jonah, leaving him to Mama and her wretched humor, but she needed to get away, fast, before she pitched to the ground. Her hand found the doorknob and twisted. She staggered in. Jonah moved to follow, but Mama's arm was in the way. "There are half a dozen bedrooms in this house, Jonah." Her voice was like metal on metal. "Pick one."

Justice shut the door behind her before she could hear Jonah's response, almost sobbing with gratitude at the refuge inside. The silence, welcoming. She fell onto the bed and pulled the sheets up over her head, cocooning herself. Safe.

Faith and the Statuette

" **A** m I the only sane person here?" Faith railed at the little black man propped up on her dressing table.
"Everybody's gone crazy. The whole world's mad. This boy
darting off from the lawyer's office and leaving his wife behind. Money to burn he got, and his face turns to ash and he
runs. And Justice, wandering around in the garden. Telling
me 'no.' " She pounded her chest. "Me! Her mother!"

The African listened quietly, enough of a gentleman to let
her belch out her frustration without interrupting. She
yanked open her underwear drawer and pulled out a glass
and the bottle of twelve-year-old she'd taken to keeping
there. Lately, she'd been drinking it like it was milk, but it
wasn't a problem. All it did was keep clarity in her head and
the ache out of her heart.

When her throat was moist, she took up her rant again.
"That boy will kill her. She's sick, and a sick child needs her
mother. But he keeps on interfering. Thinks he knows what's
good for her better than I do. That arrogance, it's the gutter
in him, I tell you. Goddamn Dominic and his bright ideas. If
he'd listened to me—"

"What?"

"None of this would ever have happened. Justice would've
married someone suitable. And she'd mind what I say, not

turn away when I talk to her. She learned that rebellion from him. He's starting a mutiny, and I won't stand for it!"

"Up to you, Faith," he reminded her. He sounded as sympathetic as she needed him to be.

"Yes."

"To keep everything under control."

"Yes!" Oh, God, so good to have someone who knew. Who understood. "Nobody knows what it's like," she moaned. She picked him up and cradled him against her breast, scotch in one hand, him in the other. Her two bringers of solace. She finished the scotch and put down the empty glass, not wanting to make him jealous.

"*I* know," he comforted. Although he was pressed against her flesh, his voice wasn't muffled.

"Yes, you do." She was so, so tired. Not taking the time to kick her shoes off, she crawled into bed and set the figurine upright upon her flat belly. So strange, how the universe worked. How the loved could be so easily lost, and the loathed loved. If anyone had told her that her bed would be empty before she was fifty, she'd have called them a fool. If anyone had told her that the void would be filled by this black-skinned being, they would have been doubly condemned.

And to think she'd almost set him on fire! She'd have laughed aloud at her own obtuseness if it hadn't been so potentially tragic. These days, there was no talk of fire, only endless conversations with this dark man who knew her every thought before she voiced it. This soul, although transported from afar across that huge expanse of water, was an echo of her own. Even her husband had not known her that well.

Oh, if only he could satisfy her physical needs as well as he could her emotional ones! If only this spirit could transform itself into a huge black bird and settle upon her outstretched body with the fluttering of wings!

He sensed her anguish and tried to comfort. "Soon, beauty.

Time in the world of flesh is not the same as time in the world of the spirit. But those times will collide. Soon."

"But I don't have time," she protested. "Being alone is worse than death. Even the dead have company." Sometimes she wondered if she'd been cursed by her rashness to suffer the same endless burning she'd threatened him with, before she'd come to know him.

"You're not alone," he corrected gently.

She brought him up to her face, staring into the light that glowed beyond his hollow eyes. He was right. She wasn't alone, not while he was there. Comforted, she placed a kiss on his bald head and pressed him against her left breast, right over her heart. Exhaustion made her eyelids heavy.

"Sleep, Faith," he whispered.

Mattie

Mattie didn't head for home until the sun was low be-hind the trees, and even then she was loath to do so, reluctant to leave what had become for her a mountain of revelation. Something in her had changed, or made itself known, so stunningly fast that it couldn't have been brought about by anything other than the hand of God. There was something irretrievably different about the color of the grass now, and the smell of the air, and the sound of gravel crunching under her wheels. Had the mountain become infused with this magic because of the presence of the monks, or had they sensed it and thus chosen it as a place to settle?

She didn't find it strange that this man had, without warning, expanded within her heart and mind to take up all the space there, squeezing aside anything else that had held residence there before. What had happened? Surely not their half hour in the grass! Sex in and of itself was never that good.

Moments before he had drawn her down onto the earth, she'd been fading away, lost to the light, just as in every nightmare that dragged her from sleep. And although every thrust of his hips had made her more impervious to fading, riveting her to a hard surface like one of her own mirrors being nailed to the wall, that was not the reason for this overwhelming desire to be with him, see him, touch him again.

Her only guilt was her lack of guilt about Blood Pye.

Surely she should feel ashamed! Surely she should feel badly for having behaved like one of those flighty women she so disdained! But as she searched about blindly in her mind like someone reaching into a dark cupboard, she could find nothing less for him than what had always been there: a deep, abiding affection. What she and Jonah had done had certainly not diminished that. What it had revealed for her, though, was that there could never be anything more.

Jonah had given her a part of him to keep safe and had taken a part of her away. The space left behind was more than adequately filled, and not only with what he'd given her. She was filled to the seams with want and need and greedy, delightful desire. As she rode, she pressed down against the padded seat of the bicycle, feeling a throbbing in her groin, urging it to grow. She pumped her legs hard, leaning into the ride, going faster than she had even when she and Jonah were racing, because maybe if she went fast enough, she could affect the pace of time through effort and wanting, speeding up the spin of the Earth, and tomorrow would be here all the much sooner.

Blood Pye

"Where you been?" Blood Pye tried not to sound annoyed; but he'd been standing in the yard in front of the candy store for an hour now, with Miss Louisa giving him bad-eye all that time, and now there was Mattie, sailing in on her bike, smiling like she had a secret. She was wearing a dress of the brightest green he had ever seen. She looked like a basket of limes. He walked up to her before she could come to a stop and put his hand on the bars. "You have me waiting here a whole hour for you. More than an hour. Where you been, girl?"

Mattie showed him all her teeth, but the grin had an edge to it that made him let go of the bike and give her room. She leaned it up against the wall and faced him, hands on her hips, hair bristling with some kind of strange excitement. "You tell me you were coming?"

"No."

"So why you expect me to be here waiting for you?"

He pointed at the sweetie parlor with his chin. "You ain't supposed to be working this afternoon?"

She shrugged. "I took a little time off. I work my ass off in there, day in, day out. You think I'm not entitled? To a little time off?"

He could have let her draw him into some talk about

whether she was entitled to or not, but he didn't have time for that. Instead, he asked again, "So where you been?"

Before Mattie could answer him, Louisa's shape filled the doorway. "Mattie, you late. Again. You think I ain't got nothing better to do, girl, than to watch the store for you? Bad enough I got to be slaving over a pot all day, making all them sweets, putting up with hot sugar jumping out at me; least you could do is—"

"Sorry, Auntie Lou," Mattie said hastily. She tried to ease past her grandmother, but Louisa wouldn't let her.

"'Stead of coming back when you supposed to, you gone gallivanting, and all kinds of scamps wandering in and out of my yard like they living here. Bringing in a plague of parasites in my yard; next thing you know, we itching all over, and things sucking our blood." She gave Blood Pye a nasty look, and he chose to ignore it. The old bitch was just being unfair. He'd been good and left Threes home this time, sort of a gesture of goodwill, and here she was, talking about parasites, like she thought *he* was the one with the fleas. It just wasn't right. Before he could find an apt retort, the old lady gave Mattie a hard, direct stare. "Where you been?"

Blood Pye laughed. "You see, girl? That makes two of us want to know."

Louisa pulled on her apron strings with pudgy hands, loosed it, and tossed it on the counter before disappearing into the back room. Before she left, she gave Blood Pye one last black look. "Two of us *want* to know, maybe," she said. "But only one of us got the *right* to ask." She kicked the door to the living area shut.

Mattie put her own apron on, humming softly to herself. It was almost as if he wasn't even in the room. Anxious to remind her he was there, he hopped over the counter and pulled her to him, kissing her lightly on the lips. She smelled good, like sunshine and fresh air.

And grass.

Blood Pye stiffened, startled. As a matter of fact, she

looked grassy. There were flecks of it on her dress and in her hair. Odd, he thought. "Fall off your bike?" he asked, giving her the once-over for scratches.

She shook her head, smiling like one of those whatcha-macallit cats. That wasn't good. That smile looked eerily familiar; it was the smile she gave her grandmother when she was just done giving him some sweetness and went back to work, trying to act nonchalant.

His brow knitted, but he dismissed the ugly thought that was making tiny pinpricks at the back of his mind. This was *Mattie* he was talking to, not one of those bony-assed skanks that liked to friend with all sorts of stray-'ways, so he bit back the accusation before it could leap from his mouth.

There was just the germ of a headache kicking up at the base of his skull. *Steady*, he told himself. He squeezed his eyes shut for a moment, trying to dredge up the calm he could project at will when one of his cocks was facing competition in the ring. Never let them see you sweat.

Maybe he was going about this all wrong, anyway. Girls didn't like it when you came down on them with that possessive bullshit, asking where they were and all. It made them eager to show you they were more man than you. To ask if Mattie was wherever she was with some*body*, that would have been borrowing trouble.

So as not to set her mood swinging in the wrong direction before he asked what he was here to ask, he kept his voice soft, cajoling rather than confrontational. "I just come because I was missing you. I ain't seen you in days. I wanted to see if you all right."

"I'm all right," she said. She didn't try to wriggle free of his embrace, but didn't seem interested in sticking close, either. He wanted nothing more than to hold on to her even tighter, lock her in so she wouldn't slip away, but he forced himself to put some space between them, leaning against the wall and watching her wipe down the counters and fiddle with the sweetie bottles. He tried to play it cool, reaching past her and extracting a pink-and-white peppermint stick and sliding the tip between his lips like a cigar.

Before he could say anything more, two or three children wandered in, pressed their faces against a glass case, and squabbled over their choices. He wanted to send the brats packing, but he held his peace, and ground his teeth while Mattie saw to them. When they were alone again, he cleared his throat. It was time to ask. He'd been trying to be real polite these past few days, giving her space, waiting for her to bring it up; but now his time was running out, and he had to act now or shut up while his life crumbled. "Baby?"

"Yeah?" Her eyes were on him, clear and direct, but barely curious.

"You remember what we talked about before?"

"We talk about plenty things."

She was just being difficult. She knew what he meant: the irritation made the green of her eyes just a shade brighter. He didn't let her play with him. "You know"—he put his hand on her shoulder—"the money. The money your father got."

Something passed across her face, like a cloud across the sun. "What about his money?"

"You been thinking any more about getting some? I told you, some of it's rightfully yours."

She made a sound in her throat. He couldn't figure out if it was a laugh or a stifled groan. "Got news for you, Pye. They read the will."

Anticipatory ants crawled all over his skin, along his neck and arms. "And?"

"And nothing."

He frowned. "What you mean?"

"He didn't leave me nothing." He could hear her patience fraying.

"How you know that?"

"I got my sources." She clamped her lips together, and he knew right then that if she was going to talk about this to anyone, it wasn't going to be him. He didn't have time to be jealous, or to wonder who. The pinging in his head was too loud for that.

No money. That rich high-brown bastard had gone and died and didn't leave his own flesh and blood a cent. Anger came first: if the fat fuck wasn't dead, Blood Pye was sure he'd have found a way to rectify the situation. Then panic sloshed over him like wild waves on a rolling deck, washing away the rage. He was a man on a sinking ship, and someone had gone and punched holes in his life jacket.

"And what you gonna do 'bout that?" he asked when he could speak.

"Nothing." She stuck her bottom lip out stubbornly, challenging him to argue with her.

He didn't have a choice. This was his goddam *life* hanging in the balance. "You ain't going over there to change that? You just got to make yourself known to the family. If they can't look into your eyes and see him, something wrong with them. Then they gonna know they owe you."

"What, I just walk up to the door and knock, and when his wife comes, I open my eyes wide and let her look in them and see her husband looking back?" Her voice was sarcastic, but there was something contemplative there, too. Like the idea amused her.

"You could do that," he said encouragingly. "You want me to go with you, I'd go with you."

"And then what? She ask me in, give me a cup of tea, and write me a check?" Her laugh was brittle.

Hold strong, he told himself. *Don't let your will slip.* He kept trying, talking steadily and evenly, so she wouldn't be skittish. "Then you bargain. You a business woman; you never bargained before? You tell her about all the years your daddy hide you away, like you ain't good enough to be seen. And all the years your sister been spending money, dressing nice, and smelling good. You tell her how her husband been coming over to see your ma, and how he never bother to give you money other than to buy yourself a pair of shoes or a new hat. How blood will always be blood, and you come to collect on yours."

This time, she didn't mock him. Her gaze was fixed in the distance, and her mouth was slightly open. She was sipping the air of her father's perfumed garden. He pressed home his advantage, gently.

"You got a right. This ain't no favor. You ain't got to let no society bitch watch you like you nothing, like you ain't got no right to be nothing. You *entitled.* It ain't *her* money she giving you. Is *your* money."

She flicked her eyes at him, and they were fever bright. "And then I give the money to you?"

Blood Pye stretched his arms out to her, pulling her against him as insurance against the tinge of sarcasm in her question. Her lips were pliant under his. And soft. Too soft, as if the blood that swelled them had rushed there under the urging of previous kisses.

Suspicion became concrete. *Not Mattie,* he thought. His stomach dropped to balls level. Who, who, who? *How?* The affront to his manhood made him sick. How long had he turned his back to allow this ghost to flit past the barriers her bulldog grandmother had erected around her? What kind of man couldn't come by any better place to fuck a woman than in the *grass?* And why had Mattie allowed it?

Their little circle had been breached. That offended him hugely. So what if he'd maybe slipped away for a session every once in a while. Those girls had meant so little to him; some of them, he could barely remember their names. But he was a man; that was what men did. He wouldn't have expected it from his woman!

He pushed hard, insistent, anxious to reestablish their couplehood. "And then *we* use the money. To invest. In *our* future."

"You want me to get money out of them just so you and I can start a chicken farm?" She was incredulous.

Chicken farm. That hurt. He swallowed hard and spoke slowly. "Not a chicken farm, Mattie. These ain't broilers we talking 'bout. We talking 'bout warriors. Champions. Bred from the best stock. We could be *so* rich."

"We could be *so* in jail," she retorted, but she wasn't nearly as aggressive as she could have been. Her eyes were on him, searching.

He didn't want to take the jail part head-on. "We could get rid of this devil thing that fall on them. And after the cocks get better, maybe we could get more land. Not a big farm or anything, but a plot in a nice, quiet place, so I could train out in the open and don't have to worry about no police strolling by. And them cocks gonna pay off big. But that ain't all. That money could buy us a house. And dresses for you, nicer than anything that old fowl your father married ever gonna wear."

"Nothing wrong with the dresses I got now," she countered. "And what you mean, a house? For who to live in? I already got a place to live. Right here."

Her attention was slipping away from the place he needed it to be. *Fast,* he told himself. *Before you lose her.* He put down the peppermint stick he was sucking on, so as to give her his undivided attention, and squeezed her hands. "You ain't gotta live here all your life. Don't you want to leave some time?"

"For what?"

"For me. You could come live with me. In that nice, big house we gonna build, soon as you do that one thing for me." He was making things up as he went along, drawing wild fantasies out of the air, but even as he spoke them, they became so clear in his mind, so real, that he was instantly convinced that they were the only right thing to do.

"Why?"

Blood Pye sighed. Why did women always have to be so difficult? "'Cause I love you, Mattie." Hearing the words fly from his mouth almost made him fall over. He didn't think he'd ever said it to anyone before. With most chicks, you didn't have to, even when you were trying to screw them. The women he usually went with knew what was what. You didn't have to pump them full of any of that love shit just to get them to drop their drawers. Usually, they were as willing as you were. But desperate times called for desperate measures.

Mattie was as taken aback by his utterance as he was. She half smiled, expecting him to laugh and tell her he was only joking, but when he didn't, her brows drew together. "What you saying, Pye?"

What was he saying, indeed? He was unable to stop the fingers of one hand from flying to his lips, as if the remnants of those words were tangible enough to be felt hovering there. He'd gone and told the girl he loved her. Had he meant it? He tried to backpedal in his mind to the moment that he'd said it. What had he been focused on, her, the money, or the man he could sense on her like a bloodhound? Was he just marking his territory, like a dog pissing on a bush?

He couldn't remember, so he repeated himself, straining to listen for evidence of truth or lie. "I said I love you. You smarter than anybody I ever met; you prettier than any girl I ever know—"

"I'm not—" she began.

"You like this bright spirit that nothing can't kill." He felt his mouth pull upward in a grin, astounding even himself at the discovery that he had, in fact, been telling the truth. Amazing, just amazing. He'd come all the way over here to talk about money, and opened his mouth, and out popped a secret even he hadn't known. "You got me like a big compass. And I turn around, and turn around, but no matter where I face, the needle always pointing your way." He waited for her to answer, biting the inside of his cheek in an effort to stop himself from shaking. Something which, thirty seconds before, had not even existed in his mind had suddenly become the only thing he wanted: for her to say the same thing back to him. When she didn't speak, he prompted her. "Mattie?"

She studied her feet. He couldn't bear seeing her long lashes shrouding those beautiful, expressive eyes, like curtains being drawn against the sun, so he caught her chin in his hand and lifted her face.

"I know you wasn't looking out for this. I know you wasn't expecting nothing like this. Me neither. But I said it and it's true. Tell me it's true for you, too." He was a man who could talk his way into anything, and talk anything out of everyone else. In that, he was like his father and his father's father. Women, cockfighters, gamblers, and men he owed money, everyone could be talked into doing what you wanted them to do if you found the words they wanted to hear and said them. Now, for the first time in his life, he was at a loss. For the first time, he didn't know what to say to get what he wanted.

She shook her head, partly in denial and partly to ease her face from his grasp. "Pye . . . ," she began. Her lashes were wet. "Why you got to tell me that *now?*"

I just found out, he wanted to say, but instead he said, softly, "You don't want to hear it?"

"Why you didn't tell me that yesterday, or last week?"

"I said it now. That ain't good enough? There ain't got no set time to say . . . that. The time you say it is always the right time. What you complaining about? It's not like it's too late or anything." This last thought wasn't an affirmation, but a prayer. *Make it not be too late. Make this man not be the reason she's not telling me what I want to hear.*

Her head fell into her hands, and she plopped onto her grandmother's wooden stool. His prayer had gone out the window unheard. This man wasn't an idle curiosity. Maybe the man had been saying to her all along what he'd just said, what he should have said long, long before, and would have, if he'd known it. And maybe she'd been saying it to him, which was why she was silent now.

He felt a pain in his heart so violent that he looked sharply down to see if he'd actually been cut. No blood stained the front of his shirt, but the pain expanded, cutting a path up to his throat and down into his gut. Giddy, he fell to his knees before her. "Not you, Mattie!" He'd have thought his mother more capable of such betrayal than Mattie.

"He saw me." Her voice was muffled behind her fingers.

"Saw you?" The pain was laced with jealousy, like acid poured into an open wound. "Where he saw you? And who's that fucker anyway? 'Cause he dead . . ."

"No, no." Her wet eyes were near black against stark white, pleading for him to understand. "He saw *me*. He proved to me that I was there. And I gave him something, and he's going to keep it safe."

Was she mad? She was talking foolish, and he didn't like it. "What you gone and give him, Mattie? Tell me. And tell me who he is, so I can go and get it back for you."

"Can't get it back," she said.

"Try me."

"Pye!" She sounded like a trapped mongoose. "You could have done something before. You leave me waiting and wondering, a year now. You come when you need me and go when you don't. You ever turn up when *I* need *you*?"

Guilt fought his jealous anger, but lost. He shot to his feet. "I don't know what shit you going on about, Mattie. But I'm your man. Whoever he is, you forget him. Whatever love you think you got for him, get it back. It's mine."

"I can't get it back." The mention of her love for this man made her more resistant, more determined. "That horse already bolted."

So angry. He was so angry it almost blinded him. He wanted to hit something, smash it, thrust it from him in the hopes that all this hurt would be cast away with it. He grabbed up a bottle of red-dyed Chinese plums and drew his arm all the way back before sending it flying against the far wall. Mattie cringed, covering her head instinctively as glass shattered outward leaving a stain on the wall that looked as though someone had been shot. A mayonnaise jar full of paradise plums followed, but the crashing sound did not nearly ease the hurt that poured out of the gap in his chest that Mattie had made.

Mattie's grandmother came charging out of the living room, barreling into him, knocking him over, cursing in her rough, mannish voice. One elbow caught him in the temple, and red and gold spangles glittered inside his head. There was a crashing of piano keys, random, and raucous, in his ears.

"Out!" Louisa shouted. "I finally had enougha you. Get your scrawny ass outta my house. And I don't want to see it again."

He looked past Louisa to Mattie, silently begging her to intervene and explain to her grandmother that this was a mistake, just an incident between lovers. That it would be all right once he made Mattie understand that he was the one she wanted, not some phantom. But Mattie was backing away, shell shock on her face.

He screamed out her name, even as Louisa steamrollered him out of the door. "Baby! I'm coming back. I gonna fix things, and I'm coming back. Gonna make everything okay, and then it'll be you and me, yeah?"

Mattie turned and ran from the room.

Jonah

The leather couch squeaked under Jonah as he twisted. Dominic's study was dark: he hadn't bothered to turn on the brass lights on the wall on either side of the huge bookshelf. The darkness around him was so dense that he was sure none of the other lights in the house were on, even though it was barely past eight and both Faith and Justice were probably still awake.

Although, as Faith had spat at him, there were many other bedrooms in the house, he didn't feel like entering any of them. Sterile, clean, and silent, they existed in perpetual stasis, awaiting a guest. Hand-crocheted bedspreads making sure that the linen sheets underneath remained unsullied. Tasteful decor and muted tones. No soul.

The entire house, he realized, was soulless. It was a giant cavity into which people crawled, but in which nobody was truly at rest. The only room in the house that welcomed him was Dominic's study. The transformation from deadness to life was evident from the moment he had crossed the threshold. Each book was possessed of its own spirit and, having been touched and consumed by its reader, also bore traces of his presence; in infusing Dominic with knowledge, they had stealthily taken something from him as well. Even his desk, with blotter, pens, and pencils still neatly arranged, spoke of him. The huge globe that Jonah had played with as a boy, searching for the names of far-off places under Dominic's paternal eye, waited in a corner of the room to be spun, and it, too, vibrated like a living thing. No wonder this was the only room in which he could seek peace.

He shifted, restless. There was an emptiness in his belly that couldn't be filled with food, and a heaviness on his shoulders that sleep could not lighten. His stomach churned, and his head was filled with the women who so confounded him.

Faith, who sat high in her web like a large, malevolent spider. Free to speak her mind now that her husband was gone. He'd always known of her contempt for him, and to tell the truth, he understood it. She had been born and bred for her role, schooled to be the wife of a rich man. She knew things about teacups and saucers, stationery, wine, and cuts of veal that he would never, and didn't care to, learn. She'd coasted through life on her light skin, perfect diction, and her husband's last name. She was what her milieu had made her. To be honest, her contempt didn't hurt as much as it should have.

But to stand between him and his wife! That was something else entirely. She had failed to speak when she had her chance, before their marriage had become a reality, so now, she should hold her peace. Their marriage was a fact—legal and consummated—and as much as Faith hated the idea, he *was* her daughter's husband. She had no right to interfere.

But Justice had become so worn away by her mother's dominance, so cowed by her mean and controlling spirit, that not even Jonah could hold sway over her actions. The sound of their bedroom door closing, shutting him out of the room they had shared, leaving him in the hallway to face the shame of Faith's triumphant smile, had cut deep. Her rejection had left him feeling lonelier than he ever had before.

He remembered something Mattie had once asked him: did he love his wife, or had he found a way to love Dominic more through her? He squeezed his eyes shut. If his mind were to have the final say, it would be that marrying Justice had brought him closer to his hero, cementing his claim on sonship, giving him the father that the boy in him had always craved. But if his heart were to speak for him, it would say that his love was real. He didn't doubt that. He'd have been crazy to ever have.

What he'd done today with Mattie hadn't changed that: it fact, it might have made it clearer. And if he loved Justice so much, why *had* he made love to Mattie? Just the thought of her brought back the feel of her skin on his and the sensation of their bodies against each other's. He knew more about Mattie after one month than he'd ever understood about Justice. He believed with his heart that the transfer that they had undergone in the forest had not taken place in his imagination. He'd seen and felt the light that had passed between them. He now carried part of her, and she carried part of him. That left him committed, by honor alone. He'd promised to look out for her, and he wouldn't break that promise, even while he was struggling to gather up the shambles of his marriage. Even though Justice had somehow sensed his infidelity and didn't seem to care. Was her absence of jealousy a good thing? Would he have preferred shock, rage, tears, if only they meant that Justice still returned his love?

So if he loved his wife, what was this thing he felt for Mattie? Was this love, too, in a different shape and form? Or had he, somewhere in his mind, merged these two sisters into a single woman, each the opposite of the other, each one half of a single coin, which, together, would be whole? Pale and dark, soft and hard, soothing and invigorating. . . .

And if he loved them both, wanted them both, and craved them both with his mind and heart, mouth, hands, and prick, well, then, what sort of man did that make him?

Mattie

He hadn't come. He'd said he would, and she'd believed him. And he'd left her there waiting in the shadow of the monastery, turning her back to it for shame all afternoon, condemned by the Holy Thursday services being held there by people praying and remembering the events of the evening before their God had died. That same God had ordained the penalty for adultery to be stoning. Was there a penalty for wanting that forbidden liaison to go on and on, so much so that a woman sat and waited for her married lover to come, even long after it became evident that he wasn't going to show? And was there a penalty for promising to meet, even against the edict of heaven, and not showing up? And if so, which of the sins was greater?

She'd barely made it past her grandmother in the store before the tears had come, and now, as she slammed the door and locked it, they were hot on her cheeks. She stumbled to the floor at the side of her bed, kneeling like a child saying bedtime prayers. Some two thousand years before, on this same Thursday night, the man-God had knelt in a garden, tears of blood on his cheeks, in anguished anticipation of the twin pains of betrayal and death. Although she didn't expect, as she wiped her face on the hem of her bedsheets, for any smear of red to be there when she lifted her head, she doubted that this betrayal she suffered at Jonah's hands hurt any less.

Had his love for his wife held sway, or had something happened? She hoped that he'd been delayed by mishap rather than conscience. Car trouble or illness, rather than the realization that his wife came first, or the discovery of a shame too great to allow him to look her in the eye again.

Not now, she prayed. *Not guilt*. Better the Commandments be erased from every holy book than this man be bound by them to not return to her. To not give her more of what she craved to steal from her sister: his time, his secrets, his passion.

That passion alone was a currency in which her father's debt could be repaid. She would be more than happy to meet Jonah, again and again, in secret or openly—she didn't care which—because with every meeting, and with every time their bodies came together, her father's offenses would become less. Having Jonah would make up for the luxuries she had been denied, and which another had so nonchalantly enjoyed.

Denied her, even though she, as firstborn—albeit by a mere few months—should have been heir, by right of birth. Her sister, this Justice, had everything, not sold to her for a mess of pottage but given away, simply because of that cold woman who carried Dominic's name and wore his ring.

What she'd always craved was not her sister's money, but her sister's *right* to exist. The right to stroll through their gardens and to eat at their heavy-laden table. The right to call her father "Daddy" in full view of others without being shushed, without causing a scandal. Second-born, Justice was, and yet those rights were hers.

Thief.

But now, Mattie had taken something of her sister's. She'd touched the same sweat-dampened skin that her sister touched, loved the man her sister loved. It almost made them even. One hasty entanglement, one sigh hissing past his lips as he poured himself into her, had made up for years of being less than, years of being the other.

Mattie laughed out loud, even through her tears. She wondered what would happen if the warm liquid that Jonah had left in her were to take root. History would repeat itself after more than twenty years, a somebody coupling with a nobody, giving birth to a secret whose name could not be spoken in polite company.

If that happened, Mattie thought, she wouldn't do as Claudine had done. No secrets. No lies. She'd give that child a name, a big, loud name, and walk to Jonah's gate and shout it out so that everyone inside could hear. Jonah and his wife, and Dominic's wife, and the gardener and the maid. And the neighbors. People would be peeping out past white-painted gingerbread shutters at this strange woman in the street and whispering to each other, wondering why this low-class woman couldn't take her fish-market behavior elsewhere.

Mattie rose from her knees, squeezing tight the muscles between her legs, even though it was far too late now: a whole day had gone by, and if there were to be conception, it already would have taken place.

She'd see him again if she had to seek him out. She'd have more. Taste more. Lure him away from the thief in Dominic's house and suck him in until the memory of Justice was a blur in his mind. For too long, the younger had enjoyed all the pleasures of life that were denied the elder.

The time had come for that to change.

Jonah and Faith

Anticipation and self-loathing made a strange, bitter cocktail that bubbled in Jonah's belly and left the back of his throat tasting like shit. Part of him was excited, determined, nervous, the way he imagined a swimmer felt moments before plunging into the water, knowing that making it to the other side would bring him victory—providing he made it past the sharks that waited to feast on him should he lose.

The other part, an equally sizeable part, was ashamed and disgusted. He'd promised Mattie he'd meet her yesterday. He'd watched that strange new glow on her face, known what it meant, and how her feelings for him had shifted, rumbling like faults below the earth's surface, changing everything. And yet he'd stood her up.

Shame.

He wondered how long she'd waited and whether at the moment she'd admitted to herself that he wasn't coming, these feelings had veered toward anger or hurt. Both, probably. Mattie talked tough, but the girl who had made herself a cushion between him and the ground was nowhere as hard as she liked people to believe. And even if when this was all over he managed to beg and obtain her forgiveness, he would never forgive himself.

As he got up off the leather couch, his joints creaked like an old man's. His back hurt, as did his neck, his legs, and his head. He'd fallen asleep in Dominic's study, with his shoes still on and his belt still buckled. Second night running.

It was Good Friday morning. He walked to the curtains and tugged one edge aside with a finger, looking out onto the street. A blanket of stillness and silence had been spread out upon the neighborhood, even though it was a holiday and all the children were home. It was no different here than it was in his home village. Good Friday, the day on which they crucified the Lord, was a day of quiet contemplation, and even the children were kept indoors if they weren't already in church. He remembered his mother screaming at him if he dared turn on the radio, or run, or whistle in the house back then: "You got nothing better to do than run around whooping like a *warahoon?* The good Lord dying on the cross, and you can't show Him no respect?"

He felt another flicker of guilt, this time for a different reason. What would Rosalie have said if she had known that her son wasn't getting all scrubbed up and taking his wife to church like the good Catholics they were supposed to be? He tried to think of a single year he'd missed before this one, but couldn't. This sin of omission was bad. Even worse was admitting to himself and God that part of the reason for his absence was fear of the condemnation he would find within the beaten-bronze eyes that gazed down from the huge cross on the wall.

Adultery. A petty sin by modern standards; even an accepted, expected one. Men strayed. The guilt that gnawed at him stemmed not from shame at the act but the realization that he wanted it again. And again. Discovering that he could love one woman so much and yet be held in thrall by the other. It remained to be seen, however, whether "the other" would have anything to do with him once the messy business he had planned for today was over, and he had time and opportunity to talk to her again.

"I'm so . . . sorry," he apologized to the empty street beyond the window. He wondered if he rehearsed, repeated it to himself a hundred times, or a hundred times a hundred, whether the cumulative effect would be enough to merit him absolution.

But he'd done what he'd done not out of callous disregard for Mattie, but through necessity. After that ghastly scene in the garden, he'd dedicated his every waking moment over the next twenty-four hours to saving lives, his and Justice's. For Jonah, this Easter would be one of hope. Come Sunday, his dead marriage would take its first breath of new life, rising from the grave, bigger, brighter, and better, because by then he would have moved it far from all this decay. Once he took Justice away from this charnel house of bad memories and prejudice, musty old values and suffocating control, she would awaken, as Christ had, from the dark domain to which she had exiled herself.

Excited, he left the study and hurried toward their bedroom. Justice had locked herself in all day yesterday. He longed to see her face. He ached to touch her, if only lightly, just to reassure himself that her skin was still warm.

"Jonah." Faith's voice was clipped and cool, acknowledging him as she would a stranger passing by in the street.

He'd been hoping that she'd have slept late today and that his purpose would not have been thwarted so early in the game by her appearance. "Faith," he murmured, trying to keep his voice from joining his heart in his shoes. This was not the time to engage her. Today, he was rescuing his wife, and every second spent getting tangled in Faith's spiteful web would mean unbearable delay.

But Faith stopped at the foot of the stairs, preventing him from slipping past. She was draped in foamy white, a bathrobe that looked more like an evening gown: satin like spilled milk. The scent of her perfume clung to the back of his throat. One hand was placed on a newel post; the other held the small, crude statue, the one that Dominic had loved and she had loudly hated. He was momentarily distracted by the sight of it, and the continuing strangeness of her carrying it around as she had these days: part weapon, part shield.

"Where d'you think you're going?" she asked.

"To see my wife." He held her gaze steadily, even though the venom there made him cringe.

"She's asleep."

"I plan on waking her up."

"I won't allow it." Faith clenched the post, nails curling around it.

He had to struggle past his frustration, to hang on to the hope that had infused him all day before. Since first light yesterday he had been gone, charging out of the house, fueled by the determination that by end of day he would find someplace suitable for him and his wife to live. Finding a home in a day had seemed a near impossible task; but he was, after all, a businessman, and Dominic had taught him well. He'd pulled in every favor, made two dozen calls, and returned home last night with a set of keys in his back pocket. Now he was getting Justice, and they were leaving. Forget their clothes, forget their books, forget her trinkets. That would all come after. He was taking his wife. Today. "Step aside, Faith," he said.

Her smile didn't show any teeth. "Listen to me. Whatever you think you are, remember that my daughter and I are better. However smart you are, I am smarter. Don't expect to spirit my daughter out of my home, from right under my nose, without me doing something to stop it!"

Jonah gaped. She knew! He wondered for a bewildering moment whether her spite had given her unnatural powers to look upon his face and draw an understanding of his unspoken thoughts, but before he could dismiss the thought as foolish, she spoke again.

"Remember, those 'friends' you think are yours were my husband's first. Remember they owe their loyalty to me, not you. Were you stupid enough to believe you could set a house hunt in motion in this town and it wouldn't get back to me?"

Betrayal stuck him through in a dozen places. He wondered if he was dwindling physically at her malice or whether it was only his self-esteem that had shrunk. He should not have been surprised: after all, Faith was right. The men he dealt with were Dominic's friends, not his. Just because he and they had business in common, traded anecdotes over brandy, and swapped stories about the market didn't mean they respected him enough to keep their peace. Somewhere, in the privacy of their offices, or while they recounted stories of his naivete to their wives, they would be laughing. Whatever told him that he would ever be, in their eyes, anything more than Dominic's little social experiment?

His chagrin must have showed on his face, because Faith's smile dissolved into one of mocking pity. "I see you understand." She made a sweeping gesture with her arm, indicating that he should walk before her, away from the stairs—and Justice.

The silence that lay upon the neighborhood congealed within the house, unpierced by the groan of defeat that never made its way past his lips. What was it that Mattie had told him? Try as he might, he'd never be Dominic. She'd been right, but she hadn't seen the whole truth: not only was he not Dominic, he was not, and never could be, Dominic's kind. He looked down at himself: expensive clothes rumpled and creased from having been slept in, looking like a wrinkled second skin. A skin that never quite fit.

They had taught him in school that a man could be anything he wanted. That no matter where you started, and who you were when you began, whatever you wound up being at the end of your days, failure or success, was entirely up to you.

Liars.

You were what others saw you as. You were a composite

of skin color and texture of hair, rank, bloodline, and geography, and nothing a man did to better his standing could ever achieve more than a superficial elevation. You got to a place where people listened because you had power, helped you because you had money, admired you because your hair was good and curly, rather than hard and niggery; but deep in their hearts they knew you were an upstart and a pretender, and laughing behind your back was the best you deserved.

This time, his groan was audible, barely so, but loud enough for Faith to hear. "It's not your fault," she told him, almost kind now that she had won. "It's the way we are. It's the way we live. We came and met the rules; we didn't make them up. And they're going to be around long after you, I, and everyone else are dead and gone." Her lips pulled back in a ghastly parody of a smile. "Okay?"

If only she knew how ugly she looked, he thought, she wouldn't do that. Her very ugliness shocked him. In spite of their differences, he'd always thought her a beauty. But her face now had a hollowness to it, the life and light having slowly ebbed, leaving something barely animated, an unlit candle. His eyes locked into hers, but although he could see her clearly—more clearly than ever before—there was no evidence that she saw him. He had the fleeting sensation that *he* was the unlit candle or, at least, one that had flickered out before her chill wind.

Now he knew. Understood fully what Mattie had felt, that fear of being unseen. Of being there, yet not substantial enough to be seen by someone who didn't care to look. The panicked thought came to him that he might have absorbed this fear through Mattie's mouth when he'd loved her out there on the grass. That maybe the part of her that he'd taken was a portion of her own private terror, which now lived and grew inside him like a virus.

If you took her fear from her, he asked himself bitterly, *what did you give her? Your courage? Your strength?* There he was, being cowed by this woman who felt nothing but disdain for him. Willing to let her turn him into her own lowly vision of him. Willing to walk away from his wife, who was upstairs dying slowly of a venom her mother had injected in her from birth. Was that what a man did? Let a woman claw at his balls and then slink away thinking that he deserved his own castration?

Jonah turned so swiftly that he threw Faith off her balance. In an effort to steady herself, she flung out the arm holding the statue, and it rapped the baluster sharply, catching in the elaborate design. There was a loud crack as the statue's head was torn from its shoulders, and a dull sound as it hit the parquet and rolled. With a soft cry Faith dropped the body and leaped after the rolling head. Without stopping to help, Jonah sprinted toward the top of the stairs.

"Jonah!" Faith screamed hoarsely at him.

His head spun around. Her voice was raw with a mixture of rage and grief. She held the severed head in her palm like an injured bird.

"Get back! What d'you think you're doing? I said get back!" She leaped after him, faster than he expected she could run, and her free hand caught hold of the tail of his shirt. His own momentum brought him down. Her nails scraped his skin, and he swatted her hands away, unwilling to exert any more force than that. But Faith was persistent. Using her handhold, she dragged herself up onto him, onto his back, hissing like a hellion.

As he tore one arm away from his neck, the other came up in a wrestler's hold. There was pressure on his windpipe. "Enough, Faith," he managed to say. He knew he was big enough to free himself; but doing so would mean hurting her, and that he wouldn't do. Instead of standing up and tearing her off him as a large bear would a wildcat, he shook himself, trying to dislodge her more gently.

"Why don't you just go away? Why d'you keep pretending that you're wanted?"

"Justice wants me." He prayed that was still true.

"Justice doesn't know"—she panted with the effort to cling to him—"what she wants. She's a child."

"She's a child because you kept her a child. And her father. And me. We're all to blame. But not anymore. She's leaving with me."

"And you think that will make her better?"

"It has to." Both their voices were getting steadily louder, and he wondered why Justice hadn't come to the door, if only to see what the commotion was all about. Nobody slept that soundly.

Before Faith could spit out a rejoinder the doorbell chimed. Almost comically, they both stopped struggling, locked in an incongruous embrace, heads up, to listen. The sound came again.

"Answer the goddamn door, girl!" Faith screeched into the stairwell.

Jonah took advantage of her distraction to shrug her off. He stood up, panting, more from emotion than exertion. "Teresa's not here," he reminded her. "She's gone to church."

The doorbell stretched out into one continuous, annoying note, like a bee trapped inside his skull. Faith stood up, still clutching the wooden head, even through all their struggling. "You answer it, then."

He was at Justice's door, one hand on the knob. The buzzing of the bell became louder, filling the house. "I don't live here anymore," he told her. He managed a smile. "You forget?"

Blood Pye and Faith

Blood Pye felt his thumb going numb in the doorbell. That was what rich people were like. Happy to keep you waiting at the fucking door if it suited them. Well, he was waiting, all right. He'd wait all day if he had to. And if his thumb got tired, he'd just change hands.

He scratched the top of his head with the other hand, feeling stubble growing in. Usually, he shaved his skull meticulously, but he'd been too tired lately, too distraught over the small tragedies he found in his stables every morning, to bother. Look at what he'd come to, he mused. Things were really bad if a man didn't have time to make sure he was clean and presentable.

And now, this thing with Mattie. A double blow. Him discovering that he loved her—*loved* her, like they talked about in cinema shows—on the same day she turned out to be going after some other son of a bitch. He hadn't slept in two nights: every time he remembered the look on Mattie's face that day, every time he remembered her surprise at his revelation and her perplexity at her own, he'd groaned and turned over on damp sheets. He'd spent the last two nights veering sharply between fishing for good reasons not to turn up here and working himself up into a lather, rehearsing over and over what he would say when he did.

He looked down at his feet, where Threes perched contentedly, unaware of his master's distress. "That's the way it is with women," Blood Pye advised him. "They real, real contrary. Never know what they want. Who they want. One minute they bitching because you never turn up and you spending a few hours here and there with another woman, next minute putting horn on you with some other fella. You could imagine that?"

Threes looked up at him in consolation, a near smile on his face. Blood Pye went on vehemently. "And Mattie. Mattie of all people. Always acting like she so picky with her men. Took me three whole months to get her panty off. And some man come out of nowhere . . ." It hurt too much for him to go on. He stopped talking and rested his forehead against the door.

Mattie's infidelity had done nothing to make him love her less. Being here today proved it. If she was afraid to, or ashamed to turn up and ask for what was rightly hers, he would do it for her. That was what being a man was about. Sticking up for your woman. Doing the painful things, the hard things, that she couldn't. Even if, at the end of the day, she just took the money and said "thank you," and didn't spare him any for his cocks. . . .

The door flew open, and Blood Pye had to throw his hands out to stop himself from hitting the landing. He righted himself, struggling to get over his surprise. A tall, wild-looking, high-brown woman stood there. Her hair was in disarray, her face contorted. Her silly-looking white housedress made her look as if she'd fallen asleep in her ball gown. Only her skin tone told him that she had to be the lady of the house and not some lunatic maid.

"Ma'am," he said.

"Who the hell are you?" she began, but then a movement at his feet drew her gaze downward, and she let out a scream. "A rat!"

"Mongoose," he corrected irritably. What the fuck was it with these women? He scooped Threes protectively into his arms and asked, with as much politeness as he could muster, "I could come in?"

Her eyes flicked down him, from the *grain-grain* stubble on his scalp, along his best shirt and tie, to his only pair of leather shoes, and contempt curdled her face. "Why should I let you in? What do you want?"

What did he want? Money, naturally, but now that she put the question so baldly, he wasn't sure that an equally bald response was the best way to go. He cleared his throat, which seemed to have a hair stuck down it. "I got business to discuss with you," he said. "Your husband's business." And then he added hastily, "God rest his soul."

Her sour expression did not relax. "And you come on whose behalf? This is a public holiday. Couldn't this business wait until next week?"

Blood Pye shook his head. "This business urgent, ma'am. Concerning your family. There's things I got to tell you concerning you and your daughter, but I don't think you better listen standing up. You look a little . . . fragile . . ." She looked as strong as an old mule, but he thought diplomacy was best. "And I just thought that maybe . . . we could sit." The acid in her look made him stumble a little, but he stuck to his resolve and held her stare.

Then something funny flashed across the woman's face. She blinked at him, and her mouth fell open. Typical. Just because your skin was black, they looked at you like you were a new species. Her head dipped, and she looked hard at something she clutched in her hand, and then back at him, eyes full of pained shock. *Fainting spell?* he wondered. He watched her warily, lest she came crashing down on him. If she looked like she was heading in that direction, he was sure as hell stepping aside. She looked like the type, if he tried to catch her and his hands brushed a tit or something, who would scream bloody rape.

Her eyes dragged along his body again, to his feet and back, and Pye squirmed. The bitch was off her head, he decided. Or drinking. He sniffed the air discreetly, but couldn't pick up a thing.

After several long seconds, she said, "The big rat stays outside."

"The mongoose goes where I go," he told her.

Mattie and Louisa

Mattie hated seeing her grandmother cry. The last time Louisa cried had been the last day Dominic had come to see her mother, before Claudine had let the cancer take her. "She waiting to see him one more time before she die," Mattie remembered Louisa weeping in the kitchen. "Now he come, she gonna go." Louisa had been right. Claudine had slipped away that very night, with a contented sigh on her lips.

Now Auntie Lou was standing on the sidewalk outside the store, which was open for business, even though it was Good Friday and most of her young clients were in church cooling their heels, or confined to the indoors by their parents until three o'clock, because it simply wasn't decent to run and laugh and play until after the Lord's Passion was over. She wasn't blocking Mattie's way, as she had a month before, on the morning of her father's funeral, but her gusty sobs kept Mattie riveted to her bike, unable to ride off.

"She's a thief," Mattie tried to explain. "Everything she got should be mine."

"She's your sister," Louisa protested. "And she's not to blame for all this. Blame your father. Or your mother. Both of them rest in peace, please God. She ain't never tried to hurt you. She don't even *know* you!"

"It's not just about her. It's about him, too. I just want to see him again. He was supposed to come yesterday; he promised, and he didn't. I just want to see—"

At the mere mention of Jonah, Louisa let out a wail. "What it is about my girl children? Your mother, and you, never know how to pick a man. First you with this nasty chicken seller . . ."

"Blood Pye's a cockfighter," loyalty propelled her to say, "and he's not a bad person." And he loved her—or thought he did. Even though she didn't, and couldn't, return the feeling, she was honor bound to defend him. He didn't deserve her grandmother's contempt.

"If he ain't a bad person, then what you gone and done with this other man? And why him? He your sister's husband. You put God out your thoughts, girl? Adultery is a terrible sin—"

"And guess who I learned it from," she began to retort, but a sharp slap from Louisa's heavy hand cut her off before she could say any more.

"Show some respect for the dead," Louisa sputtered, even though moments before she herself had put blame on Claudine's shoulders. "Don't talk about your mother like that. And besides, you ain't gone and picked out just any married man. You gone and picked your brother-in-law. He's family, girl, and that make it double worse."

"He's not *blood*," she retorted.

"It don't matter." Auntie Louisa dabbed her eyes with a colored bandana and sighed from deep in her chest. "And what you gonna do when you get there? Bang on the door and tell him to come out? You think that will help you get him? That ain't how you do things. You can't even go about your crime under cover of darkness and hope God don't see you. You want to walk into his yard and make a scene?"

"I don't want to make a scene."

"What you think it will be? They all gonna be happy to see you? Your mother spend her whole life keeping her secret close to her chest just so these people, who ain't never done you nothing, could go about their lives and be happy. Why you want to change that?"

Yesterday, she'd been willing to sit and wait, just like her mother had, until Jonah came to her again. Meet him in secret, love him in secret. Enjoy every stolen morsel and be grateful for however long it lasted. But all night she'd lain awake thinking about him, growing more angry with him for not honoring his promise to meet her, and more resentful of Justice for having him there whenever she wanted. By morning she could see clearly that hiding wasn't fair. Not to her. After fighting all her life for her right to be seen, here she was, willing to slip deeper into the shadows, just so she could keep a man who wasn't hers.

Today, she had to go there. To see him, and be seen. It was the right thing to do, freeing herself from the need to hide. After today, she would never hide again. And she wasn't even afraid. Somehow, at the monastery, Jonah had taken away her cowardice, either by drawing it into himself or by driving it away. But where before every fantasy image of making herself known to her father's family had, since childhood, been laced with stomach-churning fear, today she knew she could make it real. "I've got to go."

"And crush your sister's heart."

"And make her share. Not her money. Not any of her fancy things. Share the right to *be*."

"You *got* the right to be. If God didn't want you to exist, he wouldn'ta made you. Why you gotta look to somebody else to give you permission to exist?"

Louisa was making her head hurt. Speaking truths Mattie didn't want to hear. Making sense. She knew that if she stopped to listen, she would see the wisdom in her grandmother's words, and her intent would be stillborn. And every moment she wasted arguing was a moment that stood between her and her father's house, which, after a lifetime of waiting, she would storm like castle ramparts. Crash in and shout out her name. After that she would be finally free. No more fading away. After that, Jonah might hate her. Not that she had any intention of making known what they had done together, but because when she was finished, her sister, his wife, would know that she was not the only child, and her vision of her father would be forever changed.

If only she could have them both. Make her presence known and still have him, steal him, keep him. If there were a way, she'd find it. She threw her leg over the bike and settled into the saddle.

"Pray for me, Auntie Lou," Mattie said.

Faith and Blood Pye

An uncanny feeling of dread crawled over her skin, like tiny, sharp-clawed spiders snagging their way up her legs, and arms, and spine. Unbelievable. She glanced down to the severed head she held in her palm and then to the man standing before her. At the point of its beheading, had the spirit of the statuette been catapulted out of its wooden confinement, to materialize in flesh and bone at her door?

The skin: tar black. Not shiny and gruesome like Teresa's, but matte, a hand-buffed glow. The African nose, and African lips, and the strangeness about them that had so repulsed her in the statue, but which had become so familiar to her in the time she spent with it that the repulsive had become enthralling.

The shoulders, broad and hard, even under the fabric of his shirt. The waist, small, trim, narrow but manly. Her eyes drifted below the belt he wore—even from this distance, she could see that it wasn't real leather—and lingered briefly. The statue's exaggerated penis, which had so offended her, came to mind, and she knew her face grew hot.

She chastised herself silently for being a fool. This man was not her statue. That was impossible, denied by every law of physics. *But he promised,* she reminded herself. *He promised he'd come. He said it would be soon.* But this couldn't be he. Her African was a warrior. Noble, strong, wise, perceptive. The man before her was a nobody, dressed up in a polyester shirt and synthetic tie that probably passed for decent where he came from.

She caught the man's quizzical expression on her face and struggled to gather herself together. She remembered too late that she was still in her dressing gown, and her hands flew up to cover her chest. "Who are you?" She let her belligerence form a natural barrier around her bewilderment.

"Blood . . . ," he began, and halted. "Reuben."

"Which is it? Blood or Reuben?" What kind of person had a name like *Blood?*

"Reuben," he said. She wondered if he had just made up his mind. "Hinds."

She racked her brain for a reference, but the name meant nothing to her. "And you have information regarding my husband?"

"Your daughter, too. Both of them."

Reuben Hinds was straining to see past her into the house, and reluctantly, hooked by the mere mention of Dominic, she twisted her body slightly, just enough to let him past, but not close enough to touch her as he did so.

You're crazy, she admonished herself. Letting this large, strange-looking man inside. Carrying an even stranger animal on his shoulder, to boot. It was missing a leg. A civilized person would have had a creature like that put down ages ago. She wondered briefly if it had fleas, or ticks, or something she'd never seen before and wouldn't know how to kill if it crawled into her flooring. What kind of parasites did mongooses carry?

She was even crazier to have stopped to answer the door at all, given that her son-in-law was upstairs trying to steal her daughter away from her at this very moment. Take Justice to a new house, in her condition—was Jonah mad? This house was all that Justice had ever known. And this self-righteous interloper could find nothing better to do than uproot her at her most fragile moment and tear her away from everything familiar. She'd stop that from happening if she had to barricade the doors and call the police.

"Let's get this over with," she said crisply, and led him to a small anteroom off the hallway. It wasn't really *all* the way into the house, she reasoned. More like a convenient place to hang car keys and set wet umbrellas to drain. But it had a narrow love seat. She pointed at it. "Sit." He sat gingerly. "And keep that thing off the upholstery."

She folded her arms and watched him sharply. She felt better standing. This way, he didn't look so tall. Her glance flicked in the direction of the stairs leading to the bedrooms. All was silent. *Soon, soon,* she told herself. First, her husband's business. What could this stranger possibly have to say about Dominic that could affect her and her daughter? The idea of this man having been in contact with Dominic before his death, or even presumed to be involved in his business, made her angry. Pearls before swine.

"Has my husband left a bill unpaid?" That was just like Dominic. Forgetful. Nonchalant about financial affairs. Another trait Jonah had chosen to mimic. Was she the only one in the house with a head for money?

He shook his head. "No, ma'am."

"Because if he did, you'd better have brought the bill with you."

"Not a bill, ma'am."

He didn't volunteer any more information. Instead, he let his eyes roam around him, from the door to the plants to the curtains at the window and the scroll-worked trim along the edge of the flooring. Faith was familiar with that look. It was the look poor people got when they tried to calculate your worth and gauge just how much they would be able to squeeze out of you. Her lips pursed.

"Talk," she said crisply. "I'm a busy woman."

This time, he looked directly at her. He had eyes that were blacker than sin, unlike her statue, who had hollows for eyes, which went on and on and reflected nothing.

It is *him,* she realized, and her spirit soared. He had now what he'd been lacking before: a pair of eyes that had enough life in them to hold his light. The spirit had been made flesh, and those awful hollows were filled.

There was a new audacity in his stare, and she hoped to God he hadn't sensed the flood of warmth that rushed through her. The hand holding the wooden head was clammy, and she wanted nothing more than to cast it away from her. There was no need for it anymore. Its animus was alive and seated before her.

Eventually, she set it down upon a wrought-iron plant stand, wedging it between a clay pot and the wall. It was nothing but dead wood now; it could rot there for all she cared. She dried her palm surreptitiously on her dressing gown. The man was still staring, and the bastard had the audacity to be amused.

"You could sit, too, you know," he told her, sliding over on the love seat to give her room. Still smiling.

Inviting her to take a seat on her furniture, in her own house! Arrogant, as always. Making fun of her, as he did when he wasn't being wonderfully gentle. "I prefer to stand," she said.

He nodded slowly, empathetically, and kept on staring. He held the dirty beast in his lap, stroking it as one would a cat: slowly, sensuously. It arched its back to meet his hand, fur electrified.

She wondered if her body was visibly flushed. If her face and neck were giving her away. Again, her convictions veered. *This is ridiculous. This man is nobody, means nothing. Statues don't come alive.* She wished she had a shot of brandy to take the edge off her nerves. *This is no prince-warrior, no African soul unleashed. He's just another low-class, rag-picking hustler, sniffing out a target.*

"Speak," she said harshly. Her voice caught, rough and rasping. "Or get out."

"It's kind of a long story." His tongue flicked out like a snake's—no, not that fast. Slowly, thoughtfully. Seductively. It slid against his full lips, leaving them glistening. "I could get a drink of water before I start?" he asked.

"No," she said.

Jonah and Justice

Unsurprisingly, the door to their bedroom was locked. He tapped lightly, a soft sound that he only half expected her to hear. "Tish," he called.

It seemed that everywhere he went, he slammed into a locked door. The room he'd thought was his, the neighborhood he'd grown into, and the people he'd thought he could trust to disentangle themselves from the sticky red tape of the social order. He wondered idly if just leaving the house was the answer. He was a businessman: he'd learned enough under Dominic to run the business; maybe he knew enough to start one of his own. Total liberation, complete separation. Maybe that was it.

His whole body felt heavy. He wished he could sit. If he'd had the time, he would have, camping out cross-legged before the door, waiting patiently, directing all his energies through the panel of wood between himself and his wife, until, unable to resist his silent entreaties, she would succumb to his will and come to him. But whoever was ringing the doorbell had given him only a brief reprieve. He'd be a fool to think that Faith's momentary distraction would be anything more than just that. He might fail in his attempt to take Justice away, but he was prepared to go down with all weapons drawn.

The door flew open, startling him. Snatched from his

reverie, he steeled himself against what he was about to see: Justice, even more frail than she had been two days before, if such a thing were possible. Paler than she had been, with blue veins beating gently at her throat and temple. Hair tangled, unwashed. Fading.

She was upon him with the swiftness of a ghost, gliding up to him, within inches of his face, as solid a presence as the door had been. When he saw her, he gasped.

She was beautiful. Still thin, as light and fragile as balsawood, but her skin had a glow about it, as if kissed by the sun, in spite of the drawn curtains and dim light. Her hair was clean, and soft as a cloud, infused by the same strange new life that flooded her cheeks. Her eyes, gem-bright and ocean-deep, were greener even than Mattie's had become seconds before she'd squeezed them shut, trembling under him.

"Justice?" He stepped over the threshold, one hand reaching out to reassure himself that she was not a figment of his own cruel imagination. His fingers encountered marvelous flesh. Closer still, and she didn't resist him when he pulled her against his chest. She was lighter than air.

How had this happened? *What* had happened? For days, weeks, he had watched her wither, each day less a part of their world than she had been the day before. He had a hideous memory of her as she had been the last day he'd seen her, on her knees scrabbling in the dirt like a woman deranged, eating lily bulbs, cramming them into her mouth like cloves of garlic. Now, miraculously, she'd gone from *that* to *this*.

Hope swelled inside him. Justice could be rescued. There was still time—ample time to get her away from the rank air of this place. Almost weak with relief, he kissed her brow and murmured against her skin. "We have to go, Tish," he told her. "We have to get out of here. We don't have to stay here anymore. Nothing to keep us. We can move out today, just get a few things and leave. I got us a house. If you don't like it, we can fix it up. If you still don't like it, we can get another one. Just leave with me. Today." He knew he was babbling, but he was too anxious to allow her time to protest.

He held her by the hand and dragged her over to the dresser, tearing open drawers and tossing underwear onto the bed. "Just let me get us packed. One bag each for now, and we can come back and get our things later."

She watched him silently while he pulled out two small cases, the ones they had bought for their honeymoon, and frantically began stuffing clothes into them. He remembered her collection of glass animals and hesitated. Justice loved them as she would have if they were alive. He knew she'd hate to leave them behind, even for a few days; but time was of the essence, and to transport them, each would have to be carefully wrapped and packed.

He turned to her. "Maybe you can just take one today. Or two. And I can come back tomorrow and get the others for you. Okay, sweetheart?" He was speaking as he would to a small child. "Which do you want to take?"

It was only when he caught her eyes on him, wide and intently focused on his mouth like a lip-reader, that he realized she hadn't spoken a word since he'd rushed in. He set down the glass turtle he was holding and rushed back over to her. "Justice, are you hearing me?"

She nodded, slowly.

"You understand what I'm saying to you?"

She nodded again, and then opened her mouth. Her voice sounded as though it had been stored away somewhere, and she'd just taken it out, dusted it off, and was trying it for the first time in ages. "I'm hearing."

"And you'll come with me? To the new house? Then we can start again. Whatever it takes to make you feel better, I'll do it. We just have to leave, today."

"I'm ready to go. It's time."

He scooped her against his body, shaking with relief.

There had been no need to argue or struggle to persuade her. She was willing to come with him, thank God. "You have no idea how glad I am to hear you say that. I love you."

She tilted her face to his, letting him kiss her without complaint. Her smile was radiant. "I love you, too, Jonah."

He let her go just long enough to pick up the glass turtle again and slip it into her hand, and then he grasped each suitcase. Justice had never been far from her mother. Did she really think it would be so easy? As anxious as he was to get her out, and get her out now, he just had to warn her: "Your mother doesn't want you to go. She's right outside, and she's going to fight to make you stay. Can you handle that?"

"I can handle anything now."

"You can see her in a few days, as soon as we've settled down. As soon as you start feeling better. But until then . . ." He paused. Faith was lethal. A greedy, crawling vine that had begun strangling Justice since the day she was born. But Justice was as dependent on that constraint as a falling tree was on the surrounding plants which, while choking it, gave it the support it needed to keep it standing. Once she was away from the house and the awareness of separation set in, would she panic? "You scared?" he had to ask.

She shook her head, and a smile hovered about her lips. "No. Not anymore. I'm not afraid of . . . *anything*."

He nudged the door open with his foot. "Let's go, then."

She looked down at herself, hair falling into her eyes as she did so. "I can't go like this."

"Then throw something on." He tried to keep a note of anxiety from creeping into his voice. Faith was still distracted by her caller, but she wouldn't be for much longer. "We aren't going that far. Just put a dress on, and some slippers . . ."

"No." Her voice was remarkably firm. "I need a bath. I have to take a bath."

He set the cases down and schooled his patience. "Okay, love. A quick bath. You want me to help you?"

It was there again, that weird, ethereal smile, and a shake of the head. "I'm a grown-up, Jonah."

The assertion, coming from the wife he'd somewhere in the back of his mind always thought of as a child, made him smile, too, in spite of the urgency of their situation. He was proud of her for coming to that realization on her own. "Yes, you are."

"I can take care of myself."

"I know you can." He watched her peel her shift away from her skin and turn and walk, naked, into the bathroom. She shut the door behind her. "I'll wait," he promised, and settled in the bedroom doorway. If Faith concluded her business and returned like a Fury to challenge him again, he would be prepared. He folded his arms and squared his shoulders, trying to fill all the space between his wife and the rest of the world. Five minutes, ten at the most, and they would be out of there.

Then, a voice, distant but insistent. Children in the street? A mother calling her recalcitrant young back into the house? His attention was diverted only briefly, and then he was back to dreaming of how good it would be once he and Justice had the time and space to work their way through it alone.

But there was a loud, insistent hammering, and the voice came again. The words had become distinct, only they weren't words, but a name, being called over and over: "Jonah! Jonah!"

Mattie! What was she doing here? He felt simultaneous happiness and panic. Part of him ached to see her again; but his wife was a room away, and today was the day they escaped. Why had Mattie come? To see him, or Faith? And why today, when everything he held dear hung in the balance? He had an awful premonition of Justice coming face-to-face with the sister she had never known existed, and worse, intuiting, as she had in the garden, that this was the woman he'd been with that afternoon, the one she'd sensed on him so effortlessly. That couldn't happen. He had to stop those two worlds from colliding, even if he needed to throw himself down between them as a buffer.

He threw a hasty glance at the bathroom—all was quiet inside—and ran to the foot of the stairs, leaving the bedroom door to fall back partly into place, hindered by the cases.

Justice

Good Friday. The Day of Death that came before the Resurrection. A day she'd always hated. Every year, bar this one, Mama would make her get dressed and then tow her off to early mass, which always began with the Stations of the Cross. Shuffling along the road at a make-believe Calvary, surrounded by earnest old men and faltering old women, reeking of the kind of lavender water they sprinkled on corpses. Foolhardy young men hauling heavy wooden crosses, brows glistening with sweat like spikes glinting off a thorny crown, believing that this labor would buy their way into heaven. Young girls with their faces shrouded in black mantillas weeping for a young man murdered nearly two thousand years before. Nothing said "death" like Good Friday. No day God wrought was ever darker.

That was before she received the Understanding. That was before she Knew. The women who wept for a dead God were in fact weeping out of fear of their own demise, and that fear belonged to the foolish and the uninformed. The shadows, the silence, were good. The tomb that had followed Golgotha must have been a sweet sanctuary, if only for three short days. She shut the bathroom door and locked it. Jonah was outside, waiting for her. She'd be quick.

Her naked reflection caught her eye, and she stopped in front of the mirror, turning slowly. She was a willow, a reed, an Easter lily. Not the fat little girl Mama always enjoyed being slimmer than. Not the chubby coward Jonah had married. She was a sliver, a whisper, a ghost, able to slip from this world to the next, and back again, if she chose to. Between her thin blood and the muted excitement in her chest, she shivered. She ran the bathwater hot.

Her husband was waiting. He who loved her, even when he lay with someone else. Even days after her discovery of his infidelity, she still felt not even the faintest glimmer of jealousy. There was only indulgent understanding. There was room in that big heart for so much!

She wondered how long he'd been planning this ridiculous escape, or whether he'd planned it at all. Maybe he'd just gotten up this morning with a bee in his bonnet and raced upstairs to her. She'd heard the commotion on the stairs with him and Mama. Did Jonah think he could battle against her and win? Her mother was a woman who would turn the tide, breach hell, to get what she wanted. Didn't Jonah know that?

No, probably not. He was too kind, to simplistic. People who lived in the light were unable to recognize the darkness. He thought that two suitcases and a car ride were enough to set them both free.

"Wrong," she whispered to him. "You're so, so wrong."

She felt an ache of regret. She loved him, but not the way he did her. Not the way he thought. Not a love uncluttered by the persistent presence of her father and her need for a bolster between her and the world. She loved the boy from the sea who still believed that things didn't have to be the way they were, and that cruelty and jealousy and meanness and greed and prejudice didn't exist. She wondered if he'd ever learn the truth. She hoped he never would.

The bath was still filling, but it was already deep enough. She stepped in, cradling the glass turtle Jonah had given her to hold. She couldn't remember where her father had bought it. She'd had it ten, maybe fifteen years now. She considered pouring soap into the water, but decided against it. The color and bubbles would spoil the clarity of this perfect moment. At the bottom of the water, the glass turtle disappeared, just a trick of the light against the tile.

Oh, but the water was gentle! It came up, and up, all around her, like outstretched arms. Sweet, like rain. She lay in it, on her belly, feeling its fingers flutter against her breasts, creeping up along the tiny hairs on her body. Unhesitating, she let her face break the skin of the surface and opened her eyes. The water looked deeper than it really was; it went on forever.

She hated swimming. On family visits to the beach, while Dominic and Jonah disported themselves in the waves, swimming out beyond the breakers until the lifeguards called them back, and while her mother slathered sunblock on her fair skin and huddled under an umbrella with a book, Justice always walked along the edge, where the white froth was only ankle deep, looking for shells. Tantalized by the water, but too afraid to go in, and even more afraid of drowning by proxy: that one of her men would slip under and never surface. Water was a dangerous thing. Eternal, having no beginning and no end.

Jonah used to tell her stories of growing up on the beach, about how desperately he'd wanted to be a fish. How he'd lurk beneath the surface holding his breath, resenting the moment when he'd have to lift his head and suck the air in.

Her hair was soaked now, as the warm water rose over it. Soothing. She understood now why Jonah loved it so much. It took everything away, and promised everything in return. She felt almost sorry she'd never had the courage to learn to swim, kick out and let her body be carried by the sea. Weightless. Jonah knew how to do that well.

But there was one thing that Jonah didn't know. Something he'd overlooked. Being one with the water was easier than he thought. You didn't have to hold your breath and fight against your nature, hating the air you craved, and hating the water for not giving it to you. You didn't have to wish for scales, pray for gills, hate what you were and do nothing about it. All you had to do was welcome the wet embrace, sink yourself into it, feel it rush into every orifice, every pore. Open your eyes, open your heart, and . . .

. . . Inhale.

Mattie

In all her childhood fantasies, Mattie had expected the wrought-iron walls of her father's house to open for her as she rode up to them, like supermarket doors, recognizing her as heir and swinging apart to let her inside. Instead, they remained sullenly shut. She was winded from her long ride, cheeks flushed, pulse pounding. She set her bike against the wall, not even bothering to chain it to anything. In this neighborhood, bikes didn't disappear. In this neighborhood, people stole bigger: stocks, bonds, corporations. Birthrights.

She steeled herself to enter, patting down her dress, ensuring the hem was straight, drawing strength from the color in which she had cloaked herself. Today, she wore red. Not candy red—cherry, strawberry, lollipop red—but blood red. As red as the thin line that tied her to Dominic and to the young woman who paraded about inside this house, unaware that her poached title of firstborn was about to be torn from her grasp.

The gate opened under Mattie's hand, and she rushed in, propelled by the giddy anticipation of what she was about to do. Within the walls, the air was cooler, sweeter, perfumed by pampered trees and grass trimmed with nail scissors. She ran across the lawn that by rights should have been hers, to the doors that had always kept her and her mother out, and raised a hand to press the doorbell, but then stopped.

This was crazy. Years of being forced into the shadows had taught her to be cautious. Claudine would have severed her hand at the wrist rather than press that bell. What if her mother had been right? What if nothing came from her self-revelation but disaster?

But anticipation overwhelmed any misgivings. To be known. To be seen, finally, by these people! And to see Jonah again! He'd be there, standing in the wings while she told her father's wife and daughter her story. Silent, if he knew what was good for him, not to muddy his own waters with the revelation that he had known who she was and not said a word. But he'd be *there*, and she'd be near him.

She hammered the doorbell with her fist, once, and then again. When nothing happened, she tried the door, but it was locked. She punched it, hard enough to hurt her hand. Her gold bangle bit into her wrist. No answer. Maybe they were in church, or praying, or waiting solemnly for the Lord's Passion to begin.

Or maybe her father's wife was eyeing her through a crack in the curtains, unwilling to answer to a stranger. Not even prepared to send out the maid. Too bad. She'd come too far to be ignored. She wasn't letting anyone hide and pretend she wasn't there!

"Jonah!" His name leaped from her lips, and she discovered she liked the sound of it, out loud like that. An affirmation. "Jonah!" She ran along the front, slapping her palms against the windows, calling him over and over. Even if he was in bed with his wife, wrapped in her pale arms, he couldn't help but hear. She shouted again.

The door flew open, and she spun around to see him shoot out, running to her, calling her name in response. He grasped her by the shoulders. "What're you doing here?"

So good to see him! She threw her arms up around him, wanting to slip her face in the crook of his neck. In spite of himself, he hugged her, arms tight around the small of her back, but the contact was brief. Too soon he was holding her at arm's length, shock in his eyes. "Mattie, why'd you come?"

Her smile of delight still hovered. "To see you. To make them see me. One or the other. Both." Then, less confidently, "You not glad to see me?"

He looked as if he were running the question through in his mind, and the answer was a surprise to him, too. "Yes, but . . ."

"But what? I'm here. Like every dream I ever had. Here, in my father's garden. The one place he never let me be." She looked around herself, wishing she could take snapshots of every shrub and tree, so that even if this single penetration into Dominic's world was her last, she'd have photographs to take out and peruse whenever she desired.

"And you're going inside to reveal yourself to Faith," he stated.

She didn't like the graveness on his face, but she stood her ground. "And your wife. My sister."

His shoulders sagged. "Mattie, I'd never tell you not to do that. You know what I said. I promised if there was anything I could do to smooth your way, make you part of the family . . ."

"You could let me in."

"But not today. Please, Mattie, not today. My wife's not well. We have to leave . . ."

A shard of jealousy cut into her. Damn that nobility that put his wife first! She protested, petulant. "But I want—"

Before she could finish, and before Jonah could deny her a second time, a voice cut across them. "Who the hell is it, Jonah?"

Both Jonah and Mattie snapped around to see a woman in the doorway. Her gown hung from her body, and her disheveled hair gave her the look of a madwoman escaped from a tower.

"Who the hell is this?" the woman snapped.

Mattie swallowed hard, trying to summon up her fantasies again and use them as a script. But in those well-worn scenarios, Faith Evers was genteel, cool, even distant and contemptuous. She was prepared to brazen through any of those. But this wildness, almost a breathlessness, confused her and tied her tongue. She took a step nearer. "Ma'am," she began. "Mrs. Evers . . ."

Faith peered at her, like someone trying to put a name to a familiar face. Then her lips took on a cynical twist. "The girl from the churchyard. You hit our car." Her eyes lifted to meet Jonah's. "What, didn't you pay her off well enough? Or did you give her so much you made her greedy?"

Mattie was quick to protest. "I didn't come for money . . ."

"What, then?" Faith put her hands on her hips.

"I wanted to tell you—" She couldn't finish, because before she could search out the words, there was another shape in the doorway. "Pye!"

Blood Pye gaped. "What you doing here, girl? Ain't I tell you I gonna handle your business for you?"

Mattie felt Jonah at her side, stunned into wordlessness, but she could hear his mind churning. She glanced up to see his quick eyes run over Blood Pye's face and down his body, assessing him, like a male dog sizing up another in the presence of a female.

"You know each other?" Faith's voice had a should-have-known ring to it. "And you both decide to invade my privacy today. Is this a game?"

"You didn't have to be here," Mattie addressed Blood Pye, who was returning Jonah's stare with equal animosity. Threes balanced on his shoulder, tipping forward to sniff at Jonah. "I can do it myself. I can tell her."

"Tell me what?" Faith demanded. She looked from Mattie to Blood Pye and back again. "Tell me what?"

Jonah walked over to Faith and placed a steadying arm at her wrist. "There's something you need to know, Faith," he began.

What is he doing? Mattie wondered wildly. She didn't need help. Not from Blood Pye, and not from him. This was her story, hers to tell. "I can do it!" she shouted. In just two steps she was next to Jonah, inches away from Faith.

Behind Faith, Blood Pye hopped in agitation. "Tell her, baby. Now's the time."

"What the hell do I need to know?" Faith demanded, her voice growing shrill. Then she halted, body stiffening, eyes locking into Mattie's. They widened, and then Mattie felt a fire ignite in her blood, hissing through her veins, but immobilizing her so there was nothing she could do to scratch the itch. Her arms were heavy, her legs rooted to the ground. Hard as marble. Worked into stone. Never to fade again.

Faith's eyes, clear, shrewd, and filled with . . . recognition. "Oh," Faith said. "It's you. Dominic's child."

Faith

"Well," Faith said. She hoped her voice sounded steady, because the last goddamn thing she planned on doing right now was lose control, not in front of these people. She tried to adjust her dressing gown, regretting having put it on in the first place. That humiliating tussle with Jonah on the stairs had ruined it for good. She wondered just how bad she looked, and then remembered the bemused stares that Reuben and then Dominic's brat had given her. Probably looked like hell. But she was still in charge, and she was damned if she'd have this farce played out on her front lawn for any and everyone to see. "Maybe we can take this inside?"

The three of them gaped at her, all speechless, and their astonishment made her smile, despite the unpleasantness of the situation. What, had the girl and her rodent-loving acquaintance come all the way over here in the hopes of surprising her? Ridiculous. She could tell from Jonah's gawping that he'd known, too. Had he known her before the collision in the churchyard? Had Dominic, in the spirit of masculine camaraderie, taken his son-in-law into his confidence about the bastard he had squirreled away out east with his little trashy mistress?

Probably not. Dominic had been arrogant enough to imagine that he'd kept his secret all these years, coming in late every Wednesday from his "meetings," thinking that nobody suspected a thing. That his sterling reputation, church on Sundays, and lying excuses had protected him from discovery. Hardly likely he'd have risked besmirching Jonah's adoring devotion to him by letting that bomb drop.

In front of her, nobody had moved. "You told her!" the girl shouted at Reuben.

Reuben shook his head hard, holding the mongoose steady with one hand. "I ain't tell her nothing, Mattie. I swear. I just got here." He shot Jonah a hostile look. "Maybe somebody done tell her already. Maybe we bringing stale news."

"Faith?" Jonah was trying to keep his voice from faltering, and he tried his best not to bristle from Reuben's sideways accusation. He still had his arm at her elbow. "You knew?"

She pulled her arm away from him. Whatever was happening right now, she hadn't forgotten her daughter was upstairs. Probably hiding from him, unwilling to give in to his crazy plan to snatch her from the only place she was really safe. As soon as she got this unpleasant scenario over and done with, she and Jonah would be settling this, once and for all. So right now, being touched by him was the last thing she wanted.

She let the air out of her lungs in a gust. "I'm going inside," she announced. "If any of you want to say anything to me, you do it there. If not . . ." She made the mistake of letting her eyes be caught by the girl's green ones and halted. So like her daughter's. So like her husband's. If ever she needed proof that the rumors that swirled above her husband's head had been true, these eyes were enough. For a second, she was lost in them, seeing her husband alive in them. She broke the spell by tearing away her gaze and turning to enter.

Like statues unfrozen they tumbled in after her. "You know y'all owe her, don't you?" Reuben was saying.

"Shut up, Pye," the girl hissed.

"I'm just sayin' . . . ," he protested.

In the same anteroom in which she'd sat the young man

just moments before, she stopped. The other three almost collided with each other, like something from an old black-and-white slapstick. She faced them and folded her arms. "Five minutes," she said to the girl. "Not a second more. Say what you have to say, then leave."

She licked her lips. "I just wanted—"

"Money," Faith filled in for her.

"That's right!" Reuben said triumphantly. "Y'all owe her. She's blood."

"Not money." She shook her head. "Be quiet, Pye."

"What, then?" Faith ignored the man's indignant snort. She knew what it was like. These people always wanted *something*. It just took some of them longer to get around to it than others.

"To know you."

Faith laughed. "Know me? Don't be silly, child."

She went on, determined. "And for you to know me. That I exist."

"I've always known you existed."

"How, Faith?" Jonah spoke at last.

She gave him a withering look. "You men, you and my husband, always make the same mistake. You think your money and your business connections make you powerful. You think they make you immune, and invincible. Wrong. Money isn't power. Knowledge is. And just because I spent my days making this"—she waved her arm, taking in the room around them—"a home for my husband and my daughter"—she pointedly excluded her son-in-law—"that makes me a fool? You think that just because I spent my days entertaining other wives, and my evenings on my husband's arm, his best business asset, that I didn't know what was going on? You're as naive as he was, boy. I knew you were pulling your silly stunt today, trying to steal my daughter from under me. Why wouldn't I know something my husband tried to keep a secret for over twenty years?"

Faith returned her attention to the girl, who was looking

disappointed, robbed of the chance to tell her story. "What's your name, child?"

"Mattie. Matilda."

"Your father came up with that?"

"Yes, ma'am."

Faith snorted. "Better than Jane, I suppose. Dominic never had much of an imagination. Now you know why I did all the decorating myself." That struck her as funny, and she laughed softly. Then her eyes and voice were hard again. "And your mother?"

"Claudine." The thick lower lip trembled. "She's dead."

Faith nodded. "So I heard. What do you do?"

"I sell. In a sweetie parlor."

"Bright future ahead of you," Faith said dryly, and was pleased to see them all squirm.

There was an anticlimactic lull as the room fell silent, each one waiting for a cue from the other as to what to do next. Matilda's eyes moved wildly about the room, like those of the blind given a few precious moments in which to view the world before being plunged into permanent darkness once again. "And my sister?" she asked tremulously.

"She's not your sister," Faith was quick to point out. She wasn't having any of that. Put the presumptuous snit back into her place before things got out of hand.

"But she is!" she protested. "We had the same father. We share—"

"Proteins. Genetics. What you are, is an accident. A married man fucking some incidental woman—" Her tongue almost tripped her up in surprise. She was sure she'd never used that word before, not even at her husband's urgings in bed. She wondered if these people, by their presence, were contaminating her by their coarseness, but she persevered, barely missing a beat. "Doesn't make the result of that sweaty mess family. Family isn't where the sperm came from. Family is about breeding, and nurturing . . ."

"My father nurtured me!"

"How? Did he peel off a few bills and hand them to you now and then? Did he give your mother money to buy you shoes for school, just so she could convince herself that she was taking the money for your sake, and not because she was willing to cock her ass up in the air and present like an ape whenever he chose to drop by?"

"Faith!" Jonah burst out. "Enough!"

"Don't let her talk to you like that, baby!" Reuben said. He thrust himself forward, but Faith wouldn't give him the satisfaction of flinching. The animal on his shoulders leaped to the ground and darted under the love seat. *If it shits under there,* she decided, *I'm having it killed.* Dragging her eyes away from the brown shadow under her furniture, she focused on the girl, and ignored the two louts who fancied themselves her protectors.

"Did your father ever sit up with you when you had the cold? He ever took you to be baptized like a good Christian, taught you your catechism, introduced you to his friends? He ever walked down the street with you, held your hand, picked you up when you fell down, rushed you to hospital when you had a fever?"

Her voice was barely a whisper. "No, ma'am."

Faith brought her face dangerously close, speaking softly, but not so softly that the two men could not hear. "So tell me, dear. Exactly what is it you think makes you family?"

A diamond of a tear glistened at the corner of the girl's eye, an Faith would have felt sorry for her had she not been so repulsed and violated by her very existence. You didn't feel sorry for pests, whether or not they were God's creatures. You just gritted your teeth and dispatched them.

Matilda's shoulders hunched as her spirit sagged. "That's it, then," she said to nobody in particular. She took three or four steps toward the door, but seemed to run out of energy, and slowed to a halt like a child's toy running out of batteries.

Both men moved to her, but Jonah was there first. Faith

watched, stunned, as he pulled her to him and laid a hand in her hair. "It's okay, sweet," he whispered. "Take heart. I'll take you to her. Soon. When she's better. You'll meet Justice; I'll make sure of that."

Before Faith could protest that the girl would see her daughter over her dead body, and that Jonah had no goddamn authority to promise anything of the kind, there was a wild grunt from Reuben, and Matilda was wrenched from Jonah's arms.

"It's him!" Reuben was shouting. "It's him, right? Tell me!"

Matilda murmured something, but her voice was drowned under the sound of Jonah's body hitting the floor as, taken by surprise, he was unable to resist a full-body tackle. The men rolled, grappling. They were of equal weight, although Reuben might have been an inch or two shorter. He snarled, some rubbish about Jonah and Matilda, and her coming home covered in grass.

"Pye!" Matilda screamed. "No! Stop!"

Faith watched Jonah free himself, only to be floored again as a punch sent his glasses flying to the ground, shattering where they landed. On full defensive now, Jonah hit back, less anxious to free himself than he had been ten seconds before. Fighting in her house? Almost as ridiculous as the reason for the fight. Jonah and this little slip of a girl? She was less chagrined by the affront to her daughter's marital privilege than she was by the person he'd been cheating with. Men had affairs. Lord knew, she would be the last person to pretend they didn't. But the type of women they chose. . . .

Dominic had taught Jonah well, obviously. Or was it something innate that led men unerringly toward the lowest common denominator in their quest for a mistress? Why was it that they never searched for one from among women at their own level? Were they all like pigs, ignoring the fragrant flowers that grew above ground, to root and snuffle at the grubs and rotting vegetation that lay below it?

This time, she was the one to shout, "Enough!"

Jonah and Reuben stopped, their arms around each other in a parody of a dance, and both looked at her. Jonah was the first to disentangle himself, touching his cheek gingerly to assess the damage from the first blow Reuben had landed.

His darker opponent looked ready to take him down again; he was crouched in an attack stance, teeth bared. "She was doing fine," he was saying. "Then you come along with all your money, and give her a piece-of-shit bike, and you think you bought her. You think you can just come along and use her like her daddy used her ma."

"I never used her." Jonah picked his glasses up and squinted at them, shaking the small fragments from their frames.

"You lie! You and her father, y'all ain't no different. You think poor women's just toys you can play with and walk away. And come back and play with them again—"

"Mattie is not a toy!" Jonah roared. He threw the glasses across the room. "And I'm *not* just like Dominic!"

"That's a first," Faith began bitterly. "Sounds funny, coming from his shadow."

"I'm not his shadow anymore. I'm not *in* his shadow anymore."

She'd never seen him look so assertive, so almost grown-up, rather than boyish. Sheer dislike prevented her from giving him her grudging admiration. "You say it, but do you believe it?" Faith waved her arm, encompassing the room and, by extension, the rest of the house. "You know he's here. He's in everything. Every brick, every wall, every window. He can't breathe anymore, but this house breathes for him: in, out, in, out . . . It smells of him. It reeks of him. Our bed does. Me, too. And you. So don't think that even if you walk away today and go hole up in your new house like a coward hiding from the thunder, that you'll ever be free of him. He took you apart and put you back together, exactly the way it would please him best."

She was horrified at her own words, even as they came tumbling out of her mouth. Not that they showed disloyalty to her husband, or that they amounted to speaking ill of the dead, but because every word was a discovery in itself. "He did it to you, he did it to his daughter, and if I know my husband, he did it to this misbegotten brat and her mother, tore them to pieces and rearranged them, and made them into whatever he dreamed up in his head that he wanted them to be, and they probably loved it. They probably begged for more, just like you did, every day he was alive . . ."

It was only then that she became aware that there was no answering protest from Dominic's daughter, who had fallen silent. She looked around as the same expression dawned on the faces of both men. Matilda was gone.

"Justice!" Jonah gasped, and sprinted past. She followed, surprising herself with her own speed. The bitch had taken advantage of the skirmish to slip away. No doubt she had found her way to Justice's room by now and was regaling her with her ugly story, claiming kinship when there was none.

They didn't have far to go. The anteroom opened onto the main hall which, a month before, had been filled with the chatter of funeral guests and the stench of fish pastries. Beyond that, the stairs, and there, Matilda stood frozen. Lacking the guts to go any farther, probably. Coward.

Faith made a dismissive but triumphant sound in her throat. To have come all the way over here and run out of steam? That would teach her to waste people's time. Maybe now she, her man, and his beast would slink off with their collective tails between their legs and leave her be. . . .

Two steps nearer, and her own strength failed her. The reason for Matilda's hesitation became apparent to the two men a mere second before it did to her, and when it did, a heartsickness swept over her like curtains across the mouth of a darkening stage. Like actors in a tableau, they stood transfixed, all four of them sharing the same thoughts, clawing with their minds at the same puzzle, and arriving at the same conclusion, perhaps not understanding exactly what had happened, but knowing deep down that something terrible had.

Water curled around the curve of the stairway, each riser a small waterfall. Gently, like a forest rivulet: lazy, peaceful, streaming steadily over the edge like an ornamental fountain, widening across the tile. Matilda stared up into the stairwell, her eyes and mouth three huge circles in a child's drawing of a face, as the water pooled around her ankles.

Mattie

Mattie would never forget the bellow that tore from Jonah's throat, or the way he took the stairs three at a time, feet landing unerringly where she and the others slipped and slid in the water. She followed close but could not quite keep up.

It was uncanny. She *knew.* She knew what lay at the source of all this water. Horror and loss loomed huge in her chest as the pressure, the constant tug in the opposite direction that *the other* had always exerted on the blood-ribbon that bound them, suddenly went slack. The blood-tie rebounded like an elastic band stretched to its limit and let go, snapping into her and stinging. She'd followed that red cord like a lost hiker working her way back out of a forest by means of a piece of twine, only to find at the forest's edge that the twine was tied to nothing.

Two small, waterlogged suitcases wedged open a door. Jonah kicked them out of the way and sprinted inside. There was an overwhelming sense of femininity about the room: all pink walls, flowers, and lace. Not a trace of Jonah, other than a light scent that perhaps only she could perceive. The floor was under a sheet of water that was warm to her toes.

Farther in, another door. Jonah wrenched at the handle,

but it was locked. Faith Evers rushed past her, shoving Jonah out of the way, yanking on the handle with both hands, her voice like a shattered plate as she screamed futilely for her daughter. "Justice! Justice! Open this *door!*"

"Stop, Faith." Jonah put his arms around her waist, trying to get her away from it, but she clung like a limpet to the handle, bucking and kicking. His voice gained a rough edge. "Get away from it! I need to kick it down! You're in the way!"

Anxious to help, Mattie tried to pry Faith's fingers from around the handle, but they were like a bird's claws, holding tight. She looked around frantically for help. "Pye!"

Blood Pye had been hovering, slightly bemused, and even more reluctant to step uninvited into a lady's bedroom. At her plea, he joined them, and between them they tore the sobbing, cursing woman from the door.

"You," Jonah ordered, "hold her back."

Instead of bristling at the command from the rival he'd been grappling with a few short moments ago, Pye obediently brought his arms around Faith, who, although fighting like one demon-possessed, was no match for his strength. He dragged her to the bed and pulled her onto his lap, pinning her there. Her deranged screams were punctuated by his soothing murmurs as he clumsily patted her hands.

"Let me help," Mattie said to Jonah.

He didn't look her way. "Stand back." He lifted his foot and kicked. The door shuddered, but held fast. The wood looked like teak, notoriously strong, and the lock was brass, embedded seamlessly into its face. With each successive kick, his face grew redder with panic and frustration. It took six assaults to break the lock, and the door blew inward.

Water. Everywhere. Coursing over the top of the tub, deeper in here than anywhere else. Jonah on his knees, plunging both arms into the tub. Mattie dropped down next to him.

A drowned mermaid, her sister lay facedown. Pale, and paler still by a trick of the light on the water. Thin, floating like a slender stalk fallen into a puddle. Jonah lifted her without effort, turning her over. Her hair clung to her face like seaweed. The exact twin of Mattie's gold bangle was a wide, looping circle around the bony wrist. She tried to avert her eyes from her sister's nakedness, and as she looked away, she encountered the other's sightless pair.

Ice crystallized in her chest, flakes of frost building up one on the other. Those eyes, a parody of her own: green and gold, detailed with patience by the hand of a master artist, like stained glass windows, but those windows looked out into empty space. No garden, no laughing courtyard, but nothingness. Pupils impossibly wide, not flat black disks, but tunnels that drew her into a gaping void. That void, like one of those relentless holes in space that sucked in everything in its path and crushed it under its own weight: hope, laughter, pleasure. With everything it crushed, the void grew huger, and the only things that seemed to have survived those violent forces were despair, loneliness, and madness.

"Mirrors," she gasped, but only she could hear. She'd lived her life surrounded by mirrors. Sentries positioned around her, guarding every entrance, in case nothingness swooped down upon her to snatch her away. What a worthless joke. What a laughable delusion. God's own green mirrors, a perfect pair, were hers to examine, and what they reflected was not herself, but the distillation of everything she had ever begrudged her sister. And all that her sister, the second-born, had had in her stead had not been enough.

Instinctively, Mattie held both her hands out to Jonah and Justice, wanting to help, but not knowing how. He laid her on the floor, and the water sloshed up over her sides, to the place where there should have been breasts, but where there were only two sad bumps. He struggled to keep the water from rising up over her face, and eventually Mattie plopped to the ground, pulling the limp head onto her lap, smoothing the hair away from the open mouth to allow Jonah to fix his own mouth over it, to blow air into lungs that showed no interest in accepting it.

This was how her father had gone, Mattie remembered. With Jonah's lips fixed to his. Poor Jonah. Two tragedies, one a mirror reflection of the other. With every puff of air he forced into that dead mouth, her heart hurt. She wished she could tell him there was no need, that her sister's heart had lost its last spark of life, but the earnest intent on his face told her this was something he didn't want to hear.

Instead, she watched him as he worked, marveling at the strangeness of the multidimensional love in the room: she loving him, he loving his wife so much that her death was unthinkable. Justice loving him back, perhaps, but not so much that it stood in the way of what she had done to herself. Sister knowledge told her that this was no accident. This had been no fall. What had Justice loved more, or not loved enough, to allow her to do such a thing?

Outside, Faith's shrilling subsided to broken whimpers, and Blood Pye's voice was now more audible than hers. He spoke softly, steadily, comfortingly, telling her over and over the lie that everything was just fine. Mattie felt love for him, too, and gratitude. And pride that reckless wretch that he was, he was able to offer this kindness to a woman who thought he was nothing.

After a long, long time, too long for any rational soul, Jonah stopped forcing air into the bony chest, but did not lift his head. His lips remained fixed on Justice's in a last, lingering kiss he was too afraid to break. Mattie's fingers, which had been stroking her sister's flat hair, slid up a few inches, to encounter tears rolling down Jonah's cheeks, as warm as the water that still ran lustily into the tub.

"Oh, Jonah," she whispered. Pity and compassion. Her lap was heavy with the weight of both of them: her sister unmoving, and Jonah spread out upon her, hugging her close, sobbing, yet still not ending that death kiss. She leaned forward, curving her spine, to press her own lips to the back of his head, into his damp, crisp hair.

She waited with him.

Jonah

It was a while before Jonah realized the water was still running. The sound of the river meeting the sea. Childhood sounds, as comforting as his mother's voice. It was only when he became consciously aware of its existence that it had become distracting. He lifted his head, breaking that vain, final contact with his lifeless wife.

Mattie's hands were on him: one at the back of his head, the other on his shoulder, both light, exerting no pressure, but speaking volumes. She'd promised to keep him safe. Now she was fulfilling that promise.

He sat up, reached over, and put an end to the sound of running water. *What now?* he wondered.

"Can we"—Mattie hesitated—"get her up?"

Taking Justice into his arms was hard, even though she weighed nothing. The burden of his guilt was piled upon her chest like a load of bricks. Standing with her took more effort than anything he had ever done in his life. He'd awoken this morning hating himself for reasons that now seemed petty. Tonight, assuming he did go to bed at all, he'd fall asleep justified in that hate. He'd come to his wife as a protector, determined to take her away, to save her. He'd failed because he hadn't paid attention. He'd left his sentry post at her door and been drawn into a squabble and a skirmish. Fighting, rolling on the ground, like some boor in a bar! And all the while, Justice had needed him. He'd taken his eyes away from the prize, just for a few moments, and the Devil had stolen it from him.

"I distracted you," Mattie reminded him, making him wonder if he'd spoken his thoughts out loud. "You said you needed to be with her. I didn't listen, because I wanted . . ." Her mouth trembled. It was her turn for tears.

"No," he said firmly. This guilt was his. He wasn't sharing. "This is mine. My fault. I tried to be a man for her, and I fucked up every time . . ."

"But I shouldn't have come!" Mattie followed him, arms folded across her chest, grabbing all the blame she could carry and holding it close.

"Don't, Mattie," was all he could say.

They walked into the room he and Justice had shared—no, Justice's room. It had never been his. On the bed, Faith was limp in Blood Pye's arms. He was holding her in a light embrace; brute strength was no longer necessary. She was crying softly, like a child, into his shoulder. When she saw them, the breathy gusts became screams again, as the spectacle gave her her second wind. She flew from Blood Pye's lap, and Jonah steeled himself, thinking that she would try to snatch Justice from him; but she thrust her arms outward, more like a blind woman feeling her way than someone expecting to have her arms filled, and made no attempt to do so. Instead, she patted a dead arm lightly, like a mother waking her child up for school.

"She was mine," Faith shrilled. "You tried to take her. You, you, you!"

He stood before his accuser with Justice in his arms and hung his head. Speaking in his own defense would not only be useless; it would be dishonest.

Mattie bristled, trying to slip between him and Faith, looking fierce, her small plaits poking up about her head like detonator pins on an old sea mine. "Not him," she insisted. "Me. I came . . ."

Faith didn't seem to hear her. Her hands left her daughter's body, and she turned her wrath on Jonah, scratching at his eyes, trying to get a grip on his too-short hair and failing. "She was mine! She was mine!" Her nails were sharp, tearing at his skin, and the vehemence of her attack almost caused him to lose his balance, but he persevered, sidestepping her and crossing the threshold.

"Jonah!" Mattie tried to keep step. "Where you going?" He frowned, befuddled. Where *was* he going? What did he do now? All he knew was that he didn't want Justice to be a part of all this ugliness. He'd promised to take her far from it, and that was what he had to do. "Away," he realized. He discovered that his eyes had yet to give up their last tear.

Faith shouted after him. "You've got nowhere to go, boy. Where've you got to go? What've you got besides this?"

Nothing, he was about to admit. What did he have, now that Justice was gone?

But Mattie spoke for him. "He's got more than you think. This is temporary. This won't last." She turned to him and tried to give an encouraging smile. Her next words were only for him. "Bring her back," she said. "And we'll get through this."

Jonah looked down at Justice's peaceful face, and then looked back at Mattie, falling into the depths of her concern, but didn't move.

"Besides," she added, "you can't . . . move her." Mattie gestured to Justice's body awkwardly. "It's—"

"Against the law," Blood Pye reminded him. Jonah hadn't even sensed him approach. "You ain't supposed to do that. You got to leave her where she . . ." He was about to say "died," but faltered. Instead, he backtracked, bent forward, and began clumsily smoothing the bedsheets, fluffing pillows and making sure the hems were even. When he was done, he gestured awkwardly to the bed. "Come, man. She'll be real comfortable right here. She'll be real good."

Above Blood Pye's placations, Faith's shrieks resumed, and

the noise ricocheted in his head. Jonah hesitated. Turning back would mean returning to *that*. Stepping once again into the howling storm that Faith created within the room would be more than his soul could bear. And yet, Mattie was right. He had to take her back.

Without hesitation, Blood Pye turned to Faith and lifted his arms, like a father welcoming a child into them. "Faith, Faith . . ." His voice was so low that had the room not fallen into an anxious silence, it would otherwise not have been heard. "Shush. Come here."

Faith? The other man's temerity was beyond belief. Even Faith stared, halfway between sucking in a lungful of air and expelling another scream, and vacillated. Jonah watched the thoughts dart across her face: the grief being shunted aside briefly by this affront to the natural social order, only to be washed away as a new wave of grief sloshed back into shore. She swayed, and then crumbled like a beleaguered cliff face, falling into the waiting circle of arms.

For a brief moment, Blood Pye's presence filled the room, and then Jonah dragged his attention back to Mattie, who was, by now, standing at his elbow, whispering that he should put Justice down, please, please, Jonah, put her down.

Mattie

Seven years' bad luck. Seven times seven, more likely. Early morning sunlight made the scattered shards of glass glitter like sequins on a ball gown. The cheval glass had been hardest to break: that had taken both strenuous effort and an old brick, but finally, the frosted mirror, with its flower etchings now beyond recognition, joined the other bits and pieces on the floor.

Silently, she congratulated herself. She'd managed to smash them all, tearing them from their frames on the wall, sweeping them off the dresser and down from shelves, making sure that no reflective surface went undimmed, with only a few small cuts to show for it: two on her palm, and one on her thigh. Her palm bled heavily, but astoundingly, there was no pain.

Probably because she was all out of pain by now. She'd sat with Jonah while the police came and left, while men in rubber boots cleaned up all that water, and later, when neither of them could sleep or speak. Blood Pye had stayed, too, talking to the cops, giving orders to the workmen, and calming the maid, Teresa, who had returned from church to find her employer's home in chaos. He'd cajoled her into calming herself long enough to take care of Faith, and after Teresa had bathed her, slipped a pill or two past her lips, and put her to bed, Blood Pye had taken up a sentry's post at the top of the stairs and had remained motionless and alert.

Mattie surveyed the heaps of glass on the floor from the relative safety of her bed. She felt wrung out, battered, her energy having seeped from her like blood from the palm of her hand. But spent as she was, there was giddy exhilaration there, too. With every shattering sound there had been release. She'd used each sharp mirror's edge to saw through the fibrous mass of fear that had held her captive all her life.

It had been stupid of her, relying on reflected light to reassure her of her own existence. Handing over all that power to hard, flat, cold things that couldn't think or reason, but which were, all the same, deceitful enough to bounce back at you the image you most desired to see.

A lesser folly than the power she'd let Dominic tear from her grip. The sound of his name being spoken in her head made a wall of emotions rise inside. Old grief that became fresh with every exploration, of course, and a sense of loss. But the overarching sentiment, as domineering as Dominic himself had been, was anger. Sheer rage that had more clarity than any glass, in which she clearly saw her father, unblinkered by awe and adoration as she now was.

"Monster," she told him. It was time she addressed him by his real name. "Look what you did to us." To think that *she* was the one people called a bastard, through an accident of birth, when the man that had spawned her was so much more deserving of that name. He'd played them all to bolster his godlike self-image, and for his own amusement, like life-sized pieces moved from square to square on a giant chessboard.

His own wife, knowing how he was lying to her week after week, year after year, and keeping her silence, building up a hard, bitter layer around herself like pearl around a grain of sand, until that layer had crumbled, leaving her the weeping wreck that was probably still sleeping off pills in the palace that Dominic built.

His daughter, Justice: God alone knew what had led her to the bottom of a bathtub. She'd never even had the chance to meet her, after all those years of wondering and wishing, but she knew, either through instinct or by the whisper of the blood they shared, that Dominic had helped lure that ship onto the rocks.

And Jonah, poor Jonah, who so wanted to be strong, but who had had his underpinnings frayed away over time by a saboteur who wasn't satisfied unless *he* was the stronger. Her desire for him, and her fascination with him, couldn't blind her to his failings, but they allowed her to hope and pray that when time had blunted the edge of his grief and guilt, he would find his own feet and be the man he'd never been allowed to be.

"Turn aside," she advised him softly. "Shake the dust from your feet and walk away." She would have shouted if she thought he'd have heard her.

"Matilda!"

She started, and turned her head toward the door. For a bewildering second, she thought the muffled sound was an answer to her whisper, but the voice was all wrong. Confused, she slid her legs off the edge of the bed, but halted with her feet an inch above the ground. The dancing specks of light shimmered across the floor like sunlight on the incoming tide. When understanding hit her, she laughed. She'd all but painted herself into a corner: barefoot, and the way to the door was glass.

The voice came again: "Matilda!"

"Auntie Lou!" Relief was near delirious.

The door remained closed. That wasn't Louisa's way: she walked in and out of any room she chose. But she knocked, tentatively, as if she surprised herself in doing so.

Mattie scrambled to her feet on the bed, yelling, "Open!"

The door opened inward, pushing mirror shards aside in an arc. Louisa's gaze immediately fell to the floor, strewn as it was with spangles, and then she lifted her eyes to Mattie's, holding them steady. Mattie cringed, but didn't look away, braving the tirade that was to come.

Louisa's voice was gentler than she'd ever heard it. "You sleep, child?"

Mattie shook her head mutely.

"You eat?"

Another shake.

"You find what you was looking for, at your father's house?"

Mattie felt her lower lip tremble and clenched her jaw to hold back a cry. Find what she was looking for? She'd found a half-crazed woman whose knowledge of her existence had made a sham of all the years she'd been forced to live as a shadow. A sister who would never know her, who would never be anything in her memory but warm water and waxy skin and wedding photos in a man's album. She'd seen the weakness of a man she loved but shouldn't have touched, and the astounding strength in one she'd so recently rejected.

But had she found what she'd been looking for? That was a question she couldn't answer.

Louisa was waiting, patiently for a change, and the compassion and uncanny understanding in her eyes was Mattie's undoing. Where tears hadn't fallen before, even when she'd embraced dead Justice, they fell now. She raised her hands to her eyes to catch them before they fell to her feet. The story poured out, garbled, words tumbling upon each other in a hurry to escape her tortured mind, and from the doorway, Louisa listened, wordless, until she was done.

When heaving sobs cut off Mattie's story, Louisa crossed the room, glass crunching under her shoes like coarse-grained sugar in the teeth. "Child," Louisa said. She stood at the edge of the bed and held out her arms.

Mattie leaned forward, throwing her thin arms around Louisa's billowing flesh, sinking into her, so glad to be held, feeling the pain ooze from her, to be absorbed by the stronger, more capable older woman. She closed her eyes.

"We got to get you out of here," Louisa said after a long time. "You gone and throw all this glass on the floor. You didn't think you'da have to leave the room sometime?"

Mattie smiled against Louisa's shoulder. Her grandmother couldn't help it. A rebuke was always hovering somewhere at the tip of her tongue, waiting to spring out. She pointed to the wooden wardrobe that skewed a little to the side, on the far wall. "My slippers . . ."

Louisa didn't move, didn't lessen her grip around the thin shoulders. Instead, Mattie felt herself leave the bed, as Louisa lifted her, with much effort, and made for the door.

"Grandma!" Mattie said in surprise.

Louisa held her tighter, marching back the way she had come, and deposited her outside the door, where her bare feet were unthreatened. The two stared at each other, Louisa panting with the unaccustomed effort, and Mattie wide-eyed at her own utterance. She tried to think of a single time in her life in which she had called her grandmother anything other than Auntie Lou, and came up empty.

"You ain't never called me that before." Louisa's eyes were moist. "Just like your mother, God rest her, ain't never called me Ma."

Mattie was embarrassed, as if she'd made an unseemly slip of the tongue in polite company. "Um . . . ," she began. Louisa beamed. Mattie's tear-damp cheeks lifted in an echoing smile, and the two of them regarded each other solemnly.

Each second was a minute, each minute an hour. Then Louisa broke the silence. "Get me a broom and a dustpan, girl. Let me clean this mess up. You didn't want those mirrors of yours, you coulda sold them or something. Make yourself some pocket change. Ain't I never tell you nothing 'bout waste not, want not? But no, you gotta break 'em all up and scatter 'em all over. Waste of good, good money. And when you done get the broom, bathe your skin. You out all night, and you ain't even washed your feet since you come back in.

Go throw some water on yourself before you start stinking up my house like a little goat. You hear?"

Still smiling up into Louisa's face, Mattie didn't move. Louisa sucked her teeth loudly, struggling to wipe away the grin that was forming on her own face, and shooed her with both hands. "I talking, but you ain't moving. What, you ain't hearing me? Stick break off in your ears? Scoot! Scoot!"

"Yes, Grandma." Mattie scooted.

Jonah and Mattie

Jonah's gaze never left Mattie's face as she walked from room to room in the small house. She was naturally inquisitive, peeking behind doors, checking each window for view, and tapping her fingers along the countertops and closets, listening for a hollowness that would give wood lice away. It surprised him to discover how much he needed her approval of his choice.

"I'm tearing up all the linoleum," he told her once they were standing in the kitchen again.

She nodded.

"Putting down tiles."

"Good idea."

"Thirsty?" he asked hopefully, wanting to be a good host.

"Not very," she replied.

He poured her a glass of grapefruit juice anyway. He'd brought the fruit home from his first trip to the market since he lived at his mother's house as a boy, and squeezed them himself. The juice was the color of muddy water. His Aunt Elba, when she was still working for Dominic and Faith, had always used white sugar when making juice for the household, because that was the way Faith had preferred it, but in their own little annex at the back, she'd used brown cane sugar. Brown sugar had more vitamins, she insisted.

Even though Mattie had said she wasn't thirsty, she drank

it all in one go and washed the glass before he could stop her. "You comfortable here?" she asked.

He was glad she hadn't asked if he was happy. That would have been impossible to answer. He shrugged, and asked a question of his own. "You think Justice would have liked it?"

He watched her thick brows draw together as she pondered. He admitted to himself that it was unfair of him: Mattie had never had the chance to meet Justice, not in any real sense. She could hardly be called upon to know. He himself, over the past few weeks, had tormented his every waking moment with questions of what Justice had liked, loved, and hated, and into which category he'd fallen. To spare Mattie the discomfort, he answered for her. "Probably not. She didn't know anything other than where she grew up. She'd have made her way back home eventually. Either that, or . . ." *Or made her way to that place where we last found her,* he didn't have to say.

His shoulders shook a little. Even after the fact, he was overcome by his impotence in the face of Justice's monumental resistance. How did you rescue someone who didn't want to be rescued? How did you snatch someone from the claws of a dragon when they loved the scent of sulfur and the heat of its flaming breath?

Mattie laid her hand on his arm. "Nothing you could have done, Jonah," she told him softly. "If it wasn't that day, it would have been another day. Another time."

Her being right didn't make it any easier. He still needed to feel punished, like a penitent flagellating himself while bearing a heavy cross in a procession. "She knew," he revealed.

Mattie froze, her eyes rounding. "Knew what?" she asked, although she didn't need to.

"What we did. Behind the monastery."

"Oh," Mattie said. "My God."

He touched her lightly under the chin, letting one finger slide along her jawbone and up to her cheek. He wanted to comfort her. As much as he thought he himself was at fault, he didn't want her to bear any guilt. "Don't worry. I don't think it had anything to do with ... what she did. But she knew. And she didn't care."

"How could she not care?" The concept violated her sense of the way things should be.

That way lay hurt. The stain of adultery—there was no other word for it—was a dark and dirty one, but knowing that his wife hadn't cared enough to ask a question, demand an explanation, utter a threat, or even plead for his repentance made his marriage ring even more hollow. As much as he would have done anything to spare Justice pain, the revelation that she had, after all, felt none over his actions had injured him. Greatly.

Mattie was waiting for an answer. To stall for time, he hoisted himself onto the countertop, where he sat, his legs dangling. She came to stand between his knees, staring gravely into his face. He took two deep breaths, and then a third, before he allowed himself to speak.

"You remember once, that first time up on the Mount, when you asked me whether it was Justice I loved first, or whether I just loved her because I loved Dominic?"

She swallowed hard, tilting her eyes upward in an effort to focus more clearly on the memory. "Yes."

"Remember what I told you?" She nodded, but he repeated it anyway. "I loved *her*."

Her chin drooped. "Okay."

"But, for her part ..." He faltered. He'd spent his nights awake, lying on his back, trying to get used to his new bed, flicking through the pages of his memory at snapshots of his marriage. With hindsight came incredible clarity. At every high point in their life together, Dominic's face somehow intruded. At every junction lay his name. Even the ordinary, quotidian scenes—breakfast, church, vacations—were colored by his laugh, his presence. Justice had all but spelled it out for him once, and still he hadn't seen it, or admitted it: Jonah had been the least important member of a sticky, tangled threesome most of his life and not even known.

He tried to find his tongue again. "For her part," he started over, "things were different."

Mattie frowned. "How?"

"I was the way to him. A version of him. The twenty-five-cent knockoff."

"More to you than that," she encouraged.

"I know." The hand at her cheek fell to her waist. This was the first time he'd touched her since the day Justice died. He ached to be held, but this was as far as he could go. He still felt married: he hadn't even shifted his ring to the other hand yet. She seemed to understand, and although he could read tender longing in her glance, she never expected anything further. Whether there would be or could be more was still something he hadn't even had the energy to explore. That was a possibility he could just about glimpse on the horizon, at the end of a long and arduous road to a new understanding of himself, a definition of the life he'd live, out from under the shadow for the first time. That new life would probably involve finding a job, and friends, real friends for whom Dominic's name meant nothing. And that road was one he'd have to walk alone.

"Not alone," she told him.

He stared down at her. "Excuse me?"

"You don't have to do it on your own. No need."

He cracked a smile. She had a way of listening in on his thoughts like a bird on the windowsill.

"Remember the ancients," she said.

"Carrying the souls of the ones they loved in clay pots," he finished for her.

"I got a piece of yours . . ."

"And I have a piece of yours." The thought was incredibly reassuring.

She took his hand, the left one, spreading out the fingers,

skipping over the hardness of his ring, and placed it flat against her chest, just under the curve of her breast. He could feel the light *bup-bup* under his fingertips. His own heart tripped into double time. The thump in her chest spelled out a message, like drums across an African wilderness. He listened, his breathing slowing. If he closed his eyes and concentrated, he was sure he could bring his own drum into time with hers.

"You know what?" she spoke into the thick silence. It had grown intensely hot in the small kitchen.

"What?" His tongue was heavy.

Her eyes shone, and he was thrown back to his boyhood days on the beach. Green, green water pounding against Las Cuevas sand. "I don't need no clay pot."

His lips couldn't even form the shape of the word "why."

She increased the pressure on his fingers against her ribs. "I'm keeping it here," she said. "It's safe."

Blood Pye and Faith

After seeing about the cocks—his flock was now down to half—Blood Pye went inside and showered, brushed his teeth, and got dressed. He took great care getting ready. He'd made sure to shave his head the day before, so that if he got any razor bumps, they would be down by morning. He clipped his nails, even his toenails, which would be hidden by his new lace-up shoes, and rubbed a slice of lime under his armpits. When you went to visit a lady, you had to make sure you didn't stink her out.

"You staying home this time," he told Threes. "Sorry, brother."

The mongoose looked disappointed, but understanding. He sat on the balcony wall with his tail curled, watching Blood Pye leave, making sure he was okay until he turned the corner out of sight.

As he walked, Blood Pye thought about Mattie. He missed her, even though he'd gone to see her up to yesterday. She'd received him in her grandmother's living room like an old friend, and they both knew and accepted that he wouldn't be making a trip up those stairs to the bedroom again. He didn't even try to press for it, knowing deep down that something in her was changed for good, especially after that shit went down with the sister and all, and the father's wife looking her in the eye and saying, "Oh, it's you."

He wished her well. Really, he did. The day she'd told him about the other man, who turned out to be the Reyes fella, of all people, he'd shouted that he loved her. He guessed this was true, although it wasn't as if he had anything to compare it to. But with the passing of a little time and the cooling of blood, he supposed it had distilled into something quieter and yet more wholesome.

He kept what he felt for her in a warm and comfortable place, where her rejection of him as a man couldn't irk. Sure, he missed that sweet, round ass—he shook his head vigorously to dislodge the memory of it—but he was shocked to discover that even with that out of reach, there was still something there. Something pleasant. Friends with a *woman*. Damn!

He got out of the taxi at the Savannah, on the St. Clair side, embarrassed to tell the driver where he was really going, in case the man's face reflected what he already knew: that he didn't belong in there. So he walked in, along palmed avenues and shady sidewalks, glaring back at hostile dogs that followed his progression from behind their fences, gingerly cradling a bunch of flowers that some crooked sonofabitch florist had dug out his eye for. To think you could charge so much money for something that grew in the *dirt!*

He walked unhesitatingly up to the door and poked at the doorbell. This time, there was no waiting. The dark, round-faced maid yanked it open and stood a step or two above, looking thoughtfully down at him.

"Hello . . ." He tried in vain to remember her name. "Teena?"

She didn't help him out by telling him if he was right, or correcting him if he wasn't. "You come to see the madam?"

For a few moments he wondered if she recognized him from his last appearance at the house, and whether she was contemplating showing him the side entrance even if she did. He nodded, keeping her calm with an unwavering smile.

"Wait." She disappeared for several long minutes and then returned, surprise stamped on her face. "Mistress Evers say for you to come in." She stepped away from the door to let him by, and Blood Pye headed for the anteroom in which he and the lady of the house had had their first encounter.

"No," the girl said before he could drop onto the love seat. "This way."

Bemused, he followed her, across the hall that was wider than his own house, past the stairs all that water had sloshed down the last time, and through a short passageway lined with naked African statues. These left him a little taken aback. Faith Evers didn't strike him as the kind of lady to muck around with *those*.

She was sitting in a drawing room, the prettiest room he'd ever seen, with rattan fans swirling overhead, chairs with curly legs, and a view of the whole yard. The first thing that struck him was how skinny she looked. Her hair was neat, rolled at the back in a kind of swirl, but he could tell from the roots that she was due for the hairdresser any day now. Her lipstick was bright orange and made her lips flash like hazard lights as she spoke.

"Reuben," she said. Her voice sounded like a cool drink. Different from the piercing grief-torn shrieks he'd calmed before.

"Faith," he answered. He supposed he could have gone the "Mistress Evers" route, but after helping her across the valley of the shadow, he figured he'd earned the right.

The twitch at the corner of her eye was barely perceptible. "May I offer you something?"

The last time, she'd refused him a glass of water. Best to start there, he thought. "Some water would be nice." And then, his bravado flagging slightly, he added, "It don't have to be cold. Tap water will do."

Faith turned to the maid, who was still in the doorway, hopping from one foot to the other. "Two scotches, Teresa." She glanced briefly at Blood Pye. "Ice?"

"Please."

Teresa nodded and disappeared. The room was quiet.

"I suppose I should thank you," Faith said. She sounded surprised.

"No need," he dismissed the thought, but waited for her to do it anyway. She didn't speak again.

She was staring at the bunch of flowers dangling at his side. Remembering they were for her, he handed them clumsily over, and the cellophane rustled as she sniffed them. She let them fall into her lap as he took a seat. When the scotch came, they sipped at it companionably, not needing to break the silence.

"I suppose you're here for your girlfriend's money," she said when they had both set their empty glasses down.

He shook his head vigorously. "No. I know y'all are decent people. I know y'all going to work things out between you."

She shrugged, but didn't deny it.

She was still waiting, so he filled the void. "I come to see how you doing. How you getting along."

She was thoughtful. "Well, it's a bigger house than I realized," she managed to say.

He knew what she meant. "You scared to be alone?"

"No. Not scared. I have good neighbors."

"So you doing okay." He was glad. She looked fragile. There was no trace of the wild, hard-assed bitch he'd come up against before. He wondered how long *that* would last.

"It's just the sameness. Every day, every single day, is the same. I make sure the house is neat, and that the meals are served on time, but it's not much if there's nobody here to appreciate it."

"Bored?" He knew what that was like. He was an active man. Stasis was death.

She laughed. "Yesterday, I bought crochet needles."

"Used them?"

"God forbid."

"So what you . . ." He hesitated. He wondered if he was being intrusive. "What you going to do?"

"Valium and scotch," she said, "can heal a multitude of

ills." She put the flowers down and got to her feet, walking over to stand above him. She bent forward, placing her hands on her knees to steady herself, until she looked him in the eye. "But it doesn't make you a complete fool."

The glint in her eyes was so unsettling, he wondered if he should make a run for it. Maybe make-up and a hairdo had only masked her madness.

"I know you're not him," she whispered.

Not who? he wanted to ask, but couldn't squeeze a word out.

"When I saw you, I thought you were him. I knew it was crazy, but I wanted to believe. But I know these things don't happen. I'm a grown woman. I know magic doesn't happen."

He tried to ease to his feet without bumping into her.

"But it doesn't matter," she was saying. "Not one bit."

"Maybe I'd better be going, Faith," he whispered.

She stopped him with a hand on his arm, fingers digging deep. "Don't go!" She pushed him back into his seat and dragged her chair over until they were face-to-face, separated by barely eighteen inches. "Talk to me." In her face there was lonely eagerness.

He swallowed hard, willing himself to be calm. He pitied her. As a matter of fact, he was halfway clear to *liking* her. She smiled expectantly, like a little girl waiting to be told a story, and his self-confidence swelled again.

"Another drink?" she asked.

He shook his head. "Not right now," he told her. "Maybe after we talk."

"Yes," she agreed. "Talk to me."

She was quiet, she was alert, and she was listening. Things were going to be okay after all. Barely able to contain his exhilaration, he leaned forward in his seat until they were almost touching. "I was wondering . . ." He locked her eyes with his and took a deep breath. "You ever thought about going into the cockfighting business?"

He flashed her a wide grin.

CANDY DON'T COME IN GRAY
Roslyn Carrington

ABOUT THIS GUIDE

The suggested questions are intended to enhance your group's
reading of Roslyn Carrington's CANDY DON'T COME IN
GRAY. We hope the themes of race, family and infidelity have
been thought provoking. It is also our belief that issues of racism
within the black community must be dealt with openly and
honestly in order to bring about true healing.

DISCUSSION QUESTIONS FOR
CANDY DON'T COME IN GRAY

1. *"You got the right to be. If God didn't want you to exist, he wouldn't'ta made you. Why you gotta look to somebody else to give you permission to exist?"* Louisa seems to have the easy answer to Mattie's disappearance dilemma, but Mattie isn't so sure. Do you think she was crazy? What did the concept of existence mean to her, and why was she incapable of looking to herself for proof of her own existence?

2. Jonah was swallowed up by the Evers family and then spat out after Dominic's death, much like his Biblical namesake. Why do you think he was so slow to act in order to save himself? Shouldn't he have realized that he was part of a society that merely tolerated rather than accepted him? Couldn't he have asserted himself earlier? Why didn't he do something about Justice long before he made his first attempt?

3. Do you think that part of Faith's hostility toward Jonah stemmed from a subconscious recognition that to Justice, he was merely a stand-in for and a conduit to Dominic? Did she see her daughter as competition for her husband's affections?

4. Why do you think Mattie is finally able to call her grandmother "Grandma" instead of the more public "Auntie Lou"? Do you think this stems from a shift in her concept of family? Like the author's previous novels, *A Thirst for Rain* and *Every Bitter Thing Sweet*, *Candy Don't Come in Gray* is about the individual's sense of self in the context of family. Where should one end and the other begin?

5. *Were they all like pigs, ignoring the fragrant flowers that grew above ground, to root and snuffle at the grubs and rotting vegetation that lay below it?* Do you agree with Faith, that men usually have affairs out of their class? If so, why? Still on the subject of class, do you think that Jonah was ill-equipped to handle many of his social problems because of his origins? In other words, did Dominic have certain social

sensibilities and capabilities bred into him over the generations, which Jonah lacked? Is upward mobility absolute, or
does heredity play a part in life's success?

6. Do you think that if Justice had lived Jonah would have been
   perfectly content to keep Mattie as a mistress, much as
   Dominic had kept her mother before? Do you believe that
   habits, situations, curses, and blessings cycle through the
   generations, and that he would eventually have followed
   Dominic's well-worn path?

7. Jonah had access to many means of transport at the Evers
   house, and yet he loved that bike. What did it mean to him?
   What did Mattie's home and her grandmother symbolize for
   him? Why wasn't he afraid to be recognized when he was out
   riding with Mattie every afternoon? After all, he was a fairly
   well-known businessman. Do you think he was trying to pre-
   cipitate a situation within a marriage in which he no longer
   felt loved?

8. Why was Blood Pye so easily able to give Mattie up? Was he
   serious about her in the first place? And what do you think
   will happen between him and Faith? Are his interests romantic or merely mercenary? True, he is after her financial
   backing in order to save his business, but he did bring her
   flowers. . . .

9. What is this deep resentment—and later fascination and de-
   pendence—that Faith feels for her statue? Does she see in it
   reminders of African qualities that she hates to acknowledge
   in herself and her husband? If so, why does she seek out these
   qualities after Dominic is gone?

10. Was Dominic the monster that Mattie later saw him to be?
    Was he really manipulative, cold-blooded, and selfish? Or
    was he just a man straddling two worlds, and trying to stay
    happy in both?